NAD

of

NADIDÉ

A Defiant Rose
in the Thorny Shadow
of the Turkish Junta

NAD

of

NADIDÉ

A Novel

WAGIH ABU-RISH

K.P.H.
KIRKLAND
PUBLISHING
HOUSE

Published by Kirland Publishing House in the United States.

ISBN: 979-8-9859152-1-1 (paperback)
ISBN: 979-8-9859152-0-4 (hardcover)

First Edition

www.wagihaburish.com

To all those who genuinely have and will fight against dictatorships of any kind.

MAIN CHARACTERS

NAD or NADIDÉ

FAREED—Nad's boyfriend

DR. FIONA BURKE—Fareed's mother

DR. AMEER SHAHEEN—Fareed's father

AYSHE HIKMET—Nad's mother

GENERAL ALI HIKMET—Nad's father

MAJOR ATA ASLAN—Nad's contender

LEILA SHAHEEN CHAKIR—Fareed's cousin

TOLGA CHAKIR—Leila's husband

DANIA—Fareed's ex-girlfriend

SORRAYA—Engineering building cleaning lady

DENIZ and NAZ—Nad's best friends

SIMRA—Nad's deceitful friend

MURAT—Simra's fiancé and collaborator

GENERAL EVREN—Head of the junta

COLONEL BEIKAL—Head of junta secretariat in Istanbul

AMBASSADOR PETRY—British ambassador in Turkey

AMBASSADOR McCRAY—Irish ambassador in Turkey

THE TYPICAL BEHAVIOR OF DICTATORSHIPS

The Edicts and Actions of Dictatorships
Are Arbitrary
Even When They Pertain to
the Separate Affairs of the Heart

CHAPTER 1

I t was a crisp and sunny April day in 1981 London. Fareed and his mother Fiona were walking down a narrow street, window shopping.

"Fareed, look at this gorgeous human being. She is a physical specimen of grace and perfection," said Fiona. A good-looking young woman walked toward them, on the other side of the street.

Fareed watched as the dark-haired woman, dressed in a white sundress, passed them.

"Oh my God. Look at this behind; it is perfectly contoured and shaped," Fiona went on, nudging her son. "My, my, this is the kind of look you should be going after!"

It didn't matter that Fareed had a girlfriend, Dania. Fiona thought she was spoiled rotten with a condescending attitude toward others, especially those with lesser means. Fiona got to dislike her more when she found out that Dania had physically abused her housekeeper of seven years.

"Mother, why are you saying this?" Fareed said, exasperated.

"Don't you think Dania is a stunning-looking woman?"

"Yes, I think your girlfriend is incredibly beautiful; it is her attitude that bothers me. I don't think she is all there on top." Fiona tapped her temple to prove her point. "Look again at the grace of this young lady. If I had not gone into neurosurgery and were a man looking at her behind, like you should be doing, I would have chosen colon/rectal instead."

Fareed sighed. "Mother, how could you think this way? You are a doctor!" He had been a few months over two years old when his parents Fiona and Ameer moved to London. Ameer had negotiated a deal whereby he and Fiona were equal deputy heads of the department, with him performing his sub-specialty as a vascular neurosurgeon and she doing the same as a skull-base neurosurgeon. The two became famous practicing together, operating frequently as a team in London. Their success ratio while operating together was noticed, and recorded by many hospitals and medical schools.

Fiona stopped walking and looked Fareed in the eye. "What you don't know is that I am not talking as Fiona Burke-Shaheen; I am talking as your alter ego!" She smirked.

"If this is the case, you must not think highly of me. You know me well," said Fareed.

"I do, I do think highly of you, I am just joking," said Fiona.

They turned to watch the young woman, who was now arguing loudly with a young man. She slapped him on the face, saying, "I told you it is all over. I don't want you to call me anymore. Stop following me. Why can't you understand simple English?"

"She really smacked him," said Fiona.

Fareed, in an attempt to challenge his mother, said, "No, Mother, she does not know how to really slap a man. She ought to do it as if she is making a one-handed basketball dunk. She should step with her left, push with her right foot, and then swing high with her right arm and come down on him as hard as she can. This way, she would muster three to four times the velocity, compared to slapping him flat-footed."

"What? What are you talking about? Show me," said Fiona.

Step by step, Fareed proceeded to demonstrate to his mother, on a public street, how to slap a man. After Fiona expressed her satisfaction and mild admiration, Fareed said, "I hope you are not going to try this on Dad!"

Fiona turned around to face Fareed, her expression stern. "Your father and I have never laid hands on each other. Ameer was and continues to be the love of my life, and a gentleman of the first order. I don't want you to question this fact whatsoever."

Fareed tried to cover up his indirect insult, almost changing the subject. "I didn't mean that; it is just like he is not as engaged as you are. You take four days off to fly to Beirut to visit me every four months and you take two days off when I visit you here in London. He has never taken any days off except on one occasion."

"I don't know what your argument has to do with spouses physically abusing each other. All you are trying to do is change the subject of Dania. Nevertheless, let me answer you openly: Not all people are alike. Your father becomes very animated and performs exceedingly well in a couple of venues. They don't have to be the same venues you or I excel in. You seem to take after your father except when dealing with Dania," said Fiona.

Fiona and Fareed went into a shirt store, where Fareed bought four shirts. Afterward, they went to a nearby restaurant to have lunch.

"You talked about two venues where my father feels comfortable," Fareed began. "What are those?"

"Let me tell you about one, and don't you mind the other. When your father operates, it is just like looking at a maestro conducting a philharmonic orchestra. I know you are not a physician but every one of his colleagues is in awe of him and a few are jealous of him."

"What is the other venue?" asked Fareed.

Fiona tried to avoid answering Fareed, but he continued to insist.

"Listen Fareed, let us not talk about it. The more I answer you, the more you want to ask. Let me tell you about something that relates to you. I hope you are being careful with Dania. I want to let you know that your father and I did not have sex till after we got married. We were in Boulder, Colorado, where I told your dad that I was willing if we agreed to get married in advance, but your dad insisted that we wait. He then proposed to me to get married in three days. We got married and became intimate only afterward."

"So, what is the second venue in which Dad excels?"

"I don't feel like telling you. If I were to tell you, I know you would not be satisfied and would continue to ask questions," said Fiona, taking a bite of her salad.

"No, no, I won't. I must confess I am curious. I would not have known if you did not tell me how good he is as a surgeon. If you tell me, I won't ask any more questions about this," said Fareed.

Fiona looked at him with eyes widening. "I think I am going to regret it, but you asked for it. Your father is even better in the bedroom than he is in the operating room," she said, looking at Fareed straight.

"Why did you have to spell it out?" Fareed snapped.

"I knew it. You never stick to your promises. It's okay, this is the last time," said Fiona, winking.

CHAPTER 2

In her youth, Fiona had enrolled in the school of medicine at University College Dublin, and graduated as a physician seven years later. She then trained in general surgery and performed exceedingly well. It was her luck to be instructed by a visiting professor from the University of California, Los Angeles (UCLA). Impressed by her general surgery acumen, he asked her if she would consider applying to the UCLA neurosurgery fellowship program. She did and was comfortably accepted. The second physician accepted into the program that year was Ameer, a Palestinian physician who had just finished his general surgery in London.

Judging from his background, Ameer had to overcome greater challenges than Fiona. He had originally come from Jaffa, Palestine, and left Palestine with his family. Arriving in Lebanon as refugees, they ended up in a camp in Sidon, Lebanon. He finished his high school studies in a United Nations refugee school in the same camp.

Despite Ameer's humble clothing, he stood out. At 6'3" and

with unusually handsome looks, he was constantly being eyed by the girls. He decided to himself that education and education alone was his best avenue to leave behind his refugee status. Becoming a doctor was the crème de la crème of all professions, he told himself.

Ameer, through the Quaker church mission in Lebanon, was given a scholarship to enroll in the medical school of the American University of Beirut (AUB). There he excelled and from there he graduated as a physician, which led him to be enrolled into the surgery program at the University of London. In London, through his training, he developed the habit of taking down the names of famous physicians and famous medical programs around the world. It was the UCLA neurosurgery fellowship program that attracted his interest. He applied and was accepted, having been recommended by every one of his professors.

At orientation, he was introduced to Fiona, his same-year fellow. Ameer instantly noticed Fiona and Fiona noticed Ameer.

The first two weeks at UCLA, there was little contact between Fiona and Ameer. Only when one of the third-year fellows managed to have coffee with Fiona did Ameer decide to do something about it. As Fiona sat by herself in the hospital coffee shop, he approached her and asked her if he could bring her tea. She right away said yes.

That was the start of their relationship. From tea, it developed into wine and drinks. A year into the relationship, the thought of marrying Fiona was constantly on the top of Ameer's mind, and having children together felt like it would be the fruit of their deep affection for each other.

"Our only child will be named by me and raised Muslim if it

happens to be a boy. If we have a girl, you will have the privilege of naming her and raising her Catholic. If I happen to be the lucky one, I will call him Fareed," said Ameer.

"You are a mad Palestinian, I know that," Fiona said, laughing. "I accept. She will be our Claire."

"Or would you rather name and christen our son, instead?" wondered Ameer.

"No, Claire it will be, after my mother."

"It may surprise you, but I would rather have a Claire," said Fareed.

"And I would rather have a Fareed, a spitting image of his father," answered Fiona.

On Monday, they got married at 10:49 in the morning. That evening, Fiona and Ameer confined themselves in their hotel room and made love all night.

———

One week short of nine months from their marriage, Fiona and Ameer had their one and only child. By prior agreement rather than after the fact, it was a boy who was named Fareed.

Fiona and Ameer had two concentrations in life: Fareed, and neurosurgery. Although it had not been discussed between the two, they subconsciously wanted to provide for Fareed what their families had been unable or too challenged to provide for them. Above all, they wanted to make sure that his education was well planned and well nurtured. Other than sending him to top schools, they provided Fareed with tutors to teach him French and Arabic. English was not a challenge since his schooling took place in London. Fareed proved to be an accomplished student and a recognized athlete.

At the age of eight, Fareed had read very little about Islam and less about Christianity. Fiona reminded Ameer many times that he needed to educate Fareed in his faith, Islam. Ameer promised but always got busy with neurosurgery. In the end, it was Fiona who had to study the teachings of Islam on her own, to relay them to Fareed.

When Fareed was sixteen, Ameer and Fiona agreed to have him go to boarding school in Lebanon. There he started and nurtured new friendships. He preferred school life in Lebanon over that of London. The comradery was warmer and the friends greater in numbers. He often stayed at his friends' houses and was treated kindly by his classmates' parents.

Fiona and Ameer had planned to try to send Fareed to Stanford University in Palo Alto, California, yet Fareed wanted to study engineering at the AUB. His parents grudgingly accepted his choice. Here, he had corrected his Arabic—which he had previously spoken with an Anglo-American accent—and spoke as if he had been raised in Lebanon all along. Nevertheless, he spoke English with a slight Irish dialect that was clearly short of being a brogue. It was also here that he met Dania.

Dania was beautiful and rather charming, worth pursuing a relationship with. He took the initiative and called Dania to ask her out for dinner.

She instead invited him to go to the mountains, pick fruits at her family's orchards, and then have dinner before returning to Beirut. Some fruits were in season and the flowers were mostly blooming. Dania had prepared appetizers and arak, the Lebanese national drink. It was a high-end brand, after Dania's family name.

Fareed had not previously associated the brand to the family.

From the size of the extensive orchards and the popularity of the liquor brand, he realized that her family was exceptionally rich. He also figured that she wanted him to know that she came from wealth, which he did realize, in short order.

Under the shade of an apricot tree, she unbuttoned her blouse, ostensibly to take off the crucifix around her neck. "It's giving me a rash," she said. Fareed could not help but observe the large and firm bosoms Dania carried. They were exciting and enticing. She, after removing the crucifix, did not bother to button her blouse. Fareed could not help it. He kept looking at her bosoms.

"You are just looking," she said. "Do something."

Fareed grabbed her and kissed her, massaging her through her clothes. When Fareed helped Dania slip off her skirt and started massaging her breasts and down to her thighs, she removed Fareed's hand.

"You know I cannot do this. I cannot make love to a Muslim. I cannot marry a Muslim, unless he converts," she said.

Fareed stopped altogether, surprised and shocked at the whole thing. She had led him to that point physically, and intentionally stopped to lecture him about her dos and don'ts. She could see that he was taken aback. He slipped her skirt and bra back on and buttoned her blouse. She stared at him without saying anything.

He looked at her indignantly and said, "Listen, Dania, you fixed so many appetizers. I am totally full. There is no need to go out to dinner. We can return to Beirut early." He was seriously angry at the whole episode, and at her for being less than straightforward.

"There's no need to change the schedule," she said. He insisted.

They did return early, but not before he asked her to drive to her house. There, he told her that he would take a cab and that she did not need to bother to drive him to his apartment.

The relationship cooled off and neither one contacted the other.

———————

Within weeks there was a panel discussion, "The Relationship of Science and Reason to Religion," with Fareed being one of the panelists of six. Fareed was among the three who represented the argument that science and reason should override any religious belief. The other three, two Christian clerics and one Muslim cleric, represented the idea that faith would cease to be faith when it subjugated itself to science and reason. Dania attended the discussion. Fareed did well, and his group's views seemed to have had higher acceptance among the audience.

At the end, Dania went to Fareed. "Shame on you. So, we had different points of view, does it mean you don't call me? You are acting like a spoiled kid. I am hoping you will call me next week. We don't have to lie down under an apricot tree. We can lie down under a jujube tree," she said, trying to make a light-hearted comment and referencing a tree known in Lebanon for sharing love. "Fareed, call me. Please don't spoil it. You know I like you a lot."

Fareed liked the flavor of her invitations and her clear humility under the circumstances. He called her the following week.

Their relationship grew stronger and stronger, both emotionally and sexually. She dropped the notion of Catholic-to-Catholic sex. Dania made it clear to Fareed that she did not mind having sex with a Muslim, yet she added that she could not risk becoming pregnant by one. Dania said that her reservations could be eliminated by Fareed converting to Catholicism.

It was clear to Fareed why she wanted him to be Catholic. "You want me to become Catholic in order to satisfy your parents in case we get married. I cannot be a fake Catholic unless I am fake altogether. In that case, if we ever get married, I will cheat on you because I will be a fake husband. From now on I will remain Muslim, and you will remain Maronite Catholic, no matter what you say or what I say. So best, if you want us to continue, you should say nothing about this subject. Just hold your peace."

Fareed's language and tone surprised Dania. She said nothing then or thereafter about her desire for him to convert. Her resignation helped the relationship improve, and the two became close lovers.

It was on a weekend when her parents were staying at their mountain residence and Fareed was staying with Dania in town. He noticed her Filipino maid, Imelda, limping badly. Fareed made a point of looking at Imelda closely. He noticed several bruises behind her ears and on her cleavage. He did not want to look closer, not wanting to appear as if he was staring at her well-endowed breasts. When Dania was in the bathroom, he asked Imelda to come closer. He then looked behind her ears, to find out that there was at least one serious cut. Fareed said nothing.

When he saw Dania the next time, he asked her about Imelda's limp and bruises.

"Oh, that's nothing," Dania said quickly.

Fareed eyed her suspiciously. "I've attended a presentation about house help abuse in Lebanon. I think you've beaten Imelda up."

Dania leveled him with a scowl. "You dare to accuse me! What must you think of me?"

Fareed didn't have an answer.

———

A month later, Fareed again stayed with Dania over the weekend. Imelda had forgotten to put pomegranate seeds on the mashed eggplant. He heard Dania scolding Imelda in French in the kitchen. He was surprised. Imelda spoke Tagalog, English, and Arabic but not French. Why speak to her in a language she couldn't understand?

When he entered the kitchen, Dania kept scolding Imelda, not having heard Fareed come in. He stood there amazed at the whole scene, especially when he saw Dania carrying a stick, about to beat Imelda.

"Don't do it," said Fareed in a loud voice.

Dania looked at him, huffing. "No, no, I did not plan to beat her up. I don't do that."

Fareed took the stick from Dania's hand. He could see that the ridges on the stick matched the marks he had seen behind Imelda's ears the previous month.

"No, Dania, you do beat her up. I saw the marks behind her ears. They came from this stick. I think you were about to beat her right now if I had not come into the kitchen. And you scolded her in French when she does not speak one word of it. What is this all about?"

At the AUB, he confided in his best friend, Sammy. Sammy was more realistic than Fareed yet more indignant. For the first time, Sammy told him that he did not care for Dania. He told him that Dania represented to him what was ailing Lebanon—a rich class that not only disrespected the poor, but almost did not recognize that the poor existed.

"Look, Fareed," Sammy said, "Dania is stunningly beautiful, and you are in love with her. You have to make a decision, and I believe you will make the right one, not now but after you see more of this kind of ugly attitude and behavior."

That did not sound good to Fareed. He was in love with Dania; he was looking more for a resolution whereby he could change her behavior and feel good about it afterward.

Dania slept at Fareed's apartment that evening, to the dismay of Sammy. Sammy had wanted to sleep over at Fareed's since he was driving Fareed to the airport the following day. It was Fareed's turn to fly to London to see his parents, which he did once every four months.

The next morning, Sammy picked Fareed up and drove him to the airport. The last thing Sammy told Fareed before he dropped him off was, "I hope your mother puts some sense into you. I don't believe Dania will change her behavior any. I believe it is all an act."

CHAPTER 3

A week later, after shopping and lunch in London on that April day, Fiona and Fareed returned to find Fareed's father at home. The three enjoyed the evening, and as Ameer finished his second Scotch, the conversation got warmer and more animated. The evening took them to a fancy restaurant, where they continued the conversation.

"Fareed, I need to share with you that your father and I are going to donate our time and cover the expenses of operating on four Palestinian refugees per month, from the same refugee camp where your father was raised," Fiona began. "We just got the approval of the Lebanese government. Your dad started the whole thing after operating on the Lebanese minister of finance a couple of months back. The minister facilitated the deal," said Fiona.

The evening went well and all three enjoyed each other's company.

At home, as Fiona and Ameer headed to their bedroom,

Fareed looked at his mother, smiled, and said, "I hope the room is big enough."

———

Two days later Fareed went back to Beirut, but not before he and Fiona needled each other further. In the process, Fareed confided in his mother that Dania had admitted to punishing Imelda on three different occasions.

Fiona said, "Fareed, don't speak in code; you mean she *physically abused* Imelda on three different occasions. Isn't this what happened?"

Fareed nodded. "Yes."

"This bitch," muttered Fiona, but chose to say nothing else.

———

In June, two months after Fareed had returned to Beirut, it was Fiona's turn to visit him. Her four-and-a-half-hour trip did not feel boring. As usual, she used the time to review her upcoming surgeries. When she got out of customs, she looked for Fareed but could not spot him. He was the one who was supposed to pick her up at the airport.

Instead, another young man approached Fiona. "Dr. Shaheen, isn't it? I am Sammy, Fareed's friend," he said.

"Sammy, hello, we have met before. How are you? I recall we met on one occasion. Where is Fareed, is he okay?" said Fiona.

"No, no, there is nothing wrong. Fareed is okay. He just got held up and I am here instead," answered Sammy.

"How about Dania? Fareed said she would pick me up when he happens to be busy," said Fiona.

Sammy paused for a few seconds. "He could not make it because of Dania."

"What is the matter?"

"I really don't know. All I know is that it is something to do with Dania," Sammy answered.

On their way to Fareed's apartment, Fiona learned that Sammy was Fareed's classmate and that the two had got to know each other through their political activities. Sammy was a member of the Syrian Popular Party and Fareed, although not a member, was a supporter of the same party. When they arrived, Sammy carried Fiona's bag and opened Fareed's apartment. As the two entered the foyer, they saw Fareed had taped a note onto a chair, placed to face them as they got there.

> *I am at the Melkite Catholic convent in the Zitouna District. I should be back within three hours, or you could come by, and we can all proceed from there to have an early dinner.*

"Do you want to meet Fareed at the convent?" he asked Fiona.

"Why not? I am Catholic, and I have never been to a Catholic church or convent anywhere outside Ireland."

———

When Sammy and Fiona arrived at the convent, Fareed emerged from behind a cordoned-off area. He was immediately followed by another nun.

"Mother, Sammy," Fareed said, happy to see them both.

"I am Mother Fatima," the nun behind him said.

"This is Sammy, and I am Fiona Burke-Shaheen, Fareed's mother," said Fiona. She turned to her son. "Why are you here, Fareed?"

"It is Imelda, Dania's maid. She beat her up badly this time," said Fareed, his voice low.

"Good God, this is the fourth time, and maybe there were more that we don't know about." Fiona's words were tinged with anger. "Where is she? Can I examine her?"

"Are you a nurse?" asked Mother Fatima.

"No, I am a physician," said Fiona.

"Oh, thank God, thank you blessed Mary; we cannot call a doctor every time we treat one of the unfortunate creatures. Yes, yes, please come in." Mother Fatima directed Fiona to where Imelda was.

Fiona examined Imelda, who was lying in bed, to find out that it was harsh abuse she had suffered at the hands of Dania. She was bruised all over and had a black eye.

Fiona looked at Mother Fatima. "Fortunately, nothing is broken, although she has been beaten badly. I will prescribe a sedative and an ointment." Fiona looked at Fareed and asked him to give Fatima twenty pounds for the medicine. "I am not going to say a word here, Fareed, but believe me, I have a lot to say at home."

As Fiona and Fareed were about to leave, Imelda appeared challenged trying to raise herself off the bed. Imelda looked at Fiona and pointed to her slacks, signaling that she wanted them slipped down. Fiona tried to slip them down gently. When Fiona lowered the slacks to Imelda's knees, all three were shocked at what they saw. There were two dozen fresh cigarette burns on both thighs, all the way to her panties.

"Fareed, please go out to the reception area," Fiona snapped, having forgotten to ask him out beforehand.

After Fareed left the room, Fiona slipped Imelda's panties off to find more cigarette burns on her genitalia. "Dania did that to you?" asked Fiona.

Imelda nodded, her lips pressed together.

Mother Fatima looked at Fiona shaking her head. "If I were not married to the Lord, I would go to her house and bash in her head."

"This is the work of a depraved animal, not that of a human being," said Fiona.

Fiona and Fatima left the room, after Fiona prescribed an antibiotic and anti-burn ointment. Fiona left for the reception area to speak to Fatima privately after trying to soothe Imelda's feelings. Both were steaming. Fiona also wanted to talk to Fareed. Seconds after Fiona attracted Fareed's attention, in came Dania.

Fatima looked up. "Help me, Lord, control my emotions."

Fiona said to Mother Fatima, "I can assure you that I am married to Ameer Shaheen; I am not married to the Lord." In a quick second she recalled what Fareed had taught her about how to slap a man. She followed Fareed's step-by-step instructions, slapping Dania as hard as she could. "Take the cross from around your neck; you are not a Christian."

Dania was on the floor looking at Fiona with shock. "You have no right to slap me! Imelda is my maid and I can do to her whatever I please. She was sleeping with the delivery boy."

"She is an adult, and just as you sleep with my son, she has the right to sleep with anyone she fancies. If she is to be denied, you also deserve to be denied. Anybody that sleeps with you deserves to have his penis cut off."

Fareed looked at his mother in astonishment, as if to say, *You are talking about me!*

Mother Fatima and Fareed looked away from Fiona, having witnessed her extreme anger. Fareed had never seen his mother that mad or use the kind of language she used with Dania. As she composed herself, Mother Fatima changed her stance and gazed at Fiona semi-approvingly, trying to conceal her full approval.

"Fareed, Sammy, let us get out of here. I wouldn't want to spend another second in the same room with this derelict," Fiona said, pointing at Dania and then shaking hands with Mother Fatima.

When they got to the apartment, Sammy wanted to leave, watching Fiona in a sour mood. Fiona insisted that Sammy stay. No sooner than they got into the apartment, she held Fareed by the arm and said, "When are you going to man up and use your revolutionary fervor where it belongs? You let a bimbo like her drag you into the most demeaning situations. Look at you trying to take care of a poor and abused creature, her housekeeper, for the last seven years. What will happen to you if you get married to her? You will become the diaper and trash boy! Wake up. You have a human lemon on your hands, a real psychological misfit!"

CHAPTER 4

The following day, Dania went to see Fareed at the AUB. She ran into him in the open, under a cedar tree. "She had no right to slap me. I can do with Imelda as I please," she told Fareed.

"Dania, this is not about my mother. It is about you and your attitude toward housekeepers or anybody you deem to be below your class," said Fareed.

"Your mother accused me of not being Catholic. Who is she to judge me? And you, what do you have to do with Imelda? After all, you are Muslim, and Imelda and I are both Catholic."

Fiona arrived, listening to Dania's refrain about her and Imelda being Catholic and Fareed being Muslim. Fiona and Fareed planned to go to lunch together.

"Four months ago, you wondered why Fareed could not convert to Catholicism," Fiona said, interrupting Dania. Fiona could not help but notice Dania's hypocrisy; Dania had wanted to convert Fareed to Catholicism to serve her purposes, but now she wanted to affirm him as Muslim to contrive a new and self-serving argument. "You argued that because I am Catholic and the one who raised him, he was supposed to be Catholic, all for you to marry him without inducing your clan's objections. Now since the situation has changed, you no longer want him to be Catholic. How convenient, how diabolical. I am afraid this shift in attitude will not work. He was raised Muslim and he chooses to remain Muslim, regardless. Fareed must also choose, either his father and me, or you. We cannot accept or tolerate any of this abuse toward others—and in the process, expect my son to clean up after you and accommodate your eccentricities and abusive behavior, to put it mildly. I never want to see you ever again. Do you hear me?" Fiona grabbed Fareed's arm and pulled him away, walking crisply.

Fareed showed no resistance. "I understand what you are saying, Mother. I am with you. Let go of my arm; we are leaving together."

———

That evening Fiona cooked dinner for Fareed and Sammy, who was about to arrive. As his mother cooked, Fareed told her that he trusted Sammy all the way, and that Sammy was more shocked than even they were at Dania's behavior toward Imelda. "He actually never liked Dania, from the very start. He was the one who told me about the Melkite Catholic convent. You don't need to worry, Mother. You can talk about Dania's behavior in his presence. He is extremely circumspect," said Fareed.

When Sammy got to Fareed's apartment, Fiona began, "I want to apologize to both of you for slapping Dania. I was totally incensed. Imelda may have permanent scarring on her genitalia. I have already talked to Dr. Malak at the AUB, and he is going to treat Imelda pro bono, and if Dania resists, he will have no choice but to report her situation to the police."

"No, Mother. Don't do that. I will talk to Dania over the phone, and if she does not heed our advice, she has nobody but herself to blame. As much as I dislike it, it is over between us," said Fareed. Sammy grasped Fareed's shoulder in a gesture of comradery and support.

"Fareed, I know that you care for Dania a lot, but she is not stable," Fiona said. "Just think if you were to marry her, you would worry about her abusing the children. This will ruin your life. I have already talked to my sister, Emily, and she will assist you with enrolling at University College Dublin. I don't think Dania will ever leave you alone."

"No, Mom, I don't want to leave the AUB, but if I do, I will transfer to Boğaziçi University in Istanbul. It has a remarkably similar curriculum to the AUB," said Fareed.

———

After Fareed called and told Dania about the plan to treat Imelda, he said his goodbyes and wished her well, in a formal and crisp fashion. From that point on, Fareed refused to answer Dania's phone calls. He heard that she went to the AUB looking for him. She had told a friend of hers that she didn't intend to give up on Fareed, even if she had to stalk him until he responded to her persistence. That conversation, among others, was relayed to Fareed and Fiona.

"Fareed, she's a stalker," Fiona said.

"She'll make your life at the AUB intolerable," Sammy added, on Fiona's side.

The prospect of Dania's unwelcome pursuit was a catalyst in Fiona relenting and accepting Boğaziçi University, instead of University College Dublin.

"Listen Fareed, you don't have to abandon the idea of visiting your aunt Emily; I am suggesting you spend the summer with her in Dublin. You know that she has no children of her own and she considers you the best and most gratifying substitute. She really loves you and cares for you and considers you as her own."

Sammy agreed with Fiona and Fareed grudgingly said yes. Over the next four weeks, until he finished his finals, Fareed managed to avoid running into Dania. In the meantime, Dania tried her best to get back with Fareed, but he adamantly resisted, with obvious pain and wistfulness. He was on his way to visit his aunt, with a stopover in London. Time away at a new place would do him some good.

————

When Fareed arrived in London, his father was ready for him. Ameer was good at handling such matters, but he rarely got involved and felt sanguine about relegating all his fatherly responsibilities to Fiona. Ameer arranged a dinner for the two of them. There, he tried to soothe Fareed's feelings by talking about his own experience.

"We did not have much dating at the refugee camp. I had gone out with half a dozen girls before I met your mother, all in London, but none developed into a strong relationship. It was your mother who could have broken my heart, but she seemingly would have broken her own in the process, and here we are today. Your mother and I want the best for you. I know that you will suffer in the meantime, but time will take care of things, and you will be able to look back and appreciate the wise decision of ending your relationship with Dania. I am here for you whenever you need me," said Ameer.

Fareed appreciated his father's concern and warmth. It was the only time Ameer and Fareed had spoken on a personal and deeper level. It was always Fiona who expressed herself to Fareed, but before any of their conversations got serious, most of it was expressed back and forth in jest, with nuances of competition between the two.

At Dublin's airport, Fareed was met by Emily and her husband, Michael. Emily met him with open arms and engrossed warmth. Emily wanted to develop a warmer relationship with Fareed. She chose, in the presence of Michael, to let Fareed know that he was going to inherit half of their estate; the other half going to Michael's nephews and nieces. Fareed was appreciative yet his mind was on the loss of Dania. Consciously, he knew she was seriously defective, but subconsciously, he cared and longed for her.

CHAPTER 5

Months passed. It was August 1981. Spending ten weeks in Dublin and London managed to help Fareed endure being without Dania. His conscious desire to let go of her helped a great deal. She was still on his mind, but gradually less frequently. He occupied himself with thinking of his studies and preparing for life in Istanbul, almost one year after a military council—the junta—overthrew the duly elected government. Based on the news media reports, he was not that concerned about the political situation in Turkey.

He was more concerned about finding all the supplies available in Lebanon and those provided to him by his mother, from London. He made sure to stock up on his favorite candy, marron glacé, an exquisite product of chestnut candied in sugar syrup. He preferred the French version. Fareed used to eat it after his basketball games. He bought his two Lebanese friends studying at Boğaziçi University a box each of marron glacé and stocked up with another three for himself.

Before he got on the plane, he took out all the literature he had about Boğaziçi University, having intended to go over it thoroughly on the two-hour-plus flight. He would have rather flown economy but chose to fly first class due to his height.

There were only four occupied seats in first class. He sat in 3-C, an aisle seat on the right. To his right was an older passenger. Within a minute, another passenger boarded, a young woman who sat across the aisle from Fareed. She took 3-B without Fareed having noticed her.

As Fareed started looking through the university brochures, the gentleman to his right looked at him. "You go to Boğaziçi? I did not see you among the group."

"Which group are you talking about?" said Fareed.

"I am Dr. Berke, the dean of engineering," he said, extending his hand toward Fareed.

"How interesting, I am Fareed Shaheen. I spoke with you two weeks ago, to finalize my admission. Do you recall? Thank you for agreeing to my starting this school year on such a short notice."

"It looks like you and I are the only ones from Boğaziçi in first class. There are over fifty in economy; they were taking courses at the University of Manchester for the summer, mostly English language," said Berke.

The young lady across the aisle said, "I too. I go to Boğaziçi."

Berke said hello in Turkish. Fareed looked at her; she was a stunning beauty. He extended his hand to shake hers. "Hi, I am Fareed Shaheen."

She did not reciprocate but responded with a faint hi, without looking Fareed straight on. She continued to go through her fashion magazine. Fareed pulled back his idle hand slowly, disappointed.

Dr. Berke, having noticed the lack of exchange and the spurned look on Fareed's face, said, "Having looked at your AUB grades, I know you are an excellent engineering student. Tell me about yourself, your likes and dislikes, your hobbies and your sports."

"Well, I play basketball; I swim and I jog. As to my hobbies, I am a student of languages, not necessarily to learn them but to analyze their roots, their structures and how they relate to each other. I am also an amateur photographer," said Fareed.

Dr. Berke asked many other questions and Fareed managed to ask a couple, mostly about the engineering program. Within half an hour, Berke got close to Fareed and whispered in his ear, "Don't worry; she has been taking sneak looks at you every couple of minutes. I think she likes you but does not know how to send the right signal."

"I haven't taken a careful look at her. Is she beautiful?" whispered Fareed, jokingly.

"She is gorgeous and rather tall," said Berke.

Fareed smiled, thanked Berke, and kept silent. He waited before he got up and opened the overhead compartment to fetch five pieces of marron glacé. He offered Berke one, which he declined since he was a diabetic. Fareed waited to finish his meal then went to the flight attendant, who was standing in the back of the first-class cabin. In the process he took a keener look at the girl across the aisle. He confirmed his first impression and agreed with Berke: She looked stunning.

More as a challenge than attraction, Fareed intended to know more about the woman in 3-B. He took two of the marron glacé candies and gently handed them to the flight attendant. As soon as he said, "Here are two marron glacé pieces," the flight attendant smiled then put her hand on her mouth to hide her surprise.

"I have a daughter almost your age. She is seventeen."

Fareed was taken aback but managed to recover in seconds. He knew his marron glacé introduction sequence was wrong. He realized that the flight attendant thought that the marron glacé were intended for her.

Fareed was quick. "Pardon me, you look so much younger; well, what can I say! Since you are not available, do you mind giving them to the lady in 3-B?"

The flight attendant, Marsha, blushed with full realization that she misconstrued Fareed's subject of interest, then said, "I am sorry, but I cannot serve anything not approved and supplied by British Air."

Fareed whispered in her ear, "Listen, there are only three passengers besides me. If you don't tell, I won't tell."

She smiled again, nodded, took the marron glacé, and was about to head toward the young lady. Fareed stopped her. "You need to repeat the word *marron glacé* to her, at least three times, okay?"

Marsha again nodded okay. She put the two marron glacé candies in a British Air saucer and offered them to the young lady. "Would you like to have some marron glacé after lunch?"

"I am not familiar with marron, marron what?" she asked.

"Marron glacé. It is the candy favored by the old aristocracy in France and northern Italy. It is made of chestnuts. Try it. I think you will like them," said Marsha.

Marsha gave her the candies and was about to leave. "Would

you like me to write marron glacé on a piece of paper for you?" she asked, trying to make sure the young woman would remember the name.

"No, no, I already remember the name—marron glacé," the woman in 3-B said. "Is marron with one R or two?"

"Two Rs. It is marron glacé," said Marsha.

Marsha went back to see Fareed standing in the back of the first-class cabin. Without speaking, she winked at Fareed, signaling it was a successful handout. Fareed went back to his seat and resumed his conversation with Berke.

"I forgot to mention that I am a student of social and cultural behavior. Do you see her handbag?" Fareed quietly pointed at the girl across the aisle. "I bet you she has matching luggage. This is the kind of thing I would like to look into, and to find out why they behave the way they do."

"Who are 'they'?" said Berke.

"In this case, it is the upper class," said Fareed.

"And how do you know she is an upper-class person?" Berke retorted.

"Everything about her says she is. Look at her clothing. Look at the magazines she is reading, look at her jewelry, and above all look at the level of confidence she has in herself," Fareed answered. "Would you be willing to wait with me for her luggage to come through? We can tell then if her luggage matches her handbag!"

Berke smiled and said, "You piqued my interest. I will wait with you."

Fareed and Berke changed the subject for the remaining forty minutes of the flight. Berke told Fareed that although he was also the vice chancellor at Boğaziçi University, he thought he would be teaching advanced aerodynamics this semester. Their voices were moderately loud, over the hum of the engines.

"I will be taking this course this coming semester," the woman in 3-B said, looking at Berke. "It is nice to know you are teaching it. I had one course with you before, Dr. Berke, but someone else took over for you one week into the course."

Berke told her that most of the time it was difficult for him to finish a full semester, mainly because his administrative duties were so demanding. Fareed said nothing but pleasantly took in the fact she had been following the conversation between him and Berke.

———

The three arrived at Istanbul and were waiting for their luggage. Fareed, who by now had got to know Dr. Berke better, asked him if he did not mind keeping the woman occupied when the luggage started coming in.

"I want to prove to you my socioeconomic observations that her kind would have matching handbag and luggage," said Fareed.

Amused, Berke agreed to try to keep her occupied. As soon as the luggage started to appear, Fareed winked at Berke and Berke headed to speak to her. Her luggage was the first to come out with a Turkish sticker that Fareed could not read.

Without telling Berke, Fareed managed to loosen the name tag off her first bag. The luggage matched her handbag. Fareed went toward Berke and her. "Are these your bags?" he asked Berke, so Berke would notice the luggage matching the handbag.

"No, no, they are not," said Berke after he noticed the matching luggage.

"Oh, no, they are my bags. Let them go around. I am waiting for someone," she said.

Fareed was disappointed with her answer, as he suspected that the person she was waiting for might have been her boyfriend or fiancé. He figured that she was not married since she was not wearing a wedding ring.

In no time, a man approached her. He was big, heavyset, and more than twice her age. His age and looks gave comfort to Fareed—the two could not have been a couple, he thought, but instead relatives.

She left after saying goodbye to Berke and looking at Fareed out of the corner of her eye. Fareed noticed the contact, albeit not a full contact. He showed Berke the luggage tag. It had one name on it—Nadidé—and around seventeen numbers.

Berke pointed at the luggage tag. "Look, she doesn't have her last name on the tag, and instead a code. That means she must be the daughter of a very senior government official. Besides, the gentleman who just showed up was her chauffeur–bodyguard," said Berke. "I could hear them talking."

Fareed smiled, to the surprise of Berke. When Berke asked him why he was smiling, Fareed said that he was afraid she would be met by her boyfriend or fiancé.

"Most probably she would be met by her fiancé, if she had one, and not usually a boyfriend. Turkey is not yet America or Europe. Interesting that her name is Nadidé," said Berke as he handed the tag back to Fareed.

"What does it mean? Does it mean anything or is it just a name?" asked Fareed.

Berke told him that it meant *rare*.

"This is remarkably interesting. We have in Arabic a similar name, Nadira, and it means *rare*. I bet they are related," said Fareed.

"Here you are, back to one of your interests, the origins of languages," said Berke before he bid Fareed goodbye.

CHAPTER 6

Fareed picked up his two suitcases and cleared customs. He was met by his two friends, Ramzi and Nader, both studying civil engineering at Boğaziçi University, having transferred from the AUB. After they shook hands, kissed on both cheeks, and hugged, it was Ramzi who asked Fareed in colloquial Lebanese Arabic, "How was your flight? Was the flight attendant good looking?"

Fareed had forgotten that love and sex were Ramzi's favorite subjects. He told Ramzi that the flight attendant was genuinely nice, a few years older, and had a seventeen-year-old daughter.

"Man, she said this on the flight? She must have been interested in you. Don't get involved with married women. They are more trouble than they're worth. We will find you a nice Turkish girlfriend. They are like Arab girls; they are more scheming but not as show-offish. They are usually not as smarty-pants as the girls in Lebanon."

Fareed stopped Ramzi and said, "I think I may have found the right girl. I have no plans to date but if I were to, she would be the one. I don't know her full name; her first name is Nadidé, and she must be studying mechanical engineering."

Fareed followed with telling Ramzi and Nader how she had been in first class, sitting across the aisle from him. He gave them full details of what happened between him, Berke, and Nadidé.

"Forget her," Ramzi said, waving his hand dismissively. "She did not pay much attention to you. I will fix you up with someone who will worship the floor you walk on. Look at you—tall, slim, and you take the best features of the Arabs and the best of the Irish. Let me ask you one thing: Is she tall?"

"By Middle Eastern standards, she is very tall. By American standards, she is pretty tall," said Fareed.

"I think I may know who you are talking about, very beautiful, isn't she?" asked Ramzi.

"You know, Ramzi, I am still licking my wounds over Dania. She is still on my mind although she is big trouble. Otherwise, I would have been more forward. Even if I get the chance, I don't think I will attempt to approach her right now; maybe in a month or two, if at all," said Fareed.

"Tonight, we are having dinner with our Turkish friends—you know who I mean—and they may know more about her. If she is who Ramzi is thinking about, a real beauty. Wait till this evening," added Nader.

———

That evening Fareed, Nadir, and Ramzi met with two student members of a small Turkish leftist and revolutionary party, Vatan

Partisi. One of them, Hussein Fahri, had met with the head of the Syrian Popular Party at an international leftist meeting in Europe. There, they agreed to cooperate on matters of mutual interest.

In the evening, Hussein asked Fareed if he could introduce himself, in political terms. The first item Fareed explained was that he was only a supporter and not a member of the Syrian Popular Party.

"I believe in the redistribution of income, but I do not believe in the total ownership of the means of production by the state. I think there should be an accommodation between socialism and capitalism. The latter is more efficient and the first is more equitable," said Fareed.

Hussein looked at Fareed. Smiling and with his eyes brightening, he said, "I like you. You are a romantic socialist. It is just that socialism and capitalism cannot coexist. You will find this in time. Let us first enjoy our raki and kebab. It is so nice to meet you, Fareed. I look forward to knowing you better. Nader and Ramzi think very highly of you."

"Oh, by the way, do you know an exceptionally beautiful tall girl? Her first name is Nadidé, and she is studying mechanical engineering," Nader asked Hussein.

"Why do you ask?" replied Hussein.

"Nothing special, just asking. If she is the one I am thinking about, she is beyond beautiful. I saw her talking to her friends," said Nader.

Hussein looked at Nader, rolling his eyes. "You do whatever you want. I think I know of her if she is studying mechanical engineering. My advice to you is to forget about her. She is very well known here, but she is trouble. Do you know who her father is?

She is the daughter of General Ali Hikmet. Although he is not a member of the junta, he possibly has more influence than even General Evren, the head of the junta. He intentionally lives in Istanbul, far away from Ankara, just in case the military council is attacked or killed over there."

Ramzi looked at Hussein and said, "Are you talking about Hikmet, who allegedly kidnapped eleven socialists whose whereabouts are unknown, and whom they may have already secretly executed?"

"He is the man," answered Hussein. "The rest is up to Nader."

Nader looked at Hussein and said, "No, no, the rest is up to Fareed. I have no interest in Nadidé whatsoever. I have never laid eyes on her. I am repeating what Fareed told me."

Fareed looked at them, not knowing what to say. He paused and then repeated himself: "I just broke up with my girlfriend in Beirut. I am not ready. I am numb about the whole thing."

"This is not the end of it, Fareed. This is not Beirut. Do you know how many have disappeared already at the hands of this junta? Let us take a reasonable guess, around one hundred thousand. You have to promise everyone here that you will forget about her. Nothing is worth dying for, except of course the cause," said Ramzi.

Fareed was not in disagreement except that his emotions were stronger than his logic; he was trying to prove to himself that he was not stuck on Nadidé, although the reality of his feelings belied his best intentions.

It was a pleasant meeting and Fareed enjoyed it thoroughly except for what he heard about Nadidé's father. Istanbul was not unfamiliar to Fareed. He had been there three times before, and he liked the city a lot. It was a less costly city than Beirut and the fast food was on par with Lebanese cuisine, similar but with a Turkish inclination. His pleasant thoughts about the city did not relieve him of the anxiety Hussein, Nadir, and Ramzi's admonitions caused him, about Nadidé and her father.

On the way back to Ramzi and Nader's apartment, Fareed was pensive, wondering what to do about Nadidé. Nader and Ramzi noticed him saying little but decided to say nothing. While both did not like Dania much, they knew that Fareed was still smitten with her and they did not want to compound his wistful feelings by harping about dating and love affairs.

Per Fareed's suggestion, the three roommates ate out once a day, hopping from one favorite and affordable restaurant to another. They spent ten days together before orientation started, itself a two-day affair. The second day was orientation specific to the school of engineering. Fareed was hoping to run into Nadidé, but that did not happen.

He was still thinking about her. "Since I was originally a mechanical engineering major, I'll take Dr. Berke's course in aero-dynamics," he said to himself and to his friends. It was the same one Nadidé had said she would take. It was an eleven a.m. class and would be Fareed's first of the day, on Mondays, Wednesdays, and Fridays.

———

On the first Monday of classes, Fareed went to the school of engineering half an hour early. After he located his classroom, he decided to stroll back and forth in the lobby in the hope of running into Nadidé. As he tired from walking he decided to go out to the yard, in front of the engineering building.

At the same time, Nadidé was coming into the building.

He noticed her right away. She was looking down and did not see him at first. When she did, he winked at her. She passed him without having the time to react, but she slowed down. He slowly turned around and followed her into the classroom.

She went up three steps and turned around, sitting in the third row, aisle seat right. Fareed intentionally went up the same way, tilting his head toward her as he stepped up. He smiled as he got close to her. She smiled back. He went up two more steps and sat in row five, aisle seat on the left. He could clearly see her, but she had to take a half turn backward to see him.

In less than a minute she took her first look backward. He winked at her again and she smiled agreeably.

As she was looking at him, a tall and handsome student attempted to sit next to Nadidé. She looked at Fareed again then back to the student. "I'm sorry, this seat is taken." Fareed took note of that and smiled.

And so it went, Fareed observing her through the session and she taking sneak looks at him every few minutes. Neither of them noticed that the professor, who arrived five minutes late, was not Dr. Berke. Their concentration was not on him or the first lecture, which covered only an introductory discussion of the subject matter.

The class ended and Nadidé stayed in her seat. Fareed stood up, walked toward her, and placed two marron glacé pieces on her desk. He paused as she looked at him.

He looked back at her intently and said, "Marron glacé," hoping

that she remembered the name repeated to her by the flight attendant. He turned around, walking down and out of the classroom.

She took the marron glacé in her hand, wondering for a while,
before she figured out that the marron glacé on the flight to Istanbul
was from him. After she licked and then bit her lip, pondering, she
headed out, walking slowly, nodding and smiling. As she emerged
from the classroom, Fareed was standing there. He swung his head
backward to witness her grinning at him. She hoped he had enrolled
in the aerodynamics class because of her.

Fareed turned and sped out of the building while Nadidé
walked slowly, her mood pleasant and amused. She got out of the
engineering building, heading to see her best friends, Naz and
Deniz. She sat between them in front of the building. Her expression gave her away; it projected a clear glow.

"Ah, you seem to like Dr. Berke a lot. How was he?" asked Naz.

"It was not Dr. Berke. It was another professor, much younger."

"What is his name?" said Naz.

"I don't know. He was late. He may have introduced himself,
but I did not pay attention to his name."

Deniz interjected sarcastically, "How come? You were only
interested in his looks?"

"No, I was looking at someone else. Someone I saw on the
plane from London. He gave me those—marron glacé, same as the
ones he gave me on the plane. They are a drier French version of our
Turkish *kestane şekeri*," said Nadidé.

"You never said anything about someone giving you those on
the plane!" said Naz.

"Well, he gave them to the flight attendant to give to me, and I
thought they were from the airline. I think today he wanted me to

know it was from him," said Nadidé.

"And what does this all mean?" Deniz asked.

"It means that he likes me and I like him," said Nadidé.

"Is this Nadidé talking, the same one who has not dated for the last four years? You sound like you are in a daze," said Naz.

"No, I am not. I must go. I am having lunch with my mother. We'll talk on Wednesday, same time," said Nadidé.

After she left, Naz and Deniz looked at each other in a baffled way. They had not seen Nadidé in such posture. She had invariably turned down tens of attempts by other students since her junior year in high school. The two left, promising to probe further into this transformation on the part of Nadidé.

———

On Wednesday, Fareed got to class early. He looked in to find that Nadidé was not there yet, so he stood in front of the classroom door. The same professor arrived and stood at the door, welcoming one student after another.

Nadidé arrived and went into the classroom, passing Fareed. She did not want to draw the attention of the professor and pretended she did not notice Fareed. Fareed followed her to where Nadidé was standing next to the same desk she was sitting at on Monday. When Fareed got next to her, she signaled him to sit in her desk. He did so hesitantly and slowly. She then went up and sat where he had sat on Monday.

As the session started, Fareed realized what Nadidé was doing: She wanted to relay to him that sitting the way they had on Monday put her at a disadvantage, having to turn back to look at him. Fareed turned back and smiled at Nadidé, signaling that he realized what she was doing.

As the professor turned his back to write on the blackboard, Fareed went down two steps and sat across the aisle from Nadidé. She smiled and nodded approvingly.

In the middle of the session, the professor stopped his lecture and apologized for arriving late on Monday and introduced himself as Dr. Chakir. He added, "I am sorry to disappoint those of you who were expecting Dr. Berke. He will not be teaching this course this semester; I will be his replacement. I usually alternate teaching one electrical engineering course one semester and one mechanical the other. But because Dr. Berke is now the acting president of the university, due to the president's recent medical procedure, I will once again teach two courses of mechanical engineering this semester."

He proceeded to read the roll alphabetically, in an attempt to get acquainted with his students. When he came to read Nadidé's last name, Fareed got his assurance that she was the daughter of General Hikmet; and when Fareed's name was called, he was pleasantly surprised as his name was pronounced in proper Arabic, rather than nuanced Turkish.

Both Nadidé and Fareed were in a state of befuddled amusement and anticipation, pleased they were sitting across the aisle from each other. They took turns gauging one another. Fareed's very handsome looks were a match to Nadidé's beauty. The chemistry between them was showing on the surface, projected by their expressions.

After class was over, Fareed waited for Nadidé to leave first. She hesitated, waiting for him, but when she saw him sitting down in his desk, she went out of the classroom slowly. He followed and caught up with her on her left, turned his head, and smiled at her. She responded likewise.

Fareed did not share the news of their encounter with any of his friends.

———

On Friday, Fareed once again was at his desk, waiting while looking out through the glass portion of the classroom door, trying to notice Nadidé's arrival. This time, he had one of his books on his desk and another across the aisle, on Nadidé's desk, placed there to reserve the seat for her. Fareed hoped that Nadidé had noticed how Dr. Chakir had pronounced his name. Yet he did not want to take a chance; he placed a piece of marron glacé on her desk, wrapped in white paper.

When she unwrapped the white paper, she could see a note.

> *Did you notice how Dr. Chakir pronounced my name? It is Fareed, not Ferid, like it is pronounced in Turkish! I have noticed your name. It is the same as was on the tag of your suitcase, Nadidé.*

Suddenly Nadidé realized where her suitcase tag went. On top of his sending her the marron glacé, he had also stolen her suitcase tag. She looked at Fareed and discreetly shook her index finger at him, all the while smiling. They both left the classroom in the best of moods.

CHAPTER 7

Nadidé went to meet with Naz and Deniz in the courtyard of the engineering school, where they sat around a concrete table. All three had gone to high school and graduated together. She wanted to share with them her thoughts and her new experience, but she hesitated. Naz noticed Nadidé's confusion.

"What is the matter with you today, Nadidé?" asked Naz. "You don't seem all together."

"I don't know how to say it. I met the same guy again. He is very interesting."

"This time you have met him! Good God, what happened? For you, this is consistency. It has been a long time since you looked at anyone twice! Where did you meet him, same as before in the aerodynamics class?" asked Deniz.

"Yes, he is the same one, in my aerodynamics class, Dr. Chakir's class."

"This is great. Can we say Nadidé is in love? I have decided to take the same course; I will start this coming Monday," said Naz.

"You can point him out to me."

"How come you will be taking the same class?" inquired Nadidé.

"You forget, I, your friend, am also a mechanical engineering student. Come out with it, tell us the whole story. We know about the flight from London. What else is there?"

Nadidé went ahead to repeat the same story, telling them about the series of encounters, starting with the flight from London to Istanbul, and the last one ending just minutes ago in the aerodynamics class. "He has been sending me notes with marron glacé," she finished.

"You mean, you haven't talked to him at all. What kind of nonsense is this? Have you even heard his voice?" said Deniz.

"Yes, I heard him talk to Dr. Berke on the plane and he also asked a question of Dr. Chakir. He seems to speak perfect English. His name is Fareed, but I don't know where he is from. He is not Turkish," said Nadidé.

Deniz gave Nadidé a pointed look and said, "Look, Nadidé, you sound confused. Take it easy. Naz will be with you on Monday. Point him out to her and she will give us her opinion of this mysterious guy. After all, Naz will be eager to share her opinions whether we ask for it or not."

———

On Monday, Nadidé took the same seat across from Fareed's. She asked Naz in advance to sit behind her. When Fareed arrived, Nadidé signaled him to sit across from her. Fareed snickered and smiled approvingly, without saying anything. Naz took a good and sneaky look at him. Looks-wise, she more than liked what she saw. She poked Nadidé in her back and signaled her high approval to Nadidé by first shadowing her face with her palm, referring to Fareed's looks, and then giving a firm okay with her thumb and index finger, all concealed from Fareed. Nadidé and Naz smiled broadly.

When the session was over, Fareed looked at Nadidé and signaled that he was leaving her one piece of marron glacé on his desk, then left the classroom. Naz followed everything closely. Nadidé hurried to pick up the marron glacé, then she and Naz left together. She unwrapped the marron glacé to find a message from Fareed.

I transferred from the American University of Beirut to finish my last two years here. I started studying mechanical engineering first and then switched to electrical. My name is Fareed Shaheen, just as you may have heard from the roll call. Enjoy your day, Nadidé. See you on Wednesday.

Nadidé and Naz ran to see Deniz. They both considered her to be the wisest of the three. Naz, before sitting down, told Deniz, "I saw him. He is very handsome. My God, his sparkling eyes; he must be an Arab, from his name and from the fact he was studying at the AUB."

"Okay, he is very handsome, but what do we *know* about him?" Deniz asked. "He may be a playboy trying to sample Turkish girls. No, I still say be careful. Nadidé, you just had a look at the appetizers; you haven't tasted the main dish yet, and you know the

Lebanese are known to be master playboys. They learned it from the French."

The three agreed that they needed to investigate Fareed further. Naz offered to take the initiative in the aerodynamics class.

"Naz, please don't do anything without letting me know first," said Nadidé.

"Good God Nadidé, you really like Fareed. I can tell, you are so concerned we will spoil it for you," said Deniz.

"No, no, not that; I don't want things to get complicated unnecessarily. You know, Ata is still in the picture—not as far as I am concerned, but as far as he and Father are," said Nadidé.

"I have totally forgotten about Major Ata Aslan. Have you ever indicated to your father that you were not ready to get married to Ata or anybody else?" said Naz.

"You know, my dad—he thinks Ata is the perfect candidate. He was the first in his class at the air force academy and he traces his Muslim and Turkish roots to the fifteenth century. His ancestors participated in kicking the Byzantine Empire out of Turkey. He is good looking, not as good looking as Fareed, but I don't have feelings for him. He is too militaristic. He is not my type," said Nadidé.

Deniz spoke and asked everyone just to take it easy. "Let us find as much as possible about Fareed and then we can talk about things, including Major Ata. Let us not worry about it now."

———

Fareed went to the apartment he was sharing with Ramzi and Nader. He was surprised that Nader was still looking into Nadidé's family background, and all through her father's background.

"Fareed, look at this article. It is an interview with General Ali Hikmet. Look at what he is saying: that a true Turk is a Turk that has been Muslim Sunni and Turkish, at the same time, for three generations, and that he would not consider marrying his daughter or his nieces to anybody that does not fit these criteria," said Nader.

"You are not Turkish, are you?" said Ramzi sarcastically.

"No, I am not," Fareed answered. "But I would like to learn Turkish. I am taking three courses this semester. I have plenty of time, maybe three hours a day."

"This is easy; I know three guys who work together and who teach conversational Turkish. They have an intensive program. They keep talking to you until you learn the language."

————

The following day Fareed met with the three students and decided to start having them tutor him, three hours a day, six days a week. They dubbed their style of tutoring as "Situation Language Tutoring," which meant that they would describe the situation first and then teach what to say and how to respond.

Fareed liked what he learned about their method. He bought six different Turkish language books. They started teaching him what to say when he woke up, when he left for school, and how to greet his teacher. It went from there to every conceivable situation, while at the same time he would go through some of the vocabulary and grammar books he had bought.

As usual, the three tutors started with teaching Fareed Turkish cuss words, "situation" style. The leader of the three tutors was a geology student, Nezam. He took on the task of teaching Fareed what to say to girls, depending on the situation. Nezam would describe the situation and then advise Fareed as what to say and how to answer. He got to the situation where a girlfriend would slap him or seriously insult him. Nezam told Fareed to call her, "You fossilized bitch." It was not an insult used in Turkey but Nezam, being creative and studying geology, took the liberty of contriving this term. Fareed could hardly appreciate the weirdness and the impropriety of the expression.

A couple of days later a student stopped Fareed and told him, "My name is Murat. I have talked to Nader and Ramzi. We happen to be friends, good friends. I am a supporter of Vatan Partisi. We think it is our duty to let you know that you are putting your life in danger if you happen to have anything to do with General Hikmet or his daughter. He is an extremely dangerous man, and he has vicious friends and many honorable enemies. If you do not heed our advice, you are on your own. We wanted to be fair to you and forewarn you. The rest is up to you."

Murat said no more and left. At first, Fareed took Murat's warning to heart but could not make up his mind. During the following class, he held back and looked at Nadidé twice. He left without his usual last look and wink. Both Nadidé and Naz suspected something was wrong.

Nadidé waited for the following class. She, without talking about it with her two buddies, left him a wrapped something that looked like marron glacé. She placed it on his desk. When he got there, he unwrapped it to find a piece of Turkish Delight. In it there was a note:

I don't have marron glacé to answer you. I have Turkish Delight. What is wrong? You didn't seem to be your usual self. From now on, I will use Turkish Delight—okay?

Fareed liked the fact she was inquiring about him. Her inquiry served to have him disregard the warning by Murat. He particularly liked the fact that she indicated that she would in the future send him messages. After the class was over, he left her another marron glacé with a message:

Thank you for asking about me. I fell playing basketball, and was not feeling well. I feel much better today. How are you? I have been playing too much basketball since I have not been swimming my three kilometers every day!

With that made-up story, he tried to cover up the reason behind his attitude during the prior class.

Before Fareed left the classroom, Dr. Chakir approached Fareed and asked to see him after class. On her way out, Nadidé looked obliquely at Fareed, smiled and nodded, indicating that she felt better about his condition. Chakir did not notice Nadidé's gesture.

Chakir and Fareed went to the professor's office. There, Chakir started talking to Fareed in fluent Arabic. "My name is Tolga Chakir. I am Turkish and my father is Turkish, but my mother is from Syria."

"Wow, you speak Arabic as a native—fantastic," said Fareed.

Dr. Chakir told Fareed that Shaheen was a relatively common family name in Palestine, Syria, and Lebanon. "Where are you from?" he asked.

"I am Palestinian, born in the United States. My parents were living in the United States at the time."

"The reason I wanted to talk to you is because you seem to be one of the top students in my class despite the fact you are an electrical engineering student," Chakir lied. The real reason he wanted to talk to Fareed was that Chakir had suspected there was a small possibility Fareed could be related to his Palestinian wife, Leila. Her maiden name was Shaheen. When he got home in the evening, after the name Shaheen popped up in roll call the previous week, he had started probing. He asked Leila about her relatives. Her father had only one brother and no sisters, and the two brothers had a falling out over her grandfather's will. Her father had left the refugee camp and migrated to Chile while her uncle stayed behind.

Tolga had heard all of this before but wanted to make sure. "What does your uncle do?" he had asked his wife.

"When my father died, he had stated in his will to be buried in Palestine. My mother and I did not know what to do. Finally, after ten years, we called my uncle in London and he arranged the whole thing, a village funeral. That was the only time he and I spoke. We haven't since. I don't know why we did not maintain a relationship; neither my mother nor I knew who was in the right, my father or my uncle. My uncle donated the land in contention to have a girls' school built on it, in the village. It did not seem like a case of greed, on my uncle's part," she said.

"You didn't tell me—what does your uncle do?" asked Tolga.

"Oh, I have told you in the past that he is a rather well-established neurosurgeon in London; so is his wife. I understand she is Irish," she said. When Leila noticed Tolga's engaged reaction, she asked, "Why are you asking?"

"Nothing, really. I just got a call from my own uncle, the first time in three years. So, the subject of family came to mind," Tolga said to Leila, making up a story.

————

When Tolga had his next aerodynamics lecture, Fareed and Nadidé resumed their playful, touch-free and speech-free relationship. He would wink at her, and she would smile at him. Naz was taken by the whole process.

When Nadidé and Naz met with Deniz, Naz told Nadidé, "What is this—you and Fareed have gone back a hundred years? He winks and you smile, and yet you don't even speak to each other. When are you going to say something to him?"

Deniz said, "Well, Nadidé does not like Ata, but she does nothing about it, and she likes Fareed and does nothing about it. Where does that put her, I don't know. I understand if you don't want to tell others that you don't admire them, but not telling those whom you admire that you do like them is new to me."

"I am waiting for him to say something first," said Nadidé.

"No, you are procrastinating because you don't know what to do. I am not telling you what to do. My advice is that you think about it and make a decision—your *own* decision. This is not healthy," said Deniz.

For the first time Nadidé felt she had a minor tactical impasse on her hands. In her mind, she knew she didn't want to marry Ata Aslan, and at the same time she wanted to get closer to Fareed. She surmised she was using her strange relationship with Fareed to forget about her dilemma with Ata.

———

In Monday's class, after Nadidé had spent the weekend pondering her situation, a mild relief came from Fareed. He sent her a note with a marron glacé:

> Can I call you Nadira instead of Nadidé? Nadira
> means the same in Arabic as Nadidé does in
> Turkish. Both mean rare.

As he was leaving class that Monday, Dr. Chakir stopped Fareed. "The fact you studied one year of mechanical engineering and then switched to electrical engineering intrigues me. You see, I have a doctorate in mechanical and another in electrical engineering. Do you mind if we can discuss this over dinner? My wife cooks great Arabic food. She is Palestinian."

Fareed was pleasantly surprised that Dr. Chakir was married to a Palestinian. He had not met any in Istanbul by then. He agreed.

When he got to Chakir's flat in the evening, the first thing that Chakir asked him was for Fareed to call him Tolga in social settings. That was okay with Fareed. Fareed entered the apartment to find a very good-looking woman in her late twenties—Leila,

Tolga's wife. Tolga intentionally introduced his guest without mentioning his last name.

"Tolga tells me that you are from Palestine, where in Palestine?" she asked.

Tolga interjected, "You are both from Palestine, you know Palestine is a small country. Fareed was born in the United States and was raised between London and Beirut."

The conversation shifted to why Fareed had transferred from the AUB to Istanbul. Fareed said that he had become bored. He had finished high school from the preparatory section of the AUB and after two years of college at the AUB, he did not want to spend the last three years at the same place. He intentionally avoided saying anything about his affair with Dania.

Leila backtracked to ask Fareed. "You are Fareed; what is your last name?"

Tolga suddenly asked Leila if he could speak to her in their bedroom; Leila looked at Tolga sideways, as if to say, *What is going on here?*

In the bedroom Tolga asked Leila to sit down. She kept looking at him thinking that he was going to convey some tragic news.

"Please, please calm down. I am going to tell you something rather pleasant; just control yourself. Stay calm. I think Fareed is your cousin, the son of your uncle in London. I know this because his last name is Shaheen, and both his father and mother are neurosurgeons. I looked up this information in his file but have said nothing to him. He does not know that he is your cousin," said Tolga.

"What are you saying, Tolga? Are you sure? Why do you do this to me? Why didn't you tell me in advance?" She started crying, loud enough for Fareed to hear her.

After Tolga calmed Leila down, he took her hand and said, "Let us go back into the living room or else Fareed will think we are fighting."

"Honestly, Tolga, you deserve a slap on the face," said Leila.

"I know. I was trying to surprise you and him, but somehow it got bungled. I apologize."

Tolga and Leila left the room, but not before she picked up their eleven-month-old daughter, Nermin. Leila walked slowly toward Fareed. "Excuse me, Fareed, for a second. Do you mind if I look inside your shirt? There is a small fly."

She pulled the edge of his collar away from his neck, to look for a birthmark she remembered well from her youth. It was there. She paused, breathing heavily, looking at Fareed.

"Tolga is a bastard. He should have told you in advance. He just told me. I am Leila, your cousin. Don't you remember me? You used to call me Auntie, don't you recall?"

Fareed looked at her with total amazement, stood up, and did not know what to say at first. As he eased out of his surprise, he said, "Oh my God. Now I recognize you. Oh my God!" He hugged her and Nermin together. Nermin started crying, startled at the whole thing. As Leila comforted Nermin, they all sat down with Leila tearing up.

"So, you are Fareed, my uncle Ameer's son!"

Fareed did not know what to do. He got off his chair erratically and grabbed it before it could fall on the floor, with a rattled look on his face.

Leila realized that Fareed had not had an inkling either. To Tolga she said, "You keep doing the same thing. Why are you obsessed with surprising people? I keep wondering why you behave like this!" Leila then looked at Fareed and said, "I recall so vividly when you used to call me Auntie. You started calling me that at the age of five and continued until we separated when you were eight. We are cousins, but whenever you and your parents visited Beirut, you thought you were visiting your aunt."

It took Fareed quite a while to absorb all of this and it took handing Nermin to him to soothe his anxiety. Nermin took to Fareed right away.

The conversation that evening continued for three hours. Leila insisted that Fareed come to dinner the following three evenings as she wanted to visit with him much more. He obliged her and Tolga with great anticipation.

CHAPTER 8

Nadide was thinking about Fareed's request to call her Nadira, the Arabic version of the same name. She consulted with Deniz and Naz. What bothered the three was why. When they inquired from Nadidé if she ever called him Ferid, the Turkish version of Fareed, she said she had called him Ferid one time, but thereafter she called him Fareed.

"Then insist on him calling you Nadidé; let us figure out more about his personality and let us see what he says," said Deniz.

"Actually, this kind of give-and-take will reveal more about his character. Let us see how he reacts when you do that, Nadidé," said Naz.

Nadidé left him a Turkish Delight, which contained a written message:

Just like you, I like to be called by my real name, Nadidé. Thanks.

Unlike her previous notes, it was signed for the first time,
Nadidé.

The next class, he delivered his message with the marron glacé.

*Don't do anything you don't want to do. It will end
up bothering you.*

She shared the same message with Deniz and Naz. They found
the statement encouraging and positive.

"I think he knows about the major. He is trying to use his
approval of your choices to indirectly buttress your resolve not to
marry Ata. Somebody must have told him," said Naz.

Once again Deniz saved the day. "Let us see what happens
next!"

While Fareed and Nadidé exchanged glances and smiles,
they did not exchange messages for a week. Deniz was getting
tense about the whole thing of neither one talking directly to the
other. She thought it was more than unusual; it was weird. Deniz
wondered to Naz and Nadidé if he were just playing a game and not
seriously interested.

"Maybe he has a girlfriend in Lebanon," said Deniz.

"I would not be surprised. Let us be honest. He is very handsome. I know he is Nadidé's prospect, but I cannot help it—he has a
very sexy tush. Three girls in our class alone have already approached
him. Did you see Seda? She almost gave him a kiss when she asked
him if she could whisper in his ear. No, I would not be surprised if
he has a girlfriend! They are referred to as Franco–Arab. They are
Arabs but pretend to be French, and try to act as French, especially

when it comes to dealings with the opposite sex. This is no longer a joke. We need to find more about his background. We don't want you to be disappointed. Let us think of a way as soon as possible," said Naz.

The following class, Nadidé got a new message. In it he asked Nadidé if he could call her Nad. She snickered when she first read the note, specifically at the idea that Fareed was insisting she change her name. She did not wait for the next class. She left him a note saying that she would think about it. The following class, he sent her a new note:

> *I want you to think hard about everything that has happened or will ever happen between us. You are the master of your destiny.*

When Nadidé met with Naz and Deniz next, the three of them agreed that his second piece of advice for Nadidé to be "the master of her destiny" meant he surely knew about Ata Aslan.

"Maybe he doesn't want to talk in person until you separate yourself from the prospect of marrying Ata," said Naz.

"I think this is it. Why should he waste his time on someone who is going to marry somebody else? He might be a very honorable man who cares for you, but he does not want to hurt you and torment himself," said Deniz.

"Deniz, for God's sake, say it. Say it as it is. Maybe he loves Nadidé. What is this 'care for you' business? We are mature, twenty-year-old advanced college students. We are not old-fashioned housewives," said Naz.

"Maybe Nadidé loves Fareed. You know, love through the ether! Maybe it is love at first sight. Did you hear Nadidé last time? Didn't you say that he combs his hair with his palm, as if he is massaging his brain, whenever he is thinking of an answer? This is a lover's kind of talk. Isn't it, Nadidé?" said Deniz.

"You girls, sure I like him a lot but how could I love somebody I haven't even talked to?"

"Don't give me this. You love him based on certain expectations. You already know how he looks, and you are hoping that the rest of him is as good as he looks. You also seem to like how he walks and how he treats his hair. Don't give me this," said Naz. She added, "Fareed talked to Dr. Chakir twice after class. I think Chakir may be a good source. I can talk to him. Chakir has never seen us together. How about it?"

"No, wait, let us try to come up with something else," said Nadidé.

"By the way, Nad is not a bad name. After all, my real name is Nazle and I go by Naz all the time. I never even think much about Nazle," said Naz.

The three felt challenged as they tried to advance the situation. Nadidé on her own decided to send Fareed a message to tell him that she did not mind being called Nad. She did not want him to think she was negative about all his proposals.

The following class, before Nadidé gave him her note, for the first time he walked to Nadidé and looked her in the face, his body almost touching hers. With a smile, he stood next to her with confidence, almost as if they had known each other for some time. He gave her a marron glacé and a note.

*Can we meet next to the phone booths in the lobby,
at 10:15 this coming Wednesday? We will not talk.
We will not touch. I just want to give you something.*

While surprised about his mentioning no touch and no talk, Nadidé nodded approvingly twice. She gestured him to wait. She wrote a new note and exchanged it with the old one. The note said, *Yes, yes*, mirroring her two nods. She gave it to him with a broad smile.

———

On Wednesday, he was waiting for her when she arrived. She faced him, standing ten feet from him, and smiled. There was a shelf where the students sometimes sorted their mail and looked up phone numbers in the phone directory. Fareed had an envelope in his hand. He placed the envelope on the shelf and slid it toward her. She took the envelope, which was closed but not sealed, and opened it. In it there was a single typewritten sheet of paper.

*These are some of the most beautiful women in the
history of mankind.*

> *Joan of Arc*
> *Helen of Troy*
> *Eleanor of Aquitaine*
> *Berenice of Cilicia*
> *Wallada of Cordoba*

She looked at the list but could not understand what the meaning of the list was. She gave Fareed a foggy look, trying to elicit some explanation. Fareed decided not to accommodate her. She left disappointed, and in a slightly confused mood. She was expecting something new that would have made her happy, and for her to take the opportunity to thank him approvingly. She thought that it would have been a clear step forward since he already advanced to asking her to meet him in person.

She met with her two friends.

"What is he trying to say, that you are beautiful but not as beautiful as these women were, or that he is in love with historical beauties? He is weird," said Naz.

Deniz said, "Let us take a breather. This is too much of a game for me. I think he needs to explain himself. Nadidé, you no longer should treat him agreeably; just pretend that nothing has happened and let him come to you and wonder why you have become distant. Do you agree with me, Nadidé?"

"Yes, I sure do. I think he is trying to confuse me. I don't like it," said Nadidé.

"Let us go and make copies and each of us can study it on our own; maybe we'll come up with something," said Naz.

They all agreed and made two copies.

Nadidé and Fareed exchanged no messages during the following aerodynamics class. In the meantime, Naz did research on each woman on the list. She was intrigued by the name she had never heard of before, Wallada of Cordoba.

"Look, girls, what I have found. Wallada was an Arab princess in the eleventh century, in Cordoba, Spain. But guess what—she used to go into the market in her see-through tunic. I mean, the way they describe her, it was totally see-through. You have not heard the half of it. She believed in and promoted sex between lovers, and she had a relationship with at least two lovers. Neither one ever married her."

"Where did you get all of this?" asked Deniz as Nadidé sat in a dismayed silence.

"I got it from the professor who teaches the history of Islamic Spain," Naz said.

Nadidé was mildly enraged and left without saying goodbye. She felt embarrassed and humiliated. She thought that Fareed was priming her for a sexual relationship. The next class, she left him a long note, before the class started.

> *Who do you think you are and who do you think I am? I know why you have included the name Wallada. You want me to be like her, a harlot, poetess or not! Well, that is not who I am. I am neither a poetess nor loose, like her. So, you might as well try your luck with somebody your kind. If you write to me again like this, you will not be happy at all. Wallada must already be in Hell.*

Fareed read the note. "I really screwed up this time," he murmured to himself. Shocked, he stood up, looked at Nadidé with a darkened face, and slowly left the classroom exhibiting a hurt demeanor. Naz looked at Nadidé trying to see if Nadidé was as confused as she was about his reaction.

Nadidé said nothing. As her eyelids became heavy over her bulging eyes, one teardrop came down her cheek, touching the edge of her mouth. Nadidé did not try to wipe it off. She might have been too harsh on Fareed—and she had just realized it.

Dr. Chakir came into the classroom. Five minutes into his lecture, he noticed that Fareed was not there. "Has anyone seen Fareed?" he asked the class.

Naz raised her hand. "Fareed was here earlier but he looked like he was not feeling well."

Nadidé looked at Chakir and said, "I am not feeling well either. I think I need to go home." She got up and left.

Chakir looked at Naz. "How about you, Nazle hanim?" he asked, using a formal "Miss Nazle."

"No, no, I am perfectly all right," said Naz.

After class, an unusually somber Naz went to meet with Deniz. "Today I saw a truly dejected, dumbstruck, and sad man. He looked like he was in shock, alone and forlorn. I, on the other hand, felt guilty—and, I believe, so did Nadidé. We must have screwed up somehow. We were carried away with our analysis."

When Naz told Deniz that Nadidé could not take it and excused herself to go home, Deniz said nothing for a long while. Naz asked her to say something.

Deniz answered in a hushed voice, "I think Nadidé can fix the damage. It is not the end of the world. Let us think and try to fix it. I will call Nadidé this evening. Let things simmer down for a few hours."

CHAPTER 9

The following class came about with Nadidé and Fareed in a somber mood. She took the first move. As the session started, Nadidé left a piece of Turkish Delight, including a message. It was written in large cursive style. It said, *I am terribly sorry*, and nothing more.

Fareed looked at Nadidé with a serious face and a blank look. He pointed at an envelope then left the classroom.

She picked the envelope up while Naz was looking at her curiously. The envelope contained no marron glacé, just a one-page typewritten letter.

> *I have not included any marron glacé in this envelope since there is nothing sweet about what happened in the last few days. The reason things were going the way they were is because I knew much about your family and some about you*

personally. You, on the other hand, know nothing about me or my background, other than being here to study electrical engineering. I thought a slow give-and-take would give you the opportunity to know me better, sufficiently better for us to start speaking to each other.

I cannot tell you about myself. This is not a sales job. You need to know me through my actions and interactions. I did not mean to compare your personality to Wallada's or to the personalities of any of the other beauties. I wanted to compare your beauty to their historically recognized beauty.

No, you would not wear the same kind of clothing. No, you would not have multiple lovers, and no, you would not have premarital relations with each of them. I like you as you are. I like the way you walk, the way you talk, and the way you dress. I like the way you smile at me and the way you respond to my smiles. When I do not see you, I worry and I wonder about you, and I miss everything about you, even when I learn that your absence was for no urgent reason.

I thought that you thought of me in the same manner I think of you. I may have been mistaken. For that I apologize. I apologize for not being more circumspect and for inadvertently giving you the impression that I was comparing your potential actions to Wallada's proven actions. I was only com-paring your beauty to hers and the others.

I wish you well and I wish you happiness, now and in the future, wherever you live and whomever you choose as your friend. I am truly sorry.

> *Your friend,*
> *Fareed*

When she finished reading Fareed's note, Nadidé took her sunglasses from her purse and put them on as she teared up.

Naz came to sit next to Nadidé. Naz wanted to put her hand on Nadidé's hand but Nadidé's hands were occupied, partially covering her face so as she could conceal her emotions. Instead, Naz put her hand on Nadidé's shoulder.

Fareed would have preferred not to attend class, but he did not want Leila and Tolga to inquire about him. He returned to class a minute after Tolga arrived, without looking at Nadidé, and sat silently in the upper right back of the classroom, away from Nadidé.

———

It was a hushed and anguished hour, for Fareed and Nadidé. Both looked down silently and with darkened faces. Nadidé was anxiously waiting for the class to be over, to do what was on her mind. When Dr. Chakir concluded the lesson, she stepped down and went across the aisle and up toward Fareed, while Naz was observing every move and every word.

"From now on, you can call me Nad. You don't have to call me Nadidé," she said in a low voice. She spoke to him for the first time as if she was trying to demonstrate that she was not trying to be difficult.

Naz could not hold herself. She snickered but covered her mouth right away. When Fareed heard Naz snickering, he turned his head toward Naz and smiled ever so faintly. He then looked at Nad, raising his head slightly. "Yes, Nad, that is what I will call you from now on," he said, trying to emphasize that there was a future between them.

"Besides, your letter did not include marron glacé. So, it is being rejected," said Nad teasingly.

Naz pretended she was an innocent observer; she left and tried not to look at either of them, hoping that Fareed would not detect her friendship to Nad. She went right away to see Deniz.

"You cannot believe what I saw, Deniz. They made up. You know *how* they made up? She first read his letter. I don't know what was in it, but for sure it unsettled her. After class, she walked to him, just stood there, and told him that from now on he could call her Nad and not to call her Nadidé anymore, and the rest went so smoothly. I cannot believe it! We need to celebrate. Deniz, believe me—neither she nor he had any blood in their veins until they made up. She immediately sprung rosy cheeks and you could see his face change from ashen to rosy. Unbelievable, just unbelievable. I call this true love."

Back in the classroom, Fareed asked Nad, "Will you meet me tomorrow at ten in the morning, where we met last, next to the phone booth?"

"I will meet you anywhere," said Nad.

———

The following day, they met. Fareed took a sheet from a large envelope, walked toward Nad, and handed it to her. The sheet was a picture of a few lush green leaves sprinkled over a geometrically set background of Turkish Delight, with a red rose stretching across the length of the page.

Nad of Nadidé was written just below the petals in a semi-cursive Arabesque font, with each word making a separate line.

Although it was a beautifully done design, at first Nad did not know what it meant. But in short order she realized that Fareed was comparing her beauty to the same five women he had listed as being some of the most beautiful women in the history of mankind. All of them were designated as of a certain place. Fareed designated Nad as being of herself, Nadidé.

Upon realizing the nature of the comparison, she smiled broadly and was about to leave in a most cheerful mood. After she buoyantly took three steps away from Fareed, she paused, turned around, and walked toward him, as if she planned to chest-pump him. At the last moment, she turned slightly to her right, rubbing her left arm against his right. She turned around as if floating on air and left, looking back at him, and smiling all the way out.

Fareed was beside himself. At first, he did not know what to do. He looked around and then lifted himself up onto the shelf used to sort mail; he paused in the vision of a statue he adored, *The Thinker* by Rodin.

As he was feeling proud and happy with himself, a cleaning lady appeared from nowhere. "What do you think you are doing?" she asked in Turkish.

Fareed pretended he spoke no Turkish and told her so in contrived, very broken Turkish. He wanted to demonstrate his quick-acquired fluency in Turkish first with Nad and nobody else.

The cleaning lady turned around and muttered in Arabic, "You are studying in Turkey, and you don't speak Turkish. What do you expect, for me to speak to you in Chinese?"

Fareed jumped off the shelf and asked her if she was an Arab. She told him that her mother was Syrian, and her father was Turkish, and that after twenty-five years of teaching Arabic at a high school, the government abolished the Arabic language classes at many high schools, including hers. She was now working and studying at Boğaziçi for her master's, to shift to teaching Turkish. When she recognized that he was the student she had been observing daily, she asked, "What are you doing? One day I see you smiling at her and another you give her a sheet of paper and wink at her. I know—she is gorgeous. Why don't you just grab her and give her a kiss?"

"You want me to kiss her in public, in front of everyone, here in the lobby of the engineering building?" he answered.

"You are Fareed; I heard her calling you by name. Listen Fareed, I will open classroom 32 between ten and eleven o'clock, just before you go to your engineering class. We keep it in reserve for emergencies. You can lock it from the inside. When you finish, slam the door shut."

Fareed thanked her and asked for her name.

"Sorraya," she said.

———

Nad went right away to make ten copies of Fareed's *Nad of Nadidé* layout. In her rush, she forgot to retrieve the original. She met Naz on her way out of the copy shop. When Naz finished making a copy of her research paper, the manager, who had seen her speaking to Nad, asked her if she could give the original to her friend. Naz promised to do so.

Before Naz gave it back to Nad, Naz and Deniz expected Nad to update them on the fact she decided to be called Nad. Nad didn't. When Nad was asked how Fareed was, she said that he was fine, with little emphasis.

It was then that both Naz and Deniz confronted Nadidé.

"Admit it, Nadidé, you are not only in love, you are in deep love. It is Fareed and nobody else; you don't mind being called Nad, to please him."

Nadidé had to admit that it was unadulterated love, and she could think of nobody else except of Fareed. "Please don't give me a bad time, and help me in the process," she said. They both kissed her and promised to help her all the way.

The following class, Fareed resumed messaging Nad in the same usual manner. He asked her if she could meet him at ten, an hour before their aerodynamics class on Friday, and that they would be alone in classroom 32. She signaled positively.

Realizing that Fareed had been successful in securing an empty classroom, she prepared herself. She wore full but understated

makeup and dressed smartly. Upon entering classroom 32, Nad
walked toward Fareed and faced him, smiling. He softly grabbed
her and pulled her in for a hug, so her face was on his shoulder. After
that he raised her head and pecked her on her lips. She blushed. He
then tried to kiss her on her lips in earnest.

She pulled back. "I have never been kissed on the lips before. I
don't know how to do it."

She then kissed him on his neck and as her lips slid downward,
her lipstick smeared on his white shirt collar. Fareed again placed
her face on his shoulder and hugged her tightly. They stayed like
that for a long time, over fifteen minutes. She was about to go into
a daze before she became aware of the time.

"I think we are almost late; let us go to class, Fareed," she told
him.

He told her that he would go first and for her to wait for three
minutes before she followed. He hurried to go to class.

When he got there, Tolga Chakir was, as usual, welcoming his
students at the door. He immediately noticed two lipstick imprints
on Fareed's collar. "Fareed, what is the name of the night club you
have been to?" Chakir asked in Arabic.

"Night club? I don't understand," said Fareed.

Chakir spoke lowly. "You have two lipstick imprints on your
shirt."

Fareed realized what had happened.

"Skip class, and come over later, for dinner," Chakir suggested.
"I'll review the lecture of the day for you."

Fareed followed Tolga's advice.

A minute after Fareed left, Nadidé showed up. Her lipstick was
somewhat smudged. Chakir put one and one together; he asked her

to go to his office. There she could remove her lipstick or use his wife's choice of lipstick to fix hers. She clearly blushed and accepted Chakir's suggestion. She removed her lipstick and went back to the classroom.

In class, Chakir handed her a note.

> *Fareed could not stay. He had too much lipstick on his collar.*

She realized that Chakir figured out the relationship.

CHAPTER 10

That evening, Fareed went to have dinner at Tolga and Leila's. They slowly tilted the conversation toward the subject of Nadidé. Tolga and Leila had discussed it in advance, and while they would have rather stayed silent, they felt they had to broach the issue since Nadidé was the daughter of Ali Hikmet. Leila could not hold herself back; she delved into it right away.

"Tolga tells me she is a good-looking girl. But her father is evil and dangerous. We don't want anything to happen to you. Did you hear how he sent his men to beat up a high school friend of Nadidé? The boy was a Muslim. His father was Muslim too, but his mother was Armenian Christian. To General Hikmet this is a no-no. Your mother is Irish. You fall into the same category, as far as Hikmet is concerned. I beg you, try to end it with her. It is not worth it, Fareed."

Fareed said nothing. He did not make a promise he intended not to keep. He had already become infatuated with Nadidé, and although respectful of Leila's and Tolga's opinions, he disagreed with them in this case. Just as he had felt challenged when Nad dismissed his approach on the plane, he felt the challenge by his senior relative, giving life advice. Tolga tried his luck to convince Fareed of the same, but to no avail as Fareed kept silent, indirectly turning down their advice.

Leila thought of another opportunity to try her luck. "Fareed, in two days the school paper is going to take pictures of the family. Why don't you join us? They are doing an article about each of three professors who happen to hold more than one Ph.D. at Boğaziçi. Tolga is one of the three."

In the morning Fareed and Nadidé were scheduled to meet in classroom 32. They happened to arrive at the engineering school at the same time, next to each other. Fareed stopped first. She stopped inches to his side. Fareed took the opportunity to slide his index finger down her palm and clasp her arm briefly. She loved it, and for a moment she rested her head on his shoulder.

They were interrupted by a loud argument not far from them. They let go of each other and looked at the feuding couple, two students arguing about their relationship. The male grabbed the girl by the arm. She removed his hand and said, "How many times have I told you not to touch me like this!"

She then slapped him on his face. It was an unusual and embarrassing scene.

Fareed signaled Nad to go into the building, which she did, and he followed suit. Inside, he took Nad's hand and kissed it discreetly. She loved the gesture. He signaled to her that he would write her a note.

After class, Nad received her marron glacé and the note. The note said that the slapper did not know how to slap a man, and that she could have easily slapped him three times stronger. There were also several sketches, with step-by-step instructions of how a right-handed woman should slap a man. Nad looked at the sketches, intrigued and fascinated. She had not expected to be instructed on this matter, especially by a man.

When the two met in classroom 32, they hugged, kissed on the cheeks and neck, and caressed each other's arms and torso. Again, Fareed took the opportunity to explain to Nadidé that the lady slapping the man did not do a good job. He demonstrated to Nadidé what he had demonstrated to his mother and had advised Nad about two days earlier. She told Fareed that she had studied his sketches keenly and even practiced doing the steps.

"Once you do it, it is very easy," she told him.

That evening, Fareed accompanied Tolga, Leila, and Nermin, who was in the stroller, into the engineering building's courtyard. The school paper photographer was snapping pictures of them, one after the other. He took around eighty pictures of the three of them together. He then asked to take separate pictures of Tolga pushing Nermin in the stroller.

Leila took the opportunity to open the subject of Nad again. She was walking with her head leaning on Fareed's shoulder in a gesture of loving body language, yet soft arguments volleyed back and forth between them.

"Please reconsider," she said, then pecked him on the cheek.

From a distance, Nad and Naz watched. To an observer, Leila and Fareed seemed more like lovers than close cousins. It was the impression that Naz got. Although she questioned the nature of the exchanges, she maintained an open mind. Naz looked at Nad and could almost see the blood draining out of her vessels. Nad became ashen.

"Come on," Naz said, holding Nad by the arm and walking her away to the parking area.

When they got to the house, Naz spoke to Ayshe, Nad's mother, and told her that Nad was not feeling well and for Ayshe to watch over her. After Naz finished with her appointment, she could not help but to go back and see Nad. Nad had recovered but only slightly. Naz slept at Nad's that evening.

————

In the morning, Nad looked better and could talk, but in a hushed voice. "I know what to do," she said. "Don't worry."

Naz looked at her, questioning.

"Go ahead and tend to your chores," she finished. She did not share anything with Naz.

Naz was unable to discuss the possibility that the whole thing might have been an innocent incident. "Don't torture yourself; no man is worth it."

"Close the subject for the time being," Nad said. "I'll have something to tell you later in the day." She apologized to Naz for throwing up on the way to the car the prior evening. "I am sure I will feel much better this afternoon," she told Naz.

Nad still could not believe what she had seen the prior day. She picked up the phone and called Fareed. Ramzi answered the phone and was formal with Nad. "Fareed is still in bed," he told her.

She asked Ramzi to tell Fareed that it was most important for Fareed to meet her at the usual place, at around ten in the morning.

———

Fifteen minutes to ten, Nad hid around the corner waiting for Fareed. He was there a few minutes before ten. Nad followed him into classroom 32. She smiled faintly as she entered the room looking at him. He smiled broadly. Her crisp steps could have alerted Fareed, but they did not. She headed straight to him, and no sooner than he opened his arms to hug her, she took a step with her left foot, pushed with her right, and swung as hard as she could to slap Fareed.

He lurched to the right before he straightened himself, with his hand moving to cover his left cheek, feeling the physical hurt Nad had caused him. He looked at her totally bewildered and stunned, his eyes bulging, his mouth open, his lip bleeding, and saying absolutely nothing.

Nad grew concerned. Why Fareed's sad and befuddled reaction? It was not the reaction of a guilty man.

He took two moderate breaths, closed his mouth first and then said in Turkish, "*Fosilleşmiş kaltak,*" meaning, "You fossilized bitch."

Nad was surprised that Fareed could speak any Turkish. She got confused. His reaction and his strange terminology was not what she expected. For the first time, she questioned whether she might have misconstrued the meaning of Leila's kisses. Her pent-up anger had not allowed her to dwell on anything other than taking revenge against Fareed.

She left classroom 32 huffing, not caring to look back at Fareed or trying to nurse his bleeding lip.

―――――

In a couple of minutes, Fareed managed to stop most of the bleeding. He sat down in a daze, steaming but not having any idea why Nad had done what she did.

When the time came, he proceeded to go to the aerodynamics class. Nadidé was sitting in her desk looking down. She did not look at him and he did not look at her.

Dr. Chakir slowly walked toward Fareed during his lecture and gave Fareed his handkerchief. After class was over, he went to Fareed. "Can you have dinner with me and Leila this evening?"

Fareed, challenged by his swollen lip, didn't speak; he nodded yes. Afterward, Tolga called Leila and described to her what he had seen. Nad was in a mood, on top of the condition Fareed was under. "I think Nad hit Fareed and caused the cut on his lip," he said.

―――――

When Fareed arrived at Leila's house for dinner, Leila spoke. She told Fareed what they believed had happened. He did not correct her. On the contrary, he confirmed that it was Nadidé.

"I hate to say it. I am glad this bitch did this to you. You don't have to sever relations with her. She did it herself and you should be grateful it is over," said Leila.

"It is over," said Fareed, making very few comments about the subject.

"But why did she slap you?" Tolga asked. "Did you do anything to her?"

"I don't know. I honestly don't know. It is a mystery to me," said Fareed.

"Well, it is clear. She made up with her father and his clone, Ata Aslan," said Leila.

"No, no, this makes no sense. There must be a more logical reason. She could have broken the relationship off by sending Fareed a note. She did not need to slap Fareed to make her point. This makes no sense. I think I may have an idea. Just leave it up to me to test my theory. Something you might not have thought of just popped into my head," said Tolga.

Leila had already talked to Tolga about how she argued with Fareed during the shoot. Tolga could recall how Leila used to kiss him on the cheek whenever she disagreed with him, in order to not make him feel bad. She did the same with Fareed. She wanted to placate his feelings with her family-style kisses, for Fareed to keep his trust in her.

Tolga and Leila were somewhat pleased. They thought a slap on the face and a cut lip was a small price to pay compared to General Hikmet threatening and possibly harming Fareed.

"Fareed," Leila said, putting her hands on his shoulders, "I insist that you come over for dinner every night for the week."

Fareed did not object. He craved companionship, under the circumstances. He felt betrayed and humiliated, and he yearned for the company of people who loved him and appreciated him.

———

In the morning Tolga went unannounced to the school paper. He asked to see all the pictures they took the prior day. They had taken close to one hundred pictures, and Tolga looked at each carefully. He was looking for others who might have been in the pictures.

As he got to the twenty-third picture, he could see Nadidé in the background looking at them. She and Naz were in two other pictures.

Tolga found what he was looking for; he had suspected that Nad might have seen Leila kissing Fareed, not one time but half a dozen times. He asked if the paper could produce one enlarged copy each of six of the pictures, which they did. Three pictures included Nad, two included Leila kissing Fareed, with Nermin in Fareed's arms. The sixth included the picture of a male student from one of Dr. Chakir's other courses, asking Dr. Chakir a question.

———

Nad later went to see Naz and Deniz at the same place and time. Naz looked at Nadidé and said, "What is happening between you and Fareed? I saw his lip bleeding and neither of you looking at each other. Did he try to do something?"

"I don't want to talk about it," said Nad.

"Listen Nadidé, this is serious. You can't keep it to yourself. I can see you are hurting. Grow up. Did he try to do something?" said Deniz in a loud voice.

Nadidé looked at Deniz and said, "I hit him. I slapped him on the face. He deserved it. He taught me how to hit him."

Nadidé explained to Naz and Deniz how she and Fareed observed another female student slap her boyfriend, and Fareed showed her how to slap a man. When Deniz inquired about why she hit him, she explained that he had another girlfriend.

"Nad, what we saw may have looked like it, but it may not have been," Naz answered. "Did you confirm that the girl who was kissing him was a girlfriend?"

"It was obvious! Who would kiss like that without having a close and romantic relationship?" said Nad.

"Nadidé, you don't need him. This figures—the rich Lebanese think they are French. They usually have a wife and two girlfriends on the side. All you need to do is stop dealing with him. He is not worth it. No man is worth it. But you can't physically attack people just because they are cheats," said Deniz.

"Just send him a note and tell him never to communicate with you in any shape or form. If you want, I will give it to him. This way he knows that others know about his behavior," said Naz.

"No need. He knows it is over," said Nad.

Nad and Naz went to the Friday class. Fareed was nowhere to be seen. In class, Naz displayed an angry face.

Dr. Chakir came with a press-button gadget. He told the class that he needed to share with them something that had nothing to do with aerodynamics.

"Somehow you guys think that all I do is teaching. I do twice as much research as I teach. My lab here at Boğaziçi and my outside lab both work for GE, Siemens, and the Turkish defense ministry, among others." He paused. "I devote ten minutes after each class for one-on-one question and answer. Today I will increase it to fifteen minutes. But I no longer want you to stop me after I leave class to ask me questions as I head to my labs. I usually cannot spare one single minute," Chakir said. "Let me show you what happened when the school paper was interviewing me and taking pictures of my family."

He projected on the screen one of the students from his other classes stopping him and asking him questions as he was being interviewed. He told them that the student in the picture took ten minutes of his time while the photographer was in a hurry to take his and his family's pictures. He then projected the picture of Leila kissing Fareed, with Nermin in Fareed's arms.

"I am sorry, this is my wife kissing her cousin, Fareed Shaheen. He is a student taking this course. She loves him as a brother; she has no brothers of her own. He is the only family she has. She almost raised him as an older sister would. He usually sits here up front."

Naz gave Nadidé a pointed look, almost shooting daggers toward her. Nad and Naz simultaneously looked for Fareed to find an empty chair.

Nad put her hand on her mouth to muffle her deep breathing. Her eyes started to water. She looked at Naz without saying anything. Naz gave Nad an indignant look and shook her head in regret.

———

After class, Nad went to meet Deniz. Naz followed her, ranting. "It was obvious to you, it was a romantic relationship, wasn't it! The hell with you and your conclusions. I felt worse than a cockroach. Yes, Dr. Chakir knew how to humiliate us, but unlike you, he did it as if he is the foreign minister of Switzerland. You know, you degraded yourself—and you degraded me in the process, for agreeing with you. I am not going to do it again. This is the last time."

Deniz stood up and shouted, "Would someone tell me what happened? You are talking about something I know nothing about! What happened?"

"This beauty queen hit her lover, as you well know, for kissing his own *cousin*, all in the presence of the cousin's husband, who happens to be Dr. Chakir, and Dr. Chakir pretended he was complaining about his students stopping him to ask questions, and proceeded to dress Nadidé down naked, because she deserves it and you and I are stupid enough to agree with her," said Naz. She looked at Nad straight on. "I have not, for the life of me, *ever* heard of one Turkish woman doing what Nadidé did. This is not Turkish. This is rubbish. What is wrong with just saying, 'I do not want to see you anymore'? Is the English language that limited? Give me a break!"

Deniz jumped off her seat and stopped Naz from leaving. "It is time to try to do the right thing. I agree with you, Naz; what I have heard Nad did is totally uncivilized. Let us think of what needs to be done."

Naz left after she told Deniz that she could not think of anything, but in response to Deniz's pleas, she promised to get together the following day, same time.

———

That evening, Tolga shared with Leila and Fareed what he had done in class. "Nad reacted as a spurned woman, thinking that Leila was one of Fareed's many girlfriends," he said calmly.

It was not enough to placate Fareed; Leila did not budge an iota. She thought it all happened for the benefit of Fareed.

"As far as I am concerned, she is still a bitch," said Leila.

———

Nad waited all afternoon in the lobby of the engineering building. She had gone there to give Fareed a Turkish Delight with a message.

I am stupid, and I am so wrong. If you have ever loved me, I hope you will forgive me, not to get back together but to try to be happy apart.

Fareed did not go back to the engineering building; he kept to himself. He barely spoke with Ramzi and Nader. Nad looked all over but could not find him. Nad waited for two days and left the same message on his desk. He did not sit in his usual desk; he instead went up to the corner, away from Nad.

At the end of the class, Nad followed Fareed and gave him the message wrapped around the Turkish Delight. He took it and flung it into the trash can, scoring, like basketball players do. Both Nad and Naz saw what Fareed did. So did Chakir.

"If I were him, I would not even be in the same room with you. You deserve it, Nad. Did you see how he was sitting in the corner, like a wounded lion? I swear, if it were somebody other than you, I would help him find another girlfriend."

After class, Nad and Naz went to see Deniz. Before she sat, a girl the same age as theirs approached Nadidé and complimented her on her blouse. "Where did you buy it from?"

"Mind your own business," Nad snapped.

Deniz and Naz were further unpleasantly surprised and somewhat insulted. Deniz went to the girl and apologized. Deniz asked her if she did not mind sitting with them. "I think Nadidé owes you an apology," Deniz said.

She sat down and introduced herself as Simra. She was in her final year studying psychology. Deniz apologized by saying that that Nad had gone through three rough days and that she was not thinking straight.

"I am usually not a rude person. That was not me that insulted you. I apologize profusely," said Nad.

Simra shook her head. "No harm was done." She smiled. "Although, I would still love to know where you bought your blouse from."

Nadidé looked down at her blouse and shrugged. "It was my mother who bought the blouse. If you could meet me tomorrow, around ten, I could possibly give you the name of the store."

"I will see you tomorrow at ten!" Simra left, thanking all three.

———

The following day, Simra arrived at ten in the morning. Naz was there but Deniz and Nad were not. Simra had a nice conversation with Naz, and they both knew some of the same people. Nad was the last to arrive at ten fifteen. Deniz and Naz could tell she was still in a sour mood. She gave Simra the name of the store and at the same time she saw Fareed entering the engineering building.

"Why don't you come back tomorrow, same time," Nad told Simra before she left. She took off to see if she could talk to Fareed, apologizing to Simra.

Fareed went to the phone booth area. There he ran into Sorraya, the cleaning lady. She told him that she had noticed that he and Nad were not using classroom 32.

"No, I don't think we will need it anymore. There is no relationship left to hide from anyone," said Fareed.

Before Sorraya could say anything, there was Nad.

"Why won't you talk to me? I just want to apologize. Then you can go your way and I will go mine. I know I made a huge mistake. Do you enjoy torturing me? I am in agony twenty-four hours a day. Help me relieve some of my agony. The rest may never go away. Please Fareed, just help me out," said Nad.

Sorraya took three steps toward Fareed and said, "Yalla," an Arabic word meaning *let's go—move on*. "Forgiveness is a greater relief to those forgiving than to those receiving. Do it, don't hesitate. You will feel better."

Fareed looked at Nad for the first time in days. "I have ten minutes. You can say whatever you want to say, and I will say nothing."

Fareed walked toward classroom 32. When they got in, Fareed stood erect and folded his arms dismissively, waiting for Nad to speak.

"Please don't look at me like this. You have an indignant look. I want to tell you that what I did was stupid and inconsiderate. I didn't know that I had fallen in love with you although we had very little contact. When I saw your cousin kissing you, my jealousy got the best of me. I convinced myself that she represented another romantic relationship. You cannot believe how ashamed I am of my own behavior. It was childish and immature. If you cannot forgive me now, I hope you can forgive me in the future. Please apologize for me to your cousin, Leila. I will, if you don't mind, kiss you on the cheek I slapped and say goodbye," said Nad.

Fareed looked at her sternly and said, "My cheek does not hurt. I get hit in basketball all the time. It is my heart that you broke, and which may never mend. You think you are the only one who has fallen in love. Obviously, you don't take the feelings of others into consideration. You keep talking about the wrong thing. How my heart is going to heal is the question; I really don't know. No one has been as mean and insulting to me as you have!"

Nad said nothing and walked slowly toward him, getting within six inches. She looked into his eyes and started unbuttoning his shirt. As she spread his shirt open, she kissed him over his heart.

"Is this better than your cheek?" she asked.

Fareed said nothing, standing still.

"You know, Fareed, I was a happy girl, minding my own business with almost no problems to speak of. I sometimes wonder how somebody from Palestine or from Lebanon managed to capture my heart with a few pieces of marron glacé," she said.

Fareed scoffed. "You keep talking like an engineer. Love is not an engineering course. It is a glorious feeling that touches the soul and the mind in a way nothing else matches. It is the best of human emotions. My marron glacé did not cause you to love me; *you* were my marron glacé. You were supposed to be sweeter and more delectable than marron glacé, or anything else for that matter. Instead, you humiliated me and humiliated the love I had for you."

"Let me go. Don't keep torturing me. Let me go find a new love, a simple Turkish love," she said.

"Love is universal. There is no Turkish love or American love. It is all the same," said Fareed, raising his voice.

Nad hugged Fareed and put her head on his shoulder. She started crying. "I want you to love me even if we cannot be together because I think I will love you the rest of my life. Oh God, let me go, I cannot take it anymore." She let go of him and started walking away but could barely continue. She sat in one of the chairs and continued crying. "I feel so stupid and wretched. I don't know if I will ever forgive myself."

Her tears poured down her face in clear agony. Fareed took a long step after her, grabbed her right hand with his left, and pulled her up toward him. He looked her in the eye and rested her head on his shoulder.

"Fareed, hold me tight. I hope this is a sign I am not losing you. I will not be able to bear it, especially when it is my stupid mistake. Please hold me tight. I am so sorry. Please forgive me. I was so childish. I cannot believe I did what I did."

Fareed laid his head on hers. "Don't ever accuse me of trying to torture you. Nothing hurts me more than to see you in pain. I would rather be in pain myself than to see you in the slightest agony."

Nad wiped her tears. She looked up at Fareed and said, "Kiss me, why don't you kiss me on my lips? I want to feel you, to feel all of you. Kiss me."

He first gave her two pecks on the lips, grabbed her tightly by her waist, and gave her a juicy kiss, the most passionate he had ever experienced. She reciprocated with sophistication and confidence.

A minute later Fareed looked Nad in the eye, snickering. "What happened to you? You know how to kiss as much as I do. What have you been doing, practicing with the doorman?"

"Fareed, do you want me to slap you again?! I have been watching American romantic movies," Nad said.

"I know, my love. I am just teasing. Don't you ever disappear again. I missed you so much the last two days. Next time you disappear, you will finish me."

"Never, never, never in a million years," she said. "You are mine and I am yours and I do not care what anybody says. I owe you one more apology, but I will not tell you when, where, and how." She pulled away from him. "Oh my God, class is about to start. I have one final question. You called me fosilleşmiş kaltak, a 'fossilized bitch.' I have never heard this cuss expression before; it is not Turkish. Where did you get it from?"

"I got it from someone who claimed he was teaching me Turkish. Instead, he was teaching me his version of Turkish," said Fareed.

"I don't know what it means exactly. Will you let me know later?"

"Much later."

Nad fixed her hair but did not need to fix her lipstick, as she did not have any on. She left first and one minute later Fareed followed. Nadidé was smiling and said good morning to Dr. Chakir as he received her at the door. When it was Fareed's turn, Fareed was also smiling. "Hello, Doctor."

Chakir knew something had changed. Although not a religious person, he looked up and recited a Muslim proverb, "Blessed he who does not change but does change people."

CHAPTER 11

A new chapter opened in Nad's and Fareed's lives. They both admitted being deeply in love, and they admitted it to themselves and to each other. Yet they did not admit it to the outside world despite the prodding by Naz and Deniz. In the case of Nad, her father was the problem. In the case of Fareed, her father was also the problem. While Fareed faced a slew of family and friends warning him about the beliefs and the actions of General Ali Hikmet, he did not consider them to be insurmountable obstacles but rather walls of resistance. While challenging, he considered them to be manageable.

The two seemed to have overcome their biggest emotional challenge. They were sure each loved the other and nobody else.

Ten months after he had split with Dania, she was nowhere on Fareed's mind. Nad, on the other hand, started thinking of ways to finally crush all prospects of any relationship with Ata Aslan. She had one question: How to confront her own father, the key to resolving her dilemma.

At that juncture she had a more immediate agenda. The first item was to carry out her yet unrevealed and final apology to Fareed, then to apologize to Leila; all of this to be followed by spending fun time with Fareed. The fun part was what thrusted her into postponing the more challenging tasks. She decided to wait to tackle the problem with her father, having devised no cogent plan.

Fareed told Leila and Tolga that Nad wanted to apologize to them, outside the classroom, for suspecting Leila and causing so much commotion. Leila told him, "Listen Fareed, Tolga and I spoke about it. You and Nad seem to be immersed in love. It was not long ago when I could not sleep if there was any friction between me and Tolga. You want her and she wants you and we want you to be blessed and happy. How about if I send a note to her inviting her for dinner? I will pretend it is only her invitation but will have you over after she arrives. I am now using Tolga's tactics; he likes to surprise people."

"Great, but if she asks me directly, I am not going to lie to her. I am going to tell her that I will be there," said Fareed.

"Even if she knows you will be there, arrive twenty minutes after she does. I want to give her a chance to be comfortable and casual in extending her apology," said Leila.

When Nad arrived, she was smartly dressed, with light makeup. She just about lit up the room. She truly looked radiant. At 5'8", she was two inches taller than Leila and eight years her junior, the same age as Fareed. When Leila saw her relaxed demeanor and expressive face, with a towering and lanky presence, Leila could not help but harbor a positive feeling.

In no time and after a few verbal exchanges, Leila's emotions carried her to start admiring Nad. In her mind, she not only wanted but was hopeful that her interaction with Nad would lead her into helping Fareed; she wanted to make sure that they could develop trust in each other, in order to help the situation, especially when it came to General Hikmet. She decided that instead of fearing Ali Hikmet and doing nothing, they could instead find a way to neutralize his influence on the relationship between Nad and Fareed. Leila took the initiative. Since Fareed was not there yet, the three of them conversed in Turkish.

"Fareed told us that you want to apologize to us in a fine manner. Believe me, there is no need to apologize to us. Let us just enjoy the evening and get to know each other better. Don't you agree with me, Nadidé—sorry, Nad?" said Leila.

"I will agree with you if you and Dr. Chakir prefer it this way. I still feel I owe you an apology," said Nad.

"We do prefer it this way," said Tolga. He added, "Here you and Fareed can call me Tolga. Only at the university do you need to call me Dr. Chakir."

Before long, Fareed arrived. Nadidé blossomed further when she saw him. She ran toward him and hugged him without kissing him. He held her tightly and placed her head on his shoulder. There was more than love in the air; there was warmth and deep affection.

Leila told Nad that Tolga had told her that she was almost an A student, and that he was sure once she sat for the course's final test, she would command a straight A. "I don't know how you manage with all that has happened. Anyway, I feel the future will be calmer and brighter," said Leila.

Nad spoke about her father, but she never referred to him as "General." She obliquely mentioned that he was difficult. She also spoke about her only sibling, a half-brother in Germany, who happened to be an orthopedic surgeon. She said that her mother was much more understanding and that she and her mother were friends, but that her mother did not know about Fareed.

Leila told Nad that she was about to submit her Ph.D. dissertation in civil engineering, and as soon as her advisor and mentor, Dr. Yamasaki, finished critiquing it, she would revise it and submit it to the committee, and schedule her defense of the dissertation. She told Nad that some considered her as the leading expert on earthquakes in the Middle East, specifically because she studied under Dr. Yamasaki, considered the leading earthquake engineering expert in the world.

When asked, Leila told Nad that she spoke Arabic, Turkish, English, and Japanese. Nad's favorite pastime was listening to classical music. She told them that she played the piano and violin but not well enough to be even in a junior orchestra. Leila mentioned how surprising it was for Tolga to coincidentally meet Fareed and how much she cherished reconnecting with him and having him in her life.

"I had not seen him in almost twelve years, and I have not yet reconnected with Fareed's father, my uncle. I am looking forward to that someday soon. But I guess if it were not for you, we would not have met Fareed," said Leila.

When Nad said she did not understand why that was the case, Leila reminded her that Fareed enrolled in advanced aerodynamics because of her, and if he had not, he would not have met Tolga. Nad smiled with resignation, knowing that what Leila said was true.

When Nad asked Leila if her uncle planned to visit Fareed in Istanbul, Leila answered her, "His mother was supposed to visit him every four months, like she did when he studied at the AUB. Now it is Fareed who goes back to London since Istanbul is only half the distance between London and Beirut. She is planning to visit soon. She is not as much of a workaholic as his father is," said Leila.

"What does she do?" asked Nad.

"You mean Fareed never mentioned it? She is a neurosurgeon, just like his father. They are both world famous," said Leila.

"It is nice to hear of Palestinian couples making it big," said Nad.

"No, his mother is not Palestinian. She is Irish," said Leila.

"You mean, she is Christian!"

"Yes, she is Catholic. Fareed is Muslim, like his father. Does it really make much difference?" said Leila.

"No, it does not to me, but it does to my father," said Nad.

"Oh, yeah, I heard about your friend in high school, the one with an Armenian mother. Listen to me, Nad, one way or another your father must come around. Excuse me, but this thing about being Turkish and Sunni Muslim belongs to the Middle Ages. We are all human beings and that is what counts. When it comes to your father, all his objections have to be resolved in a lump sum; they cannot be resolved piecemeal. It will take you and Fareed a lifetime to resolve them that way. Once they are bundled and handled, you can enjoy your daily routines without much concern. Life deserves to be enjoyed to the fullest."

All along, Fareed and Tolga were just listening. Both had faith in Leila; they thought she was doing a good job. Nad paused and then said, "You know, Leila, I am glad I came over tonight. I agree with you; all issues with my father must be resolved at the same time. You are right, I don't have time to resolve them separately.

Thank you for highlighting this fact."

Dinner went exceedingly well. Leila and Nad both enjoyed themselves and connected with each other well. On the way back, Nad gave Fareed a ride to his apartment. "I must say, I am disappointed you haven't told me about your famous parents, and that your mother is planning a visit."

Fareed told her that they were together not because she was a daughter of a top general. "I love you and I would love you the same if you were the daughter of a simple sergeant, and I want you to love me, not because of who my parents are. I want you to love me the same if they happened to be cleaning people."

"Fareed, you always say the right thing and sometimes you make me feel small; I love you all the same." She leaned over to give him a peck on the lips.

Nad suggested to Fareed that they go to the beach. It was music to Fareed's ears, as he missed the beaches of Beirut.

They started going to the beach once a week, where they did not swim but played in the seawater and above all felt free.

———

One day, Ata Aslan visited her father at home. He brought Nad flowers. She thanked him but showed little interest in him or his gesture, something he sensed clearly. Without sharing it with Hikmet, he put one of his privates to the task of spying on Nad.

At first, the private found nothing unusual, but one day he followed Nad to the beach. Fareed was waiting for her. He had borrowed Ramzi's fifteen-year-old car. As soon as Nad got out of her small Mercedes, she saw Fareed and ran toward him. The private observed and wrote down everything and reported it to Major Aslan.

Aslan was beside himself. His honor had been slighted, and he needed to do something about it. He himself started following and stalking Nad, all without her or Fareed noticing anything.

Many of their recreational activities were taking place directly under the watchful eyes and spurned psyche of Major Ata Aslan.

CHAPTER 12

While Nad was having more fun than she could ever recall, Simra was developing a close relationship with Naz and Deniz. The three bonded well. Nad had her mind on Fareed and all else was a distant second. Simra seemed to be more settled. She told them she was engaged and did not seem to present a social burden to any of the three. On the contrary she volunteered to be as helpful as possible. She had all the time, with one year to graduate before she planned to wed her fiancé, Murat.

Murat was none other than the same Murat who had warned Fareed against hooking up with Nad. The sinister aspect was that Simra's newly developed friendship had been instigated by Murat, who knew about her belonging to another clandestine leftist party. Simra's affiliated party refused to give itself a name, to conceal as much as possible about itself.

The purpose of Simra's involvement was to indirectly spy on General Hikmet, through his daughter. Between Murat's Vatan Partisi and Simra's clandestine party, seven of the eleven leftist leadership members supposedly kidnapped by General Hikmet were theirs. The junta had imprisoned thousands but those eleven had evaded capture. Hikmet had discovered their hiding place and seemingly taken it upon himself to apprehend the eleven and imprison them without the knowledge of the junta. They were known to have rejected the validity of any religion, including Islam, thus Hikmet's special interest, as he was an extremely devout Muslim, much to the lack of notice or detection of the secular junta.

Vatan Partisi took a defensive posture against Hikmet. On the other hand, the clandestine party sought revenge.

Although a leftist, Simra was supposed to have come from wealth, just like her three new friends. Her father supposedly owned a large metal fabricating and warehouse construction business. She had no problem joining the three in purchasing the same or more, nor was she short in spending on restaurant meals and other social activities. Just like Nad, she drove a small Mercedes. Looks-wise, while not a match to Nad, she was beautiful with a soft demeanor. Brain-wise, she was well educated and sharp. She was well versed about Turkey and the outside world. Her leftist training armed her with knowledge way above that of her newfound friends.

One day the four of them were talking shop together. Deniz said, "Listen, girls, Simra is engaged and Nad is going with someone, yet I have not met Fareed nor your Murat. How about the six of us getting together over dinner?"

"No, no; I would like to keep this as a girls' group. Once we involve the men, we will have to accommodate them more than we would accommodate ourselves. I think this is more fun. In the first place, this is one of the things which attracted me to you. I saw you sitting here day after day, without men," said Simra.

Simra's words struck a chord in Nad. Nad thought to herself. Why had they not seen Simra before? The courtyard of that specific engineering building was small and seldom had more than a few students at any one time. In short order, Nad dismissed her suspicions. She told herself that it could have been that they missed noticing Simra being there altogether; after all, Simra was not an engineering student and might have been in the engineering courtyard sparingly. Deniz kept prodding Nad that she wanted at least to have a peek at Fareed.

"I know he is very handsome and Naz has seen him many times. I want to have a look at him. I want to share with you your admiration for him. You should see yourself. Your eyes glitter every time his name is mentioned. He is surely your Prince Charming, and this means a lot to me. You and Naz are my best friends," Deniz said to Nad.

Nad promised to arrange for Deniz to have a look at Fareed.

"Just a look, Deniz. I am not going to introduce him yet. I could spend every hour with him, day and night, and I would not be bored. I really love him, but what can I do with my dad? He is obstinate and unreasonable," said Nad.

"Let me have a look at Fareed first and then I will think of something to try with your father; trust me. I'll do it," said Deniz.

That statement encouraged Nad to think of a convenient way for all three to meet Fareed. Before too long it was going to be Fareed's twenty-first birthday. Nad began to think it would be opportune for her three friends to meet and talk to Fareed, not only to have a look at him. She arranged a dinner out, for her and the three girls. Without telling Fareed or the girls that they were both invited, she and Fareed drove together. As she got to the table, all three were there.

"This is my Fareed. This is Deniz, Simra, and Naz. Fareed, I think you have seen Naz. I think she sits behind you in aerodynamics," said Nad.

Deniz could barely take her eyes off him. She thought to herself, *Nad finally found someone handsome to match her beauty.* She was elated at the match between the two. Simra took a quick glance at Fareed and gently turned her face away.

Naz told Fareed, "I am glad you continued with the second half of the course. This may be the only course that spreads over two semesters. If you hadn't stuck to the second half, you might not be here today." She was alluding to the fact that his relations to Nad only firmed up in the second half of the course.

Naz and Deniz asked Fareed several questions about Beirut, especially about it being the Paris of the Middle East.

"By all means it is the Paris of the Middle East, but it is not its throbbing heart," said Fareed.

"What do you mean?" asked Naz. Deniz posed the same question with her look.

"Well, how could Beirut be the throbbing heart with Nad living in Istanbul?" said Fareed.

"Nad is right, you are a charmer!" said Deniz. "You sure charmed our Nadidé—or shall we call her Nad from now on?"

"Or shall we call her Nad of Nadidé?" said Naz.

Nad looked at Deniz with total surprise. "How do you know that?"

"You must have forgotten—you forgot your original copy at the copy center, and they gave it to me to give to you," said Naz.

"I must not be good at keeping secrets," said Nad with a laugh.

Nad then looked around and gave Fareed a kiss on his cheek, and said, "Happy birthday, my love."

Deniz asked Fareed if he had any marron glacé for them to sample.

"I understand it is similar to our Turkish *karyoka*," said Deniz, intentionally choosing the wrong word to test Fareed.

Fareed gave them four pieces, one for each. After they tasted the marron glacé, Naz said, "No, this is very similar to kestane şekeri but drier."

All during this fun gathering Simra was quiet and inten-tion-ally chose not to make eye contact with Fareed. It was Fareed who was combing his hair with his palm, thinking.

"What are you thinking of, my love?" said Nad.

Fareed looked at Simra and said, "I was trying to recall where I saw you. You came to the apartment I used to share with Ramzi and Nader; you came with Murat."

All of a sudden, Simra got defensive. "I don't recall. Do you know Murat, my fiancé?"

"I was on the phone talking to my parents, in my room. You had left before I finished. Yes, I know Murat, but not well. I have met him briefly on two occasions," said Fareed.

Simra said nothing afterward. Fareed changed the conversation altogether.

The gathering went exceedingly well. They all liked Fareed and he liked everyone, except for Simra. He could recall when Murat forewarned him not to go out with Nad because she was General Hikmet's daughter. Murat had given him stern advice, telling him that he would be on his own if he decided to go out with Nad. He decided not to share his concern about Murat's fiancée, fearing he

would start an unnecessary suspicion on the part of Nad. He asked
Nad if she was free the following afternoon to go to the beach, a
proposal that she found most appealing.

———

At the beach, Fareed hugged Nad tightly. "If I were to ask something of you, could you give me a yes or no answer without you
inquiring why I am asking?" said Fareed.

"If you don't want me to ask you anything about it, sure," said
Nad.

"I want you to limit your dealings with Simra. I don't expect
you to follow my request blindly. You make your own decision, and
I will be happy to live with it, regardless," said Fareed.

"But why? She seems nice, intelligent, helpful."

Fareed looked at her, gave her a kiss, and said, "I wish I could
tell you. I promised someone not to say anything and I'd like to
keep my promise."

"You said it yourself, between us there are no secrets," said Nad
with a chagrined tone.

"Oh God; you are starting to sound like me, let me think about
it. I don't want you to sound like this, kind of sad," said Fareed.

He let go of Nad, turned his face to the opposite side and
started combing his hair with his hand, then turned back to face
Nad. "Yes, yes, I owe it to you. We are not supposed to keep any
secrets from each other. Early on, Murat told me that he does not
like your father's political views and that I should not be going out
with you."

"And what did you tell him?" said Nad.

"Are you crazy? I told him no. Would I have told you not to see Simra if I had told him yes? Nobody but nobody is going to come between us, not your father and not Murat. Forget it."

Nad grabbed Fareed and kissed him passionately on the lips. "My love, don't give it another thought. I don't need to distance myself from Simra but neither she, Murat, or anybody else will get between us," she said. "I just remembered there was still another form of apology I promised you. Do you recall? Well, today is the day. I will drop you in the courtyard and I will be gone briefly and then come back to apologize to you. It will be brief."

"You don't need to apologize to me. This is all history, and I don't want to be reminded of what took place then. Forget it," said Fareed.

———

Neither Nad nor Fareed had an inkling that they were being followed all the time.

This time it was none other than Ata Aslan himself. He saw how Fareed and Nad were rolling in the sandy waters. Nad's wet blouse got unbuttoned with her breasts partially visible and rubbing against Fareed's chest.

Prior to that day and during his surveillance of Nad, he had mustered the courage to visit with General Hikmet. He informed Hikmet that he had observed Nad seeing another man. The news put Hikmet in a sour mood. He felt that Nad was going against his wishes and that she was violating Aslan's trust in her.

Hikmet asked Aslan, contriving a defensive posture, "What do you want me to do? You need to find your own way to get into her heart. I am a general, not a matchmaker. As much as I want my daughter to marry you, you need to take care of her roving eyes. As a father I must deal with her lack of respect my own way. I don't know if we can call what she did acts of betrayal—probably acts of indiscretion. Officially, she is neither married nor engaged to you yet."

———————

That afternoon, after observing her on the beach, Aslan followed Nad. She was alone on her way to the flower shop where she picked up a dozen roses. He continued to follow her back to the school courtyard, where he saw Fareed coming out of the building.

Nad walked toward him and met him halfway on the main walkway, took the twelve-rose bouquet from its wrapping, and handed it to Fareed, smiling. She gave him a kiss on the mouth.

"This is my last apology," Ata overheard her say. "You can go home now, put them in a vase, and look at them to remind you of how much I love you. I will be meeting Naz inside."

Nad left smiling broadly at Fareed.

Ata was twenty yards behind Nad. He kept following her, proceeding in the same direction, facing Fareed. When he got next to Fareed, he snatched the bouquet of roses from his hand and hit him hard on the face, totally unexpected by Fareed.

Naz was coming out of the building when she saw Aslan's attack. She put her hands on her face, aghast at what she had seen. Nad was in front of her, facing her, her back to Fareed. "Look!" Naz said.

Nad looked back to see Fareed fall back, hit his head against the light pole, and then fall on the concrete, headfirst.

"Oh no!" Nad cried, alerting everyone in the courtyard. She ran to Fareed, but stopped when she saw Ata. "Major Aslan?" With her left foot forward, she pushed with her right and swung her arm as hard as she could to slap Ata Aslan.

Ata almost fell down but managed to stay up. He was shocked to experience Nad's wrath. He was even dumbstruck when he saw Nad continue to go forward, crouch, holding Fareed's bleeding head and kissing it all over, and talk to him in a hushed voice. "My love, my love."

Aslan tried to flee the scene, but Naz and four male students grabbed him and held him there. They were lucky he was wearing civilian clothes; they might not have been able to hold him if he were wearing his military uniform. The police took him in but transferred him to military police custody when they found out he was an air force major.

In custody, Aslan was granted a talk with General Hikmet. "I caught Nad red-handed walking with and kissing Fareed," he told him. "When she saw me nearby, she slapped me on the face." He did not mention to Hikmet that he had attacked Fareed.

"Are you telling the truth that Nad slapped you knowingly and intentionally?" Hikmet asked.

"Sir, she slapped me so hard, it still hurts."

———

Nad and Naz were at the hospital, where Fareed was taken into the emergency room. Nad was crying, unable to be consoled by Naz at first and by Deniz, when Deniz got there. Nad was tense and anxious, with a deep feeling of foreboding. Fareed was the only boyfriend she'd had in five years, and the only one she would call a boyfriend. For three hours she heard nothing. In the end, she stopped crying altogether. She looked as if she were in a trance.

The attending physician came out from the emergency room. "Is there a next of kin available?"

Naz stood, wiping her hands on her pants. "Fareed is a foreign student and his parents are in London." Then she pointed at Nad. "Nad is his fiancée." Deniz nodded her head in a contrived affirmation.

The attending physician told them that they managed to stop the bleeding, but they had to wait to see if there was internal damage to his brain or any of the vessels. "Go home and come back in the morning," he said. "He's in a coma."

Nad resumed crying; she put her hands on her nose and started sobbing, crouching down to the floor. Naz and Deniz helped sit her down; a nurse brought her a glass of water and a sedative. She arrived home late that night, at around eleven o'clock, after she advised Deniz to go alert Tolga and Leila Chakir. Nad wanted to shower and rejoin Naz at the hospital, expecting Tolga and Leila to be there.

————

As Nad entered the house, her father was waiting for her in the huge reception area in their palace-like home. She planned to tell Hikmet that she had been at the hospital with an injured friend, as she and her friends had agreed on. Naz had been coached to say the same, if asked by Nad's parents. Yet Hikmet did not even give Nad a chance. He looked her in the eye as he approached her and slapped her on the face hard.

"Who did you think you slapped this morning? He is an officer in the Turkish air force—a most honorable officer!"

Nad held her cheek, tears in her eyes. Her father had never abused her physically. She turned and proceeded quietly to her room, her lip bleeding.

As she walked away, he said in a loud voice, "You are not to leave this house unless I say so."

Her mother Ayshe heard the commotion and ran to Nad's room. "Why are you crying, my love?" Her voice conveyed her compassion.

"Dad just slapped me on my face. This is the first time anybody has slapped me," Nad said.

"Did you say your dad slapped you? He slapped you?! What happened? This is crazy."

"Ata Aslan hit my boyfriend Fareed and Fareed is in the hospital in a coma," Nad said.

"You have a boyfriend? Ferid?" Ayshe exclaimed.

"His name is not Ferid—it is Fareed. Yes, I have a boyfriend and I love him, and I don't love this monster, Ata Aslan. He must have been stalking me and Fareed, or else how did he know who Fareed was?"

"And Fareed is not Turkish?" asked Ayshe.

Nad raised her voice, defiant. "What does it matter, Turkish or not Turkish? I love him and I cannot live without him."

"Nadidé, my love, I am your mother. I love you. I love you more than you think. I don't want to be alienated from you, like what happened with your brother. I will not be able to take it. You are my last hope. Please understand that you are what keeps me alive. It took me five years to get over the fact your brother Ahmet separated himself from this household. Have mercy on me. I have not seen his children once. Your father broke my heart. I am sure he also broke Ahmet's heart," Ayshe said.

Ayshe went closer to Nad, who was lying in bed, and hugged her as she was crying.

Nad wiped her tears and saw her mother crying. "Don't cry, Mama. These matters must be resolved once and for all, all at the same time. It is the same story, my story and Ahmet's story. I don't care about him slapping me on the face as much as I do about his emotional abuse. It is either his way or the highway. This cannot continue. Mother, stop crying. I am not going to cry anymore. I want to go see Fareed. He is in the emergency room."

"Honey, Nadidé, don't do anything rash. Leave it up to me. I am on your side," said Ayshe.

"My name is no longer Nadidé; it is Nad."

"Nad? What for? When did you change your name? You are confusing me about yourself and about—what did you say his name was?"

"It is Fareed, not Ferid," Nad said, emphasizing the pronunciation of the name.

"Okay, okay, whatever you say. Fareed and Nad. Although I think this is not the time to change your name to Nad," said Ayshe.

"It is what Fareed likes to call me, and I am sticking to that. It will be Nad."

Ayshe nodded, saying nothing, but hurried to see Hikmet, whom she was not fond of in the first place. "Ali, did you know that Aslan attacked this poor friend of Nadidé, and he fled the scene? Her friend is in intensive care, and he may die. If he dies, it is going to be Aslan's neck but your responsibility. You promised your daughter to someone she did not and does not love and does not even respect. After what he did, it is your responsibility to fix this mess. I am going to the hospital to see the boy."

Ayshe went to see Nad and told her what she had told Hikmet. "Now you stay put."

Ayshe also tried to call their family doctor to attend to Nad's cut lip. She left a message for him and was driven to the hospital by one of their two drivers.

When the doctor called back in Ayshe's absence, Hikmet cancelled his visit.

————

At the hospital, when asking for Fareed, Ayshe was met by Tolga, Leila, Naz, and Deniz. Naz, who knew Ayshe well, told Ayshe all the details. She also told her that her friends at the engineering school informed her that Aslan was in custody of the military police.

Leila greeted Ayshe warmly. She told her that she had called Fareed's parents in London and that his mother was on her way over, and that Fiona planned to arrive in Istanbul the following day, either on a commercial flight or on a chartered flight.

"Chartered flight?" Ayshe wondered. She got curious and asked obliquely about Fareed's parents.

"Both of Fareed's parents are famous neurosurgeons. Fareed's father operated on one of Turkey's prime ministers and he only handles chronic or difficult conditions. The same applies to Fareed's mother." Ayshe was pleased and relieved that her daughter was going with somebody from a highly professional family.

They waited together for a while before Ayshe left without being able to see Fareed. Ayshe said she needed to take care of Nadidé. Then she corrected herself; she used Nad instead. The four smiled. Ayshe, in response, told them that as of today her daughter had told her that she would answer only to Nad.

Upon her return home Ayshe avoided talking to Hikmet. She went directly to see Nad. Nad had showered and simmered down some. Ayshe told her that the physicians did not have any more updates about Fareed and that Fareed's mother was planning to fly to Istanbul the following day.

"I wanted to meet her under different circumstances. Look at things now. She is coming over under the worst circumstances, and it is all because he fell in love with me. He is in a coma," Nad said with tears in her eyes.

Ayshe told Nad that she met Tolga and Leila, and that she could tell they were genuinely nice people; that they did not blame her, and they were worried about her.

"You know Nad, Leila told me about how prominent Fareed's parents are, but I forgot to ask, what does Tolga do?" said Ayshe.

"What do you mean, Mother? He is my mechanical engineering professor. He is also an electrical engineering professor. He has doctorates in both fields, and his wife will get her doctorate in civil engineering in a couple of months. She is the leading Middle East expert in earthquakes."

"*Mashallah*," said Ayshe, meaning *God's bounty*.

"Listen Mother, you need to understand I love Fareed and I want to be with him whether his father is a famous physician or a dishwasher. Do you understand me?" said Nad.

"I do, I do, but wouldn't you prefer that they are famous doctors?" Ayshe said inquisitively.

————

The following day, Leila could not reach Nad's phone since Hikmet had disconnected it. She managed to talk to Ayshe, and told Ayshe to tell Nad that Fiona, Fareed's mother, was arriving on British Air at five o'clock that evening. They intended to meet her at the airport and wondered if Nad wanted to join them.

Ayshe went to Hikmet. "Ali, Nad wants to go to the airport to meet the boy's mother," she said.

Hikmet looked up. "Nad needs to apologize to Ata Aslan and ask him if he objects to her doing that."

"Are you out of your wits?" asked Ayshe. "To have her call the man that is causing her so much pain! Are you thinking straight? Didn't you hear me as to what your clone has done? Listen, Ali, your daughter is refusing to eat, and if anything happens to her, you will have murdered her. I don't plan to let you do that. I have already lost Ahmet. I know he is not my biological son, but I raised him and loved him as if he was mine, and I have no plans of losing Nad too. I would rather lose you than her!"

Hikmet scoffed. "Why do you call her Nad? We are not Westerners."

"That is what she wants to be called. She is twenty and she has the right to be called by any decent name she chooses to be called by. You can do nothing about it. Her friends and the school already call her Nad, and if she wants to call herself by a Western name, so be it. What is the big deal?"

"Nad is not an Islamic name," said Hikmet.

"Neither is Nadidé. If we were to use the Arabic/Islamic version, we would call her Nadira. Yes, Nad knew that and relayed it to me."

Hikmet said nothing.

Ayshe hurried to her room and looked for Ahmet's phone number. Hikmet had not told Ayshe that he had a ten-year-old son from a previous marriage by the time he married her, when she was seventeen. In anger, Ahmet had separated himself from the family and gone back to Germany permanently, six years earlier. It was all due to his father's behavior and partially due to the fact Ayshe had not fought hard for him.

She mustered the courage to call him. Ahmet was most conciliatory when he heard his stepmother's voice, having woken him up from sleep.

"Listen, Ahmet, I don't want to lose Nadidé—I mean Nad. She calls herself Nad now. She is refusing to eat. If anything happens to her, I will not be able to take it. You are my only hope. Your father is as pig-headed and as backward as he has always been, and he does not exhibit any inclination to change. I want you to think about it and do something. I don't want to wait until it is too late."

"Good God. He is one of the most unreasonable men I have ever known. But what is wrong with Nadidé—excuse me, I need to get used to Nad. What happened?"

Ayshe told him the whole story, as much as she knew it, in detail. Ahmet promised to call her the following day.

———

Ahmet did call Ayshe back. He told her that two of his colleagues had accepted to fill in for him and his wife, and that he and his family would be on their way to Istanbul the following day.

Before he hung up, he asked his mother about the name of Nad's boyfriend. She told him it was Fareed.

"Fareed? This is an Arab name. My partner's name is Fareed, and he is from Lebanon. Is Fareed from Lebanon?" he asked.

"No, from Palestine but he was studying in Lebanon. Oh, oh, I forgot to tell you. Both his parents are neurosurgeons," Ayshe said.

When Ahmet inquired about Fareed's parents, Ayshe did not know their last name. She went and asked Nad.

"Nad says their last name is Shaheen," Ayshe said a few minutes later.

"You mean Shaheen and Burke? I bet that's who his parents are. She still uses her maiden name sometimes. They were my professors. They lectured our class for a whole month at Heidelberg. I recall the school paid as much as a one-year salary for just one month of their work. They are the best, no doubt about it. Don't tell Nad that I am on my way. It may be in the papers shortly and considering the reputation of his parents, it will be a big mess for the Turkish government. Shaheen and Burke are known all over Europe. Consider this—a military officer attacking and putting the son of two of the most prominent European physicians in a coma. I am sure it will be in the papers if the Turkish government does not handle it right!"

CHAPTER 13

Ahmet and his family arrived in Istanbul and checked into a hotel close to his parents' home. He called his mother and told her that he and the whole family were on their way. Ayshe was beside herself. She was elated as she had never seen her two grandchildren, a girl just turned five, and a boy, four.

She met them at the door, hugged Ahmet and then the children and could not let go. Ahmet had done a good job of educating them about their maternal grandmother, who died shortly after his birth, and explained that Ayshe was their step-grandmother.

Ahmet introduced his wife, Gisela. The children, Selim and Ayshe, introduced themselves in broken Turkish. It was obvious Ahmet intended to make a point by naming his daughter after his stepmother and avoiding doing the same when it came to his son, not calling him after his own father. The implication was clear: He was his mother's son and not his father's.

Gisela carried the two children, one at a time, and handed one after the other to their grandmother. Ayshe kissed them, rubbed their hair, and hugged them as tears came down her cheeks.

"Grandmother, why are you crying?" Selim asked.

Ahmet answered that it was because she had not seen them till now and that she wanted to see them more often. The two children felt comfortable speaking in German. "These are tears of joy," Ahmet told Selim.

Ayshe asked her mother, "Do you want us to cry?"

Gisela told her no, only older people cry like this.

Hikmet came out and saw his son, for the first time in six years. They did not shake hands or hug. Ahmet spoke first.

"I am here for Nad and Nad alone, and of course for my mother."

"You too participate in this nonsense; you call her Nad. Her name is Nadidé," said Hikmet.

"Her name is her choice. She is twenty and she has the right to decide about her name and about anything and *anybody* in her life," said Ahmet, parroting his mother's explanation. "Nice to see you," he added, avoiding calling Hikmet "Dad." "I am dying to see my sister."

Ahmet paused for few seconds then proceeded to Nad's room. He knocked on the door. Nad did not respond. He knocked again.

"Nad, this is Ahmet, your brother, open the door."

"Ahmet, is this really you?!"

The door opened and Nad hugged Ahmet and hung on to him, kissing him all over his face. He pulled back, held her face, kissed her on her forehead, and hugged her tightly.

"Let me look at your lip. Damn, it is infected. You are coming with me. Nobody but nobody will ever touch or harm you again. Get ready, pack, and let's go," he told her.

Ayshe and Gisela were waiting for Ahmet as he waited for Nad. When Ayshe showed up to check on them, Ahmet said, "Mother, we are going to be here for four nights; I want Nad to stay with us in the hotel. She does not need to face this monster every minute of her life."

Ayshe said, "Whatever you say. I have no objection."

When Nad got out of the room, she saw Ayshe Jr. and Selim. She crouched to hug and kiss them all over. Ayshe Jr. and Selim loved their aunt right away. Ahmet had never described her to them. When she finally got to kiss Gisela, Gisela kissed her back.

"You are one beautiful and graceful woman. How come Ahmet did not say much about you? He showed me your teenage pictures. I am so happy to meet you and I am sorry you are going through all this agony; it will get better. I know; I have seen many cases like Fareed's condition. They usually fully recover. I am a doctor too."

Ahmet took Nad's hand and asked everyone to follow him. Hikmet's bodyguard stood in the center of the gallery leading to the main door. The bodyguard was a 5'9", a muscular person but no match to a well-built 6'4" Ahmet.

"Get out of my way if you want to save yourself. I am the physician here. She needs to go to the emergency room," said Ahmet.

Hikmet signaled the bodyguard to get out of the way. With the appearance of Ahmet and his joining forces with Nad and Ayshe, they all noticed for the first time what looked like a restrained but not totally defeated Hikmet. Ayshe, emboldened, said to him, "I will not accept my son and his family staying at a hotel while we have ten bedrooms in this house. After all, this was my father's house, and it is now mine. You can leave and stay at the base. I don't want any conflicts. We have had enough already."

It was the first time Ayshe addressed Hikmet in this fashion, after twenty-two years of marriage, and he was insulted, as if she was trying to belittle him. Without saying anything to anybody, he packed and left for the base.

———

When the family got to the hospital, they could see Tolga and Leila. Leila ran toward Nad and hugged her.

"Don't worry, everything will be all right," Leila told Nad. "Be strong. Be strong for Fareed. He will come through. If for nothing else, he will for you. I can tell—you are his love and his life. Please take it easy. Tolga and I are here for you and Fareed. Don't you blame yourself for any of this! Blame your father and Major Aslan."

Nad was pleased that nobody was blaming her for what had happened. Her posture and self-confidence improved a lot after Leila's words.

Ahmet and Gisela were introduced to Tolga and Leila. As Ayshe held her grandchildren's hands and introduced them to the Chakirs, Nad was looking all around. She was trying to locate Fiona, Fareed's mother. Nad was very anxious to meet her.

Leila figured that out. "Nad, Dr. Burke is allowed inside." Leila asked the nurse to let Fiona know that Nad's family was there. In no time Fiona came out of intensive care.

Fiona was looking for Nad as she emerged. It was easy to tell who Nad was. Leila had described her to Fiona. Although Fiona knew of Nad, Fareed had not fully described her to his mother. Fiona sped toward Nad, her arms wide open, and hugged Nad as if she had known her a long while. Nad started crying in anguish and relief, to be received so warmly by Fiona.

"For the grace of God, look at you. I think Fareed did the exact right thing this time. Don't cry, my love. He will be all right. I have been checking on his vital signs all morning. They look exceptionally good. He will come out of it. This is my specialty and my husband's specialty," said Fiona, trying to calm Nad.

Nad kissed Fiona one more time, and then asked her, "You think I can go in and see him?"

"What do you mean? If they don't allow you to see him, we will just bring him home," said Fiona jokingly, trying to ease Nad's anxiety. Nad started laughing and wiped her tears.

Ayshe stood quietly a few steps behind Nad, not wanting to interrupt the connection between Fiona and Nad. Fiona walked toward Ayshe and hugged her. "Ayshe, it's nice to meet you. I'm Fiona Shaheen." She nodded to Ahmet.

"Mother, Fiona and Dr. Shaheen lectured my class at the University of Heidelberg, twelve years ago," Ahmet told Ayshe. "My wife and I will go in. She is a physician also. But I want them to allow Nad to go in too, if possible," he added.

The nurse called the attending physician, who allowed Ahmet, Gisela, Fiona, and Nad to go in.

Nad could see Fareed was totally out. Tears filled her eyes.

"Fareed's condition, while serious, has a great possibility of full recovery," Ahmet explained to her.

"You are truly your sister's brother. Leila and I were talking about this earlier. You flew all the way from Germany to be here for her. This is very commendable," said Fiona, patting Ahmet's back. She looked at Nad and said, "There is no damage to the brain. There was a slight hemorrhage from one of the vessels; it stopped on its own. While this is my husband's exact specialty, he operates only when the skull must be opened. In this case, we don't want to do that. Dr. Shah, an invasive radiologist out of UCLA, is the world's top specialist in this very minute procedure. I have already contacted him, and he is ready to come over, on short notice. Your brother knows what I am talking about."

Ahmet whispered in Nad's ear. "Believe me, in this case, they know what they are doing, much more than me or any doctor in this hospital."

———

While everyone in the family was busy with Fareed's medical condition, General Hikmet was worried about the situation with Major Aslan. He desperately wanted Nad to marry Aslan. Hikmet wanted to devote his time to see what to do about the major. He was also concerned that Aslan's incarceration might create trouble for him. The two of them, among others, had maintained a close and clandestine relationship for a long time. Their political views lay to the right of the junta, and religiously they were opposite of the junta.

The ruling junta had designated a shadow junta to take over in case something did happen to them—and in that case, General Hikmet would take over as the head of the replacement junta. Major Aslan was waiting to become a colonel before he could officially be a member of any junta. That had nothing to do with military code. Those were guidelines set by the junta itself. They did not want junior officers, with limited influence, to be involved.

General Hikmet went to the military prison to visit Aslan.

Publicly, Hikmet was scolding and criticizing him. Privately, they were trying to work out a way to get Aslan out of prison. Hikmet wanted to act before the military court system started processing the case. After Hikmet consulted with his own secretive ultra-right group, he reluctantly agreed to arrange an escape for Aslan, with the objective of reaching Germany under an assumed name.

In short order, Hikmet managed to plant a guard in the prison. That guard arranged for Aslan's cell to be left open. Aslan wore his own uniform, which was smuggled in, for his use. He left with relative ease. But instead of heading to Germany, he went to Pendik, a city of around half a million people. It was barely twenty-five miles from Istanbul. He was given shelter there by a cousin.

———

Nad had the nurse elevate the cot she was to sleep on to the same level as Fareed's bed. She stretched her body diagonally to have her head inches from Fareed's head. She was playing Arabic music and was singing in Turkish, whatever came to her mind.

As each musical arrangement finished, she would stop and ask Fareed if he enjoyed it. Naturally, Fareed could not respond.

She followed this routine for three nights while Naz, Fiona, and Deniz alternated in visiting her. Ahmet and his wife were busy visiting with Ayshe. They would visit in the evening to spend a couple hours with Nad before their return to Germany.

After Fiona talked to Ameer, her husband, they decided to contact Dr. Shah. Shah took the next plane to London and he and Ameer flew together to Istanbul. "There will be no harm closing the once-bleeding vessel while Fareed is in a coma, if need be," he advised Fiona and Ameer. They fully agreed with him. After making all the arrangements, Shah was given the go-ahead by the medical board to perform his procedure.

It took Shah a mere two hours, and according to him it went very smoothly. Both Ameer and Fiona, who scrubbed in with Dr. Shah, agreed. Fiona did not need to ask Dr. Shah personally to explain how successful the procedure was. She knew it was successful.

"I am now very optimistic," said Fiona to Nad. "What remains to be done is for you to continue singing in Turkish. Listen, Nad, you don't have to sing to Arabic tunes, you can sing Turkish songs. I understand there are songs called Turkish Arabesque. How about singing along with those types of songs? This way you will enjoy listening to Turkish songs while Fareed may respond to their tunes."

"Who told you I was singing, Dr. Burke?" asked Nad humorously.

"Here we go again—it is Fiona and not Dr. Burke, and yes, a couple of the nurses heard you and they like your singing. They told me that you go to sleep every night singing," said Fiona.

Nad continued with her singing but now she changed to Turkish songs. The sixth night, as her voice got faint and she was about to sleep, she heard someone singing. She woke up suddenly. She looked toward the door to see who it was. She could see no one. She turned back to Fareed, whose eyes were closed but lips were moving.

Nad gasped, jumping up. "Fareed? Fareed!" He didn't respond. She ran out and called the nurse.

The attending physician asked Nad to resume singing. As she resumed singing in Turkish, Fareed resumed singing in Arabic.

When Nad raised the volume of her singing, Fareed did the same. Nad switched to English. Fareed followed suit.

Within three hours, Fareed was awake. He could recognize Nad but could not recall anything about Aslan's attack. He could recall he was handed a bouquet of roses by Nad. Nad took Fareed's hands and kissed them.

Nad called her brother, in Germany. Ahmet, who was awakened at four in the morning, called his mother. He told her jokingly that Nad was so euphoric about Fareed's coming out of his coma that he suspected that Nad would have committed suicide had the hospital prevented her from sleeping next to her boyfriend.

"Ahmet, please be prepared to visit Istanbul again," Ayshe said. "I can no longer handle your father, if things sour further. And you are right, I have never seen anybody like Nad. She cannot think of anybody but Fareed. What more can we ask for? He is so handsome, and his parents are jewels. I didn't think she would find somebody to match her looks and her grace, but she found him and more in Fareed. Please keep me in mind. I need your help."

Within half an hour, Fiona, Tolga, and Leila had joined Nad, talking to Fareed. It was the news they were waiting for. They faxed Dr. Shah to let him know that Fareed had woken up from his coma.

Fiona resumed her leading role. "Under the circumstances, Ameer will go back home. I will stay here for three more days. I want to spend time with you, your mother, and Leila. How about it, Nad?"

For three days, the four ladies would socialize and sample Turkish food, in between their visits to Fareed at the hospital. Fareed was out of the hospital a day before Fiona left. By the time she left, Fiona felt as if she had known Nad all her life, and above all, she had fallen in love with her. Yet, she kept her thoughts to herself. She did not want to give Fareed much credit, having been disappointed with Dania before. She felt passionately that Nad would be the daughter she never had.

CHAPTER 14

I t was the best of times. Nad got to know Fiona and it was mutual respect and admiration. Ayshe got to know the Shaheen family, and she was impressed with every one of them. Ata Aslan was gone. Ali Hikmet was at the base. Ayshe asserted herself to everyone and especially to her husband. Ahmet and his family were back as part of the family and supporting Nad and Ayshe.

Ayshe spent a little time with Fareed. She told Nad that this time she had found her match: intelligent, handsome, personable. She sat down with Nad and asked her whether she thought Fareed was the right one for her. Nad answered, "Mother, I cannot think of anybody else. Do you have any doubt that I love him? I cannot think of a situation where I will separate from him. He loves me a lot or else he would have never spoken to me after I slapped him and cut his lip!"

"What! You slapped Fareed and cut his lip? Why would you do such a thing?"

"Leila was kissing him, and I did not know she was his cousin.

I thought she was another girlfriend and that he was nothing but a playboy, trying to take advantage of me. What is worse is when Tolga showed Leila's picture in class and told everyone that she was his wife and Fareed's cousin. I felt so obtuse. I despised myself until Fareed forgave me," said Nad.

"Oh, Nad, I am getting to respect this young man even more. You are lucky he forgave you. You would have really hated yourself for a long time if your stupidity had caused you to break up with him. Since you mentioned this, do you think you can arrange for the three of us to have lunch together?" asked Ayshe.

"Mom, what is on your mind? You must be thinking of something," said Nad, tilting her face and giving her mother a gaze.

"Nad, don't get suspicious. I like Fareed a lot. I just want to know him better since you will be spending most of your time with him."

———

When the three of them got together, Ayshe took center stage by needling Fareed. She did not want to show that she admired him. The first thing she asked Fareed was if he objected to calling him Far instead of Fareed.

Fareed smiled and said, "I am afraid I do object, and would prefer it if you would not . . . 'Far' means *rat* in Arabic and you would not want your daughter to be going out with a rat, would you?"

"How about if I call you Reed?' said Ayshe in a cajoling tone.

"I get it, you think that since I now call her Nad, I should accept the same for me. Well, my crisp answer is that this is not your privilege. It is Nad's privilege. You see, I would not venture trying to change your name. You know what, I think you are here to give me a hard time, a lovingly hard time, but a hard time nevertheless! Somehow, you think I deserve it."

At the end of the rope and feeling that Fareed had politely limited her teasing options, she said to him, "No, you only deserve that I love you, and since Nad loves you and I love Nad with all my heart, I love you with all my heart."

"In this case love goes both ways. Since you are Nad's loveable mother, you deserve and do have my love," said Fareed.

Ayshe moved toward Fareed and kissed him on his cheek. Nad followed suit.

Naz, Deniz, and Nad got together daily. Fareed would join them from time to time. Simra would show up whenever Fareed was not there, yet none of the three friends noticed her pattern. Nad and Fareed were inseparable. That did not mean that either Ali Hikmet or Ata Aslan had given up.

———

Ata Aslan contacted the Turkish military attaché in Beirut, Colonel Taner Yilmaz. He asked him to find what he could about Fareed and his family. Between the attaché and the intelligence officer at the Turkish embassy, all they could find was positive and mostly inconsequential stuff. The attaché reported his findings to Hikmet, who was disappointed with the news. He thought about it for a while and then suggested to Yilmaz to invite the Turkish students at the AUB for dinner, to try to secure information that was not in the public domain.

Within weeks, he invited all forty-two Turkish students. Only twenty-nine showed up; many of the leftists intentionally did not. Two of the invitees knew Fareed but only Arda—on the basketball drill team, opposite Fareed—knew him well. Arda told Yilmaz that Fareed had had a girlfriend, Dania, who was very close to Fareed for two years and that Fareed had ended the relationship abruptly.

This information piqued Hikmet's interest. Yilmaz asked Arda if he could get him as much information about Dania as possible.

"Fareed was visiting from Istanbul for the weekend," Arda told Yilmaz. "The basketball team arranged a dinner in his honor. Many things were memorable about the dinner, not the least of which was Dania crashing the party." Yilmaz asked Arda if there were pictures taken at the dinner and if there were, to try to secure as many as possible.

Within a week, Arda brought Yilmaz more than forty different pictures. Several stood out. One showed Dania hugging Fareed as he held a basketball with his name and the date of his visit. There was another picture showing Fareed unceremoniously showing Dania out the door. Yilmaz sent all the pictures in a diplomatic pouch to Ali Hikmet.

Yilmaz's report mentioned that Dania had crashed the dinner, and that Fareed chose to kick her out. That did not matter. Hikmet was looking for ammunition, real or misleading. He found two perfect pictures, almost tailor made. One showed Dania hugging Fareed; the other showed Fareed holding a basketball with his name and date. The date was during the beginning of Fareed's relationship with Nad.

———

One very early morning, Hikmet went to the house and woke up Ayshe. He took out the two pictures to show Ayshe.

"Did you or your daughter know that Fareed has a fiancée in Lebanon? Here she is." He threw the picture at her. "Look at the date on the ball. This is a very recent picture. This is all your responsibility," he told Ayshe and barged out of her room.

Ayshe did not know what to do. She did not know whether to wake up Nad or not. She was not sure she needed to tell anything before she could investigate the matter. In the end, she decided to wake Nad up and showed her the pictures.

At first Nad was dumbfounded. She could not think straight. Dania was an exceptionally beautiful girl. The pictures ware fine pictures, showing the date and occasion without ambiguity. Her thoughts were confused. At first, she thought if Fareed had a fiancée, why would Fiona be so friendly to her, and why didn't Dania fly over to visit Fareed when he was in the hospital? Although Fiona had told Nad that Fareed once had a girlfriend she did not like, in the end Nad did what she had done in the past—she jumped to a premature and specious conclusion that Fareed was not only deceiving her but deceiving his own mother.

She convinced herself that he was using her as a decoy to convince his mother that he had broken up with Dania. She thought she figured that he was waiting to graduate this year and return to Lebanon to end one relationship and re-energize another.

She took the picture and drove hurriedly to Fareed's apartment. When Fareed opened the door and Nad burst in, Fareed looked at her, taken aback. "What is going on?"

"What is going on? *This* is what is going on. Last time I slapped you on the face. This time I am going to tell you, you are too repugnant an individual to be slapped. Here is what is wrong!" She threw the pictures at Fareed's feet.

Fareed looked at the pictures. "Nad, wait, I can explain everything."

Nad snatched the pictures from the floor and barged out. She left to see Naz and Deniz.

As soon as Deniz opened the door, Nad hurried in and sat at the dining table, placing the pictures on the table. "Look what I found," she said pointing at the pictures.

Deniz looked at it. "Good God, this is only two months ago."

"He fooled us all, including his innocent mother. He wanted to convince his mother that he was no longer involved with Dania because she did not like her. He showed me off to her to deceive her, and now he is planning to go back to Lebanon to marry her, after he graduates," said Nad.

Naz came out and looked at the picture and did not know what to say.

"How do you know her name?" asked Deniz.

"Look at it. It's on the back of the picture, Dania Boulos. She is Christian. Look at the cross around her neck," said Nad.

"Whose handwriting is that?" asked Naz, exhibiting some doubt about the whole thing. Naz looked at the handwriting. "Oh God, whoever wrote this must be Turkish. Look at the umlaut over the U. It could be German, but I think in this case it is Turkish."

Deniz also had her suspicions, having gone through the experience of soothing Nad's feelings about Fareed's supposed other girlfriend, who instead turned out to be his cousin. She knew then that Nad had decided on the guilt of Fareed without investigating anything. The day before, Nad had referred to her father uncharacteristically, by his first name. Today, she was affectionately calling him "Dad." "Where did you get this picture from?"

Nad told them that her father gave her mother the pictures.

Deniz then resorted to her usual role as a prudent advisor. "Look Nad, please don't confront Fareed before you figure out what is happening. It may not be at all what it looks. Let us three think about it before you say anything to Fareed or anybody else."

"What do you mean, I just came over from Fareed's. I showed him the picture already," said Nad.

"Nad, Nad, Nad, why do you keep doing this?" Deniz sighed. "Give yourself some time to think. Give us a break. You recall when you slapped him on the face? You thought he was playing around before your very eyes. It turned out to be that he was being kissed by his cousin. Excuse me, but has he ever lied to you about anything? In the name of God, pause and think. You are making us crazy. Have you thought what you will tell Fareed if you find out he is innocent of all your inflated suspicions?!"

"But this is different. We have the proof here. It is obvious. He told me that he was going to Beirut to see a sick friend. It was his best friend, Sammy," said Nad.

"Did you check if Fareed has such a friend and if he had been sick then? Nad, help me to help you. If this picture is genuine, I will be the first to tell you to dump him, but coming from a suspicious source, from somebody who hates Fareed with passion, is enough to call for an investigation," said Deniz.

Naz agreed.

"I disagree with you. I think I have the proof. Let us seek Simra's opinion," said Nad.

"Hold off on Simra's opinion. Why not check if there was a

Sammy? If he happened to be seriously sick, just like Deniz said," said Naz.

"Let us do both. I am this time resigned to the fact I no longer care for Fareed. I am convinced he is a cheat, and this is one thing I cannot stand," said Nad.

"You know, Nad, all you are doing is trying to convince yourself that you are right. This time you may not be able to have him back if you accuse him once again of an indiscretion he is totally innocent of. You would have accused him of dishonorable behavior too many times," said Deniz.

"Deniz, please don't give me a hard time. I am not able to decide whether to cry or just do something to myself. Could I have been so stupid?" said Nad.

"In the name of God, just wait. Why are you obsessed with bad scenarios? We cannot go through this all over again. Naz and I also suffer when your love life goes astray, and we feel so good when you're happy. Only yesterday, we were looking at him and admiring all those qualities—handsome, intelligent, speaks four languages. He learned Turkish for you, and his family could not be more honorable and prestigious. Just cool it, Nad. Have some considerations for our feelings. We love you and we want the best for you. Please, just let us find out!" Deniz lowered her head into her arms on the table.

Nad started crying. "I never loved anyone else. He has been my only love. I am just devastated. I may not be able to finish this year," she said.

"Stop it, Nad, you are acting childish. I am starting to get really incensed at you. We are three months from graduation. You must graduate one way or the other, Fareed or no Fareed, but hopefully with Fareed. We all love him. He has become like a brother to us," said Naz.

———

They later showed the picture to Simra. She pretended to be totally indignant. She started talking in a socialist context. She described Lebanon as a corrupt and loose country whose political and economic system was designed by France, the colonial power that had ruled Lebanon for twenty-seven years. She said that Fareed was no more and no less than the reflection of the libertine social reality of Lebanon.

It was the first time Deniz and Naz heard such a condemnation in these terms. They knew then they were listening to a politically opinionated and likely politically active person. Neither one wanted to comment. Deniz winked at Naz to wait to talk about it later. As they were meeting, Nader showed up.

"Fareed called me and wanted to know if he could come over," Nader said. He looked at Deniz. "Can I talk to you and Naz first? Fareed seems to be very agitated."

Deniz nodded.

Simra then said, "Nad and I don't need to be here when Fareed comes over. She does not need to be further humiliated. Why don't Nad and I leave and you two can talk to Fareed and let the two of us have lunch at our Italian place?"

When Simra and Nad left, Deniz was still holding the picture of Fareed with Dania. She looked at Naz. "Do you sense what I sense—it's as if Simra does not want Fareed and Nad to be together. I think she may be jealous. Have you ever met Murat? I bet he is a dumpling. All this about Lebanon is just a cover-up for Simra to promote her desire to see Nad and Fareed apart."

Naz said, "I know who to ask about Murat. We can ask Nader and Ramzi. I think they know him well."

Fareed arrived, looking disturbed with an ashen face. He asked Naz and Deniz if they had seen the pictures.

"What pictures?" Naz asked.

"Don't play dumb, Naz, you know what I am talking about."

When they told him that Nad told them the whole story, he asked, "Would you like me to share the real story with you? Because if you don't, I will leave and stop bothering you and Nad altogether."

Deniz put her hand up. "Cool it first. Then you can proceed."

He told them that he had flown to Beirut to see Sammy because Sammy was extremely sick. He had not expected a dinner in his honor. It was all a surprise to him, but not to Dania, who had gleaned as much as she could about his visit to Beirut. He explained to them that Dania crashed the party and that he had not seen her for a couple of years before then. "I kicked her out and hadn't seen her since. Wait for Sammy to come over next week. He will have all the pictures of the dinner and you will see what I mean," Fareed added.

"Would you like to have lunch with us and repeat your story to Nad? Simra will be there," said Deniz.

"No, I will not say anything in front of Simra. I don't think she likes Nad, because she does not like General Hikmet for his politics and views. I don't like him either, but I don't confuse my feelings toward him with my feelings toward Nad. This is bullshit. She and Murat want to lump Nad with her father. I think they hate both, and who knows, they may hate me too," answered Fareed.

Naz and Deniz looked at each other and agreed with Fareed. Fareed's words helped them figure out why Simra was trying to split Fareed and Nad apart. Fareed told them that he would not be seeing Nad until he had the proof in his hand, upon Sammy's arrival.

Deniz looked at Fareed and said, "Listen Fareed, I believe you, but don't disappoint us. Make sure you have the proof in your hand. I am afraid Nad, as usual, has convinced herself that you are guilty. Without solid proof, she will resist. I think the situation in her house is unsettled and confusing. Don't be harsh on Nad. Her nerves are frayed. You love her and she loves you, but she is confused. You have become like a brother to us. We too don't want to lose you." She then showed the back of the picture to Fareed. "Do you recognize this handwriting?"

"No, no. It looks more Turkish than regular Latin alphabet. It has an umlaut in one instance," he said, pointing at the U. "I bet you anything it is General Hikmet's handwriting. Why don't we go and compare it to other samples of his writings?"

Knowing that Nad was having lunch with Simra, the three left right away to Nad's house. There they saw Ayshe. Ayshe was cordial but rather cool toward Fareed. Deniz took the initiative; she asked if she could see samples of General Hikmet's writings. Ayshe brought them samples of his handwritten speeches. At first, they could not see the similarities. Fareed asked for a magnifying glass. As they magnified specific letters, they could see the distinct similarities.

The proof was damning. As Ayshe grew convinced of what Deniz, Naz, and Fareed discovered, she apologized to Fareed. Fareed looked at her angrily, after Ayshe had greeted him tepidly. He said nothing and breezed out the door, saying that he would take a taxi back to his apartment.

Nad arrived back at the house before Naz and Deniz left.

"This was your third and last time," Naz said, looking at Nad wistfully. "I have a feeling you are not going to see Fareed anymore. It is your father's handwriting on the back of the pictures. We just finished comparing the handwritings. There is no doubt." She paused, then continued, "You know, Nad, I feel like slapping you and slapping you real hard. You cannot keep doing the same thing, either jumping to wrong conclusions or falling into someone's trap. I am afraid this time, you need to resolve this problem yourself, if it is at all resolvable."

CHAPTER 15

Deniz, Naz, Nad, and Simra met for lunch. The atmosphere was tense as Simra kept indirectly encouraging Nad to break up with Fareed. Naz and Deniz had become aware of Simra's scheming. Nad had been clearly influenced by Simra's prodding and sociopolitical analysis.

Deniz's and Naz's plan was not to let Nad be alone with Simra. They projected that after several one-on-one sessions between Simra and Nad, Simra would attempt to separate Nad from her other friends, after feeling confident she had succeeded in separating Nad from Fareed.

As expected, Simra invited Nad to go with her alone to meet Murat. Deniz and Naz were ready; they had elicited an invitation from Leila for coffee after lunch at the same time. When Simra extended her invitation, Naz was quick to say, "Oh, no, we are having coffee with Leila and Dr. Chakir. They want to see Nad."

It was difficult for Simra to top a meeting with Tolga. Nad was hesitant to see the Chakirs, for fear they had heard about her feud with Fareed. On the other hand, she had mellowed and wanted to find an opening to placate Fareed in case she turned out to be wrong.

When Deniz, Naz, and Nad arrived, Leila apologized to Nad that Dr. Chakir had been held up by an experiment at the lab. Nad was understanding. "Fareed was supposed to be here," she added to Nad, "but he decided to go to Ankara for a couple of days. He called us and said he needed to clear his head. He did not sound to be in a good mood. Nad, do you know why? Did he tell you why he was going to Ankara?"

Nad said nothing. Leila had not heard about the feud but figured that there was something wrong between the two. She did not pursue the subject further.

Deniz had already recognized Simra's scheming nature and potentially harmful plans. She and Naz had no choice but to share their suspicions with Nad. As Leila went to the kitchen to finish her food preparation, Deniz held Nad's hand and said, "I know that despite what you are saying that Fareed has been your only love, you are overwhelmed by what you thought Fareed did and what all of it meant. We are convinced that it is all your father's schemes. Fareed promised to prove you wrong in a direct and irrefutable way. He intends to do so as early as next week. My suggestion is for us to ask him not to go to the trouble. I feel the more he tries to prove his point, the less chance you and him will get back together. The effort carries lots of unnecessary friction by you believing he is guilty and he fully believing that he is innocent. I hate to see either of you say or do anything to aggravate the situation and cause this love affair to end. If you believe as I do that Fareed can envision no one else other than you, and you envision no one else other than him, you need to have some trust in him and he in you."

"There is one thing which may not be as basic, but it is potentially more dangerous," Naz said. "Simra is not to be trusted. She has evil intentions toward you and your father. She is a hell-bent revolutionary and, if unable to take revenge from your father, she and her group—whomever those may be—will take it from you, to hurt your father. I would like you never to be with her alone, and I need you to promise me that you will keep this in mind. This is not a time to be cordial. It is a time to be safe. What do you have to say, Nad?"

"You're the second person to tell me about Simra," Nad said.

"Second or first does not matter. You need to promise me, and you need to act per your promise. And if you must challenge or insult Simra, then do it and don't give it a second thought. I am being serious—very serious," said Deniz.

"You are scaring me. I have never seen you this serious all my life, but I will do as you say. I trust you and Naz," said Nad.

As Leila came back, she looked at Nad and said, "I also trust what Deniz is saying."

Deniz then asked Nad not to forget and wait for Fareed's return. Leila asked if they could explain the situation to her. Nad said in a quiet voice, "I made a mistake, a serious mistake. This is why Fareed is in Ankara. Under normal circumstances, I would apologize to him repeatedly and profusely, but I am afraid I have outlived my apology welcome. I need to stew in my own juices before I can figure out what I am going to do. I owe everyone here an apology. Let me go home. I don't think I am up to having any lunch."

Naz and Deniz had seen Nad under similar circumstances

before, but they had never seen her in a sad and even forlorn state of mind. They insisted on accompanying Nad home. There, Naz managed to brief Ayshe. Ayshe could clearly see her daughter's dazed and darkened face. This time it was different in that it showed a deep feeling of loss and regret. Ayshe was taken aback by Nad's demeanor. It projected a hopeless resignation, a look of sad bewilderment. A sense of loss descended upon Ayshe.

––––––––

Sammy was talking to Fareed daily. He could sense Fareed's disappointment and distraught emotions. After he felt he was unsuccessful in alleviating some of Fareed's pain, Sammy called Fiona. He told her about the pictures and Nad's knee-jerk reactions. Fiona was furious and saddened at the turn of events. Fiona had grown to love and admire Nad, and she didn't want Fareed to go through another heartbreak. She told Sammy that she would check with him daily if he did not mind. She wanted to think things over and see what the best course of action was.

Fiona wanted to resolve the situation as fast as possible. She came up with a plan—risky, but if successful, it would take care of everything. She called Dania in Beirut.

"Would you care to meet me in Istanbul?" Fiona asked. She told Dania that she wanted her to say goodbye to Fareed in a civilized way and that she was told that she and Fareed had a bad encounter at the basketball team's dinner. "If you agree, I'll send you the plane ticket and pay for your two-day stay in Istanbul." Dania accepted Fiona's offer with some remote hope for reconciliation between her and Fareed.

Fiona then called Sammy. "Can you advance your planned trip to Istanbul and arrange a dinner with Naz, Deniz, and Nad to show them the pictures of how Fareed escorted Dania out of the basketball team's dinner?" He agreed.

———

As Fiona waited in an Istanbul hotel room, Sammy called her from Fareed's apartment. He told her that Nad was happy with his presentation, especially the picture with Fareed escorting Dania out of the gathering. Sammy had told Nad that the plan called for trying to expose Dania as an accomplice in Hikmet's scheme.

Sammy had heard the news of Dania's involvement through Yilmaz from Arda, the same Turkish student who introduced Yilmaz, the Turkish military attaché in Beirut, to Dania. Sammy told Nad that by exposing Dania, Fareed's concentration would shift from the rift between the two of them to Dania's complicity. With that shift accomplished, he and Fiona hoped Fareed would simmer down and accept Nad's apology.

He confirmed all of that and informed Fiona that per her instructions, he was supposed to be the host and the girls were to expect an unnamed friend accompanied by a guest, without having identified Fiona and Dania as the friend and the guest. He also told Fiona that he asked Nad, Naz, and Deniz not to react in any way to the presence of the friend or the guest. They were to keep silent until the friend finished her presentation.

"I will be there soon," Fiona said to Sammy.

In no time, Fiona and Dania arrived. All three girls looked utterly shocked when they saw Fiona, and even more when they recognized Dania. Fiona put her index finger on her lips to make sure they expressed no reaction. Initially, Fiona acted like a mother hen directing chicks. After she cordially made the rounds of introduction, including introducing Dania as Fareed's ex-girlfriend, she asked Dania to sit opposite her. She took a sort of professorial posture toward Dania, as if she were a law school professor teaching tort.

"Dania, do you mind if I ask you a couple of questions for the girls to know why you and I are here?" said Fiona.

Dania agreed.

"Dania, you are here because Fareed and you want to say goodbye to each other in a civilized fashion. Isn't this the case?"

Dania agreed again.

"You were Fareed's girlfriend for two years, were you not?"

"Yes, I was, and I do not know why he broke up with me," said Dania.

"You and Fareed never got engaged?"

"No."

"You know that I am Catholic, and Fareed is Muslim, don't you?" Fiona asked.

"Yes, why are you asking all these questions, Dr. Burke?" said Dania.

"And you would not consider marrying a Muslim, would you?"

"No, I cannot, but Fareed can convert."

"But neither he nor I would want him to convert, and we insisted on it, and you knew that, didn't you?"

"Yes. Why are you asking these questions in front of everyone?" answered Dania.

In a contrived fashion, Fiona said, "I just want to educate the

Turks about the Arabs. You see, the Turks are overwhelmingly Muslim. They have very few Christian Turks. They have Armenian and Greek Christians; this is different. The Arabs on the other hand have a large Christian minority, especially in Lebanon," said Fiona, trying to cover up her scheme and her barrage of questions. "Now, why did you crash the basketball team dinner party?"

"I wanted to see Fareed," said Dania.

"But he was rude, which makes me really sad, and he escorted you out, didn't he?"

"Yes, he did, and he embarrassed me in front of all his friends," said Dania.

"Tell them what you told me about this guy called Yilmaz," said Fiona.

"Well, Yilmaz, the Turkish military attaché, told me to tell any Turk who asks me about Fareed that I am Fareed's fiancée," said Dania.

"Dania, I invited you to Istanbul for two days, but I am sorry; your plane leaves back to Beirut in four hours. Sammy has hired a taxi to take you first to the hotel and then to the airport. He has been paid in full. Fareed happens to be in Ankara, and because of that we are not able to reconcile between the two of you, in order to say goodbye to each other in a civilized way for the final time, rather than the way Fareed chose—to kick you out of the gathering, humiliating you and insulting you in the process," said Fiona in a tongue in cheek fashion.

Fiona and Sammy knew that Fareed had come back from Ankara. In the end, they all figured out what Fiona had done, although all the girls were surprised Fiona had gone to such lengths and resorted to somewhat devious plans. They were all, including

Sammy, dumbfounded and lost for words.

As Sammy put Dania into the taxi, all dazed, Fiona told the girls and Sammy later that Yilmaz was once under the command of General Hikmet.

Fiona looked at Nad somberly. "I don't need to spell it out. You know the rest. Nad, Fareed loves you so much and I hope he is not stupid enough to let go. You really have hurt him deeply this time. I will leave it up to you from here on. Listen, Nad, I would be remiss if I did not tell you that you are almost perfect in every respect, yet you have one major flaw. It looks as if you cannot but be honest and loyal, which is very commendable. I am guessing that your obsession with your own honesty and loyalty drives you crazy when you even suspect another person violating his or her promises; you stop thinking and go berserk, and you have done it several times."

Nad cried and hugged Fiona and told her how sorry she was. Fiona told her that sometimes overused apologies lose their value, and she should be careful in this regard, in how she approached Fareed this time to make up with him, and how in the future she had to trust Fareed and to resist going with whims and suspicions.

"We women think that men don't cry; they do cry but most of their tears drop on the inside. My son is one of them. He is probably crying more than you were hurt!" said Fiona to Nad.

Nad went silent for a while and then stood up to go see Fareed. Deniz stopped her. She told her that it was best that she, Naz, and Sammy see Fareed first and they would call her at home later to tell her when to come over, if they could first placate him.

"Girls, I want to spend time with Nad, about an hour," Fiona said. "I may or may not love her as much as Fareed and Ameer yet, but I love her as much as I love anybody else, as much as I love my only sister. What happens next is not under my control, but no matter what happens between Fareed and Nad, I feel I found the daughter I've never had."

Fiona and Nad spent more than an hour together. Fiona told Nad not to talk about the subject at hand anymore, but to speak about something more cheerful.

"Tell me about your vacation plans. I think this is a much more pleasant subject," said Fiona.

After they discussed Nad's and Fareed's potential travel plans together, Fiona chose to talk about Turkish mosques, about their beauty and their grandeur. Nad looked at her watch and said she should leave for home to receive Deniz's call.

"Nad, you and Fareed plan to have breakfast with me if all goes well. I would like to see the three of us together. I am hopeful Fareed will be reasonable," Fiona said to Nad.

Nad said that she hoped he would be too and promised not to doubt Fareed ever again.

"Nad, listen to me. Fareed takes after his father in this sense. If my husband were to fall in love with another woman, he would ask for a divorce first before he would cheat on me. Fareed is the same way. He will not betray you. I think he would come to you and admit his new love and apologize for it before he would even touch a new lover. Do you understand what I am telling you? This is so important. Do you understand it? If you don't hear it from Fareed, it means it has not happened!"

"I understand it fully, and I will always remember it. I used to keep forgetting that I once thought Fareed was typical, but he is anything but typical and I believe every word you said about him. Thank you, Fiona."

———

Deniz, Naz, and Sammy had done their reconciliation work extremely well. They first told Fareed how Yilmaz and Hikmet had manipulated the situation, and how Dania became, either wittingly or unwittingly, part of the scheme.

After Fareed showed his anger toward Dania, they repeated what Fiona said, that while Nad was almost perfect in every respect, she had a major flaw. They described it as someone losing his or her senses upon suspecting someone they loved, especially one they loved intensely. They asked Fareed to realize that Nad had such deficiency and that he needed to accommodate himself to such emotional affliction, with the hope of helping her out of it over the years. Fareed listened to their argument and, in the end, accepted its main premise.

———

The following morning, as Fiona was waiting with anticipation and dread, Fareed and Nad showed up hand in hand. Nad started to apologize to Fiona, when Fiona stopped her.

"Don't say another word of apology. As far as I am concerned there was a misunderstanding; it is now resolved, over and done with. There is no need to rehash anything. You and Fareed are adults and should be able to resolve your own problems. As my husband says, 'We educate them to think for themselves and not for us to keep correcting them.' I don't plan to correct anybody. Do you hear me, Nad?" said Fiona.

"Yes, I hear you," said Nad.

Fareed, Nad, and Fiona spent a peaceful and warm morning together. They were by themselves and Nad's emotional outbursts had faded into oblivion. The three separated with the plan to get together in the evening.

———

While Nad and Fareed were resolving their turmoil and enjoying themselves, an old face had surfaced from nowhere. One day, before Hikmet showed Ayshe the picture of Dania and Fareed, ex-Major Aslan called General Hikmet.

"Why are you not in Germany?" asked Hikmet. Hikmet thought that Aslan had just arrived back from Germany, where he promised Hikmet he would be, away from Turkey.

"I was with my brother. He got sick and I ran out of money. I needed to come back to sell one of our properties, a large piece of commercial land, which I managed to do," Aslan told Hikmet.

Hikmet accepted the contrived story.

"I now have lots of money, and I can support Nadidé anywhere. I trust you can arrange the rest," continued Aslan.

"Look, Major, my first concern is to extract this heathen from my daughter's life. On the other hand, I don't think she cares for you. You need to look for someone else to marry. After I take care of her friend, her happiness is all I care about. I thought she would grow to love you, but she instead hates you. It is all over," said Hikmet.

Aslan hung up. Hikmet had no idea where exactly he was in Turkey, a country approaching fifty million in population. Hikmet already had Dania's pictures in his possession when he talked to Aslan. His plan was first to discredit Fareed in the eyes of Nad and then to set him up to be kicked out of the country.

———

When Nad got home, she was dying to tell her mother and show her the picture of Fareed kicking Dania out of the dinner party. Instead, Ayshe told Nad that Deniz had called from Fareed's apartment and asked for Nad to call her as soon as Nad came in.

Nad called Fareed's apartment. Deniz answered the phone in an agitated state. She said that they found the apartment door open and when she, Naz, and Sammy entered the apartment, it was a mess and it looked like there had been some kind of struggle: Two of the side lamps were broken and there was blood on the floor. Nad told her mother that she had to go and barged out toward her car. When she got to the apartment, Sammy was hysterical.

"I think something must've happened to Fareed. Why did he have to come to Turkey? Nothing has gone right for him since arriving here," said Sammy without even taking Nad's feelings into consideration.

Nad sat down and was holding her head in her hands, not knowing what to do or say. Naz said that they should call all the hospitals nearby, to check on Fareed. They started calling one hospital after another, but none had heard of Fareed. Nad called one hospital and when she asked about Fareed, the administration person said, "You mean Ferid?"

Nad lost her cool. "Why can't this country call people by their real name? His name is Fareed!" she yelled into the phone.

After five hours of calling hospitals, the police, and the ambulance service, they were exhausted. Nad went home. There she told her mother the whole story. She told her how Fiona and Dania had shown up and how Fiona took command and guided Dania in telling the truth.

"Mother, I think I will be so lucky to have Fiona as my mother-in-law. You would think that because she is a famous neurosurgeon and considering my false accusations against Fareed, she would not care to be so considerate and even a doting person. She could and she was, and I think she would behave the same as a mother-in-law. I respect her and I love her. Now, I need to find Fareed. You think somebody did something to him?" said Nad.

As they were speaking, in came Hikmet in his full military dress. "I came back to see what you and Nad have done about her Christian boyfriend."

Ayshe grabbed the file from Nad's hand and said to Hikmet, "Where is he? What did you do to Fareed, you bastard?! You are nothing but a cheap liar. You showed the picture that suited your purposes and held back all the pictures that showed the meaning of all this. You did not want to show us how Fareed kicked her out. Where is he? You must have sent your men to abduct him."

"Who are you talking about, woman? I have abducted nobody. You must be going crazy!" said Hikmet.

"No, you are the crazy one. Your Dania was here, and she confessed to everything. She told us about Yilmaz. He is your hatchet man in Lebanon, isn't he?" said Ayshe.

"Dad, Dad, where is Fareed? We just want Fareed back. His mother is here, and she will start looking for him as soon as we tell her that he is missing. If you just tell us where he is, we will go get him and we will not tell anybody. Where is he?"

"I swear on the Koran I don't know where he is, and I have nothing to do with this. But I think I know who may have done this. Ata is here in Turkey. He called and asked for your hand, and I told him no way. He may have taken revenge by kidnapping your friend," Hikmet said.

"Dad, he is my *boyfriend*. Why are you afraid to say it? He is Muslim and he is not Turkish. I love him and I cannot live without him. Can you understand what I am talking about? If one day I must choose between you and him, I will choose him. Not only do I love him, but I respect him. He is honest and chivalrous. He doesn't need to wear a military uniform to be like this. In the name of God, where is he?"

"I swear on the Koran that I will do everything possible to find your ... boyfriend. I swear, I swear on the holy Koran," said Hikmet.

"Ali, you created this mess, and you have to solve it," said Ayshe. "You are not welcome in this house until you do. I want Nad to be happy. You made her life and my life a living hell with your crazy ideas about three generations of this and three generations of that. I swear to God, I will divorce you if you keep insulting the prophet with your crazy beliefs. Many of his wives were not Muslim. He had a Christian wife and a Jewish wife."

"Mother, they call this more royalist than the king. My father wants to be more Muslim than Prophet Mehmet," said Nad.

Hikmet looked at Nad and said, "Please give me a kiss. I am your father. I am leaving now. I want to feel good. I have feelings too. I have nothing to do with Fareed's disappearance."

"If you bring back Fareed, I will kiss you on both your cheeks, I will kiss you on your forehead, and I will kiss both your hands.

Just bring him back to me. I told you a hundred times I can't live without him," said Nad, yelling.

"For more than twenty years your mother gave me a kiss every time I left for work; now nobody is willing to even give me one kiss, even my own daughter. I promise that I will do my best to bring your boyfriend back. I do love you and I love your mother. I need you to know that," he told Nad. Before Hikmet left, he looked at Nad and added, "If you want to be called Nad, I will call you Nad."

After he left, Nad hugged her mother. "I think Dad means it this time. I have never heard him swear on the Koran without meaning it. He still prays five times a day. He now accepts my chosen name."

CHAPTER 16

Ayshe headed to the hotel where Fiona was staying. Fiona was surprised to see Ayshe but was most welcoming.

After they greeted each other, Fiona looked at Ayshe as if she was surveying her. "I did not have a chance to say it the first time we met; when I look at you, I know where Nad got her beauty. You are one very good-looking woman and you carry yourself with utmost grace. Now, what good news brings you here?"

Ayshe did not even say thank you to Fiona. She asked her first to sit down, which Fiona did. She told Fiona that Nad should have come to see Fiona on her own, but she was too distraught to think straight.

"Don't tell me. My stubborn son brought up the issue of Nad's suspicions and reverted to being mad at Nad?" Fiona wondered.

"No, it is more serious than that. Fareed is missing, and they found signs of struggle in his apartment and traces of blood," said Ayshe.

"Missing? What are you talking about?" said Fiona in a quivering voice. "How? You mean he has been kidnapped or worse yet, somebody may have done something to him?" Slamming a report she was holding on the table, Fiona continued, "Who would want to harm him? I cannot believe it. If it is not one thing it is another. It is all my mistake; I pressured him to leave Beirut, God have mercy. I can only take so much of this."

"Dr. Burke, Nad and I thought of my husband at first, but we are both convinced he had nothing to do with it. Otherwise, I know nothing else. It is all so confusing," said Ayshe.

Nad called Tolga and Leila. She told them about the fact that Fareed was missing and about the condition of his apartment. Immediately the three rendezvoused in the lobby of Fiona's hotel and headed to see Fiona to let her know. They were surprised to see Ayshe there. When Nad saw that Ayshe had gone to see Fiona, she in typical form erroneously surmised that the news had gotten worse. She immediately asked if Fareed had been harmed.

Ayshe answered, "Nad, in the name of God, control yourself. Don't make everyone more nervous than they already are. Nothing has changed in the meantime. We have heard nothing positive or anything negative."

Sammy arrived and heard the tail end of the conversation. He spoke to support Ayshe. Trying to ease everyone's feelings, he told them that the blood found in the apartment consisted of only three drops, and that it could have been from a small cut while Fareed was shaving. Tolga suggested that they all head to Fareed's apartment, to start the process of looking for him. Ayshe told Tolga to take Nad with them, and for her to stay with Fiona and for each team to update the other every half hour.

"I feel we need to know each other better despite the difficult circumstances we are in," Ayshe told Fiona. "I consider Fareed to be like a son to me. He is two months older than Nad. I want you not to hesitate to ask me for any kind of help. Consider me as your sister. I hope you feel the same way. I want to help but I need guidance from you. You are his mother."

Fiona hugged Ayshe. "You and Nad are so dear to us. You have been most kind. Please don't mind my expressions of exasperation earlier. Let me call Ameer and tell him what happened. He is not a very animated person except in emergencies, and God knows this is the utmost emergency."

"I think we all can use some advice. Go ahead and call him. It may be that we are alarmed for nothing. I will be in the other room," said Ayshe.

The phone conversation with Ameer was the tensest he and Fiona had ever had. Ameer wanted to fly over immediately, but Fiona convinced him otherwise and asked him to find replacements for her for at least one month.

Then Ameer said, "When you find him, let him come back with you to London. We can't take it anymore. It is just too dangerous. They are too militaristic in Turkey. Let them have their daughter and let us have our son. The girl is a jewel, but nobody is worth causing harm to our son."

Fiona asked her husband to stay positive and said she would keep him abreast hour by hour, if necessary. Fiona asked Ayshe if she could meet with General Hikmet. Ayshe called her husband and told him that Fareed's mother wanted to meet with him. He told her that she was welcome.

When Fiona met with Hikmet, she never had taken a more serious position in her forty-nine years of life. She informed Hikmet that Fareed was practically a citizen of four countries: Ireland because she was Irish; British because the whole family had acquired British citizenship; America because Fareed was born in the United States; and Palestine because every Palestinian anywhere in the world is considered a citizen of Palestine. She told him that if Fareed was not found within a couple of days, she intended to have every one of those countries be involved in this case, and to be involved at the highest level of government.

"My husband and I operated on one British prime minister, six lords, three members of Parliament, and two royal family members. And we operated on one Turkish prime minister and one Irish cabinet member. When I am threatened to lose my son, I will call in my chips, and I do not care who pays the price—and if you, General Hikmet, have anything to do with his disappearance, I think that I am able to see to it that you will pay the same price," said Fiona to Hikmet.

Hikmet assured her that he had nothing to do with her son's disappearance and that he had been shocked as everyone else when he heard the news. He added that he did not want to lose his daughter either, and although he did not consider Fareed the right prospect for Nad, considering the circumstances, he would do anything possible, security-wise, effort-wise, and financially, to find her son. He told her that he prayed five times a day and that he swore on the holy Koran that he did not know, nor did he have anything to do with Fareed's disappearance. "Dr. Burke, it is true that I have always wanted a different setup for Nadidé."

Fiona stopped him. "You mean Nad!"

"Have it your way—okay, Nad. I have always wanted Nad not to have anything to do with your son. If I wanted to break my daughter's heart, you think I would not have been able to kick your son out of the country? I could and I can, and I can even use a military plane to fly him out. I had my chance. I embellished the story about his ex-girlfriend, and I failed. I will make it up to her from here forward. I hope she can see the light, but I will do nothing else. You think I don't miss my son, Ahmet, every single day? I confess, I am old-fashioned and stubborn and what I am telling you I have never shared with anyone else. I know that you grieve for your son's absence, as I grieve for being alienated from my only son and his children. May God forgive me."

Fiona told Hikmet that she had read the Koran, in English, over twenty times, simply because she and her husband wanted to raise Fareed as a Muslim, and because of that she felt she ought to know the Koran well.

"I love the Koran; I think it is very poetic. And if you want me to recite verses from the Koran, all in English, I can do so very easily. My favorite Koranic saying is the one that says, 'Whoever slays a soul, unless it be for mischief in the land, it is as though he slew all men.' Tell me General Hikmet, did Fareed do any mischief?"

Hikmet was impressed with what Fiona told him. He asked her if she did not mind him embellishing some facts. When Fiona asked what he meant, he told her that he hated to do it but if he were to tell the armed forces that Fareed was his daughter's fiancé, he could have them involved in a big way.

"Go ahead, General. You have done this before. You tried to make Dania as my son's fiancée when he was not even going out with her. At least now, we are talking about two who are going out together and in deep love with each other. Please go ahead. It is your suggestion and your decision, and I am not involved in it," said Fiona.

"You know, I really respect you. You are tough but kind. Nad loves you a lot, not a usual thing if you know what I mean," said Hikmet.

"Sure, I know what you mean. It is an old-fashioned mother-in-law syndrome. I believe in this modern era, the kind of relationship you are describing has outlived its usefulness," she told Hikmet.

Fiona left Hikmet's office fully satisfied that he was not involved, and that he was willing to help in a big way. She rejoined all four girls, Naz, Nad, Deniz, and Leila. Leila took the initiative. She told Fiona that she and Tolga wanted her to move in with them.

"It is not only for us, but also for Nermin. She does not have a grandmother on either side. I know you are young, but Nermin does not know that, and she loves Fareed so much. You should see her hang on to him," said Leila.

"If this is the case, I will be more than happy. God knows I also need a shoulder to cry on and a child to cheer me up," said Fiona wistfully.

———

Fiona moved in with Leila and Tolga. Their house became sort of a command center. Fiona told them that they needed to reach out to everyone who might be able to give them any clues and that she was leaving all contacts with the Turkish government up to General Hikmet.

"I know he is sincere, Nad. He said he was going to tell the government that you are Fareed's fiancée in order to have them fully involved, including involving the armed forces," said Fiona.

Nad ran toward Fiona, hugged her, and said, "I don't know if I deserve to be treated like this, after what I did to Fareed. I will never doubt Fareed ever again. I want to apologize to everyone here for my stupid behavior. Please forgive me," said Nad.

Fiona asked Nad to stop asking for forgiveness as this was an old story. She asked that they make a list of anybody who would be able to help. When Fiona mentioned Simra, Nad jumped out of her chair and said, "No!" Fiona and Leila were surprised at Nad's strong reaction.

"Is there something I don't know?" said Fiona, looking at Nad.

"No, nothing important. It is just Fareed does not like Simra. He thinks she is not straightforward. That is all," said Nad, not wanting to go on a limb.

None of the three followed up on Nad's partial explanation. Fiona scratched Simra's name off the list. Sammy inquired if Murat had been contacted. There, Nad could say nothing short of revealing her inner thoughts about Simra and Murat. She told everyone what Fareed had told her, that Murat hated her father and wanted to harm him, directly or indirectly, "Maybe through harming me, and possibly through harming Fareed. Does this make sense to anyone?" said Nad.

Fiona looked at Nad, her eyes widening with amazement. She said nothing but was obviously disturbed about what she just heard. She changed the subject intentionally and told them that she had already contacted the foreign secretary of the United Kingdom and the prime minister of Ireland, and that she was waiting to hear an answer from the American ambassador in Turkey. As they were meeting, the British embassy in Ankara called and asked Fiona if she could meet with the ambassador in Ankara, in two days. She agreed.

All the while, everyone was impressed with the energy and systematic planning undertaken by Fiona. She asked Leila if she or Tolga could recruit a Turkish–English secretary to help out pending Fareed's return. Tolga recruited one of his trusted students, a half English and half Turkish young research assistant. The first thing Fiona told the assistant was to be as secretive as could be and not to take any of the documents outside the Chakirs' home.

The British consulate in Istanbul picked her up for her flight to Ankara, and in Ankara she was met by the ambassador's assistant, to be driven from the airport to meet with the British ambassador. Fiona said nothing to the assistant. After she met the ambassador and thanked him for agreeing to see her, he said, "You must know especially important figures back home. I received close to an order from the foreign office, not a request, to see you," Ambassador Jeffrey Petry said.

"When you save lives, people tend to remember you. This includes your uncle, Sir Norman Petry," said Fiona.

Petry seemed further impressed at first. Fiona explained to the ambassador every detail about the disappearance of her son. She told him that she did not suspect General Hikmet. He was surprised that she knew the man who British intelligence considered to be the most influential person in Turkey, short of General Evren, the head of the military junta.

It became obvious that the ambassador was miffed at the command-like request from the foreign office. He was not about to elevate Dr. Burke to the level the foreign office had described. The ambassador went around and around describing the difficulties they could face in matters such as her son's situation.

The meeting did not go well at all. Petry promised to see what he could do—almost a polite dismissal, as Fiona perceived it. Fiona was in no mood to waste time. She disliked Petry's attitude and lack of interest. She shook hands with him and asked to be driven back to the airport. She had no plans to let go of the potential to have the British embassy's help. She was planning to call her contacts and to put pressure on Petry.

On her way out, Petry asked Fiona, "When did you operate on my uncle, Dr. Burke?"

"I didn't. It was my husband," said Fiona.

"Oh, there is another Dr. Burke?"

"No, it is Dr. Shaheen," she said.

Addressing Fiona by her married name, he said, "Dr. Shaheen, well, would you thank your husband for me?"

"It is Dr. Shaheen and Dr. Burke. I use my maiden name because my medical degree is in my maiden name. He is not Irish or English, he is Palestinian–British," she said.

Still maintaining his stiff upper lip, he said, "Oh my, a Palestinian man and an Irish lass. You should consider yourself lucky."

"Why is that?" Fiona exclaimed.

"You know what they say about a combination like this, between a Palestinian and an Irish person; they say that their children explode at birth," Petry said sarcastically, referring to the fact that both the Irish and the Palestinians are known worldwide as stubborn rebels.

Fiona, shocked, turned around to look at Petry straight in the face, indignant. "I thought you were a gentleman. Not even a vegetable wholesaler at the Spitalfields Market would use such language!"

Petry was surprised at Fiona's reaction, which made him realize that his comment was crude and out of line. He grew concerned that his language could be repeated to Fiona's backers at the foreign office, whom he had not specifically identified, with potentially serious consequences.

"I am sorry I said what I said. It was a crude statement. I beg your pardon. I don't know what came over me. Will you accept my heartfelt apology?" he asked.

Fiona thought for a few seconds. "I will if you promise to help find my son, and I want you to mean it—no more of this sophisticated English double-talk!"

"Oh, you are one tough educated woman. I admire your fearless determination," said Petry.

He picked up the phone and called Major Vincent Hinton, chief of British intelligence at the embassy, who covered all intelligence affairs regarding Turkey. After introducing Hinton to Fiona, Petry told Hinton that the matter of Fareed Shaheen was most serious, per the designation of the foreign office. After getting off the phone with Hinton, Petry told Fiona that the only way he would communicate with her would be in person, and that she would have to visit Ankara as frequently as once a week, if need be, but for a starter Fiona needed to meet with Major Hinton. Fiona agreed. After she met with Hinton, she told Petry, "I know why you want to see me in person; you are spying on the junta and the junta is spying on you, and you are listening to each other's conversations. I trust you are serious. I detected a belated seriousness in the tone of your voice, just now in this office. I will be seeing you next week."

Fiona shook Petry's hand and left. Petry said nothing, twisting his face in admiration.

———

When she got back together with everyone, Fiona told them what had transpired with Petry. She described how he insulted the Palestinians and the Irish and how she took advantage to reverse his attitude completely.

"Everybody listen, when this is over and you come to visit us, I will show you the Spitalfields Market; this is a promise," she told all.

As she finished talking about her spat with Petry, she told them that the specific comment by Petry about the Irish and Palestinians reinforced the fact that looking for Fareed took precedence over anything and everything in her life, including her career, and for her to be confident about all steps and desired results, she would be directing all undertakings, including assigning the different helpers specific and detailed tasks. Everyone seemed to agree. They all nodded approvingly. Nad took special note of Fiona's leadership and assertiveness.

The Irish ambassador, Sean McCray, called Fiona and told her that he had heard from his foreign secretary and that he would do whatever necessary to help with finding Fareed. He also told her that her best bets were the Americans and the British, in that order. Before he hung up, McCray paused briefly and asked her if she could have dinner with him and his wife that evening. She was more than happy to do so.

When Fiona arrived, Ambassador McCray was most welcoming. "I wanted to tell you this in person. You don't know who is listening to whom nowadays; your best bet is to play the British against the Americans. There they tend to compete. By competing, they produce better results. The Americans believe Turkey is their exclusive sphere of influence. The British, on the other hand, think that their past qualifies them as experts in the region."

Fiona thanked the ambassador for his advice and thought he was coaching her beyond the call of duty. He in return told her that his cousin was a classmate of hers at University College Dublin, who spoke highly of her. As she was leaving, McCray looked at her and said, "The Irish government does not have much influence except through the United Nations, but if you care to keep me in the loop, I can try to influence events from behind the scenes."

Fiona said that that she would and thanked him warmly.

When she got to meet with the American ambassador, Malcolm Hester, she brought up the fact that her son was American, and that Fiona and Ameer were permanent residents of the United States. The American ambassador promised to help and asked her if General Hikmet would not mind calling him. He was eager to have his help recognized by the junta, and he thought that Hikmet was surely the right conduit.

Fiona called General Hikmet and relayed to him an inflated request of Hester. She asked Hikmet if he would not mind visiting the ambassador and she would accompany him. Hikmet demurred at first but said, "Why not. I will make an exception in this case if he agrees to meet me in Istanbul. It is usually the ambassador who visits me!"

After Hikmet and Hester greeted each other at the American consulate in Istanbul, in a most stiff and official manner, Fiona said to Hester, "To follow up on our first meeting, I must say that we are not American citizens, and it is only our son who is; yet we are, as I said, still permanent residents of the US, and we contribute one week of our work every year at UCLA, where we both trained and met. Feel free to check with Dr. Oseberg, head of neurosurgery at UCLA."

"Dr. Burke, your credentials and your world status and that of your husband preceded your visit. You need say no more," Hester said. He told her that British ambassador Petry had already briefed him on her visit to Ankara and suggested that the two ambassadors cooperate. Hester then added, "This is not a complex matter. Apparently, there has been a kidnapping. It is our mission to know who the kidnappers are and where your son is, in order to rescue him."

Despite Hester's kind words, Fiona could detect that Hester was not planning to cooperate with the British.

Hikmet noticed that Hester was more attentive to issues of American–Turkish relations than to Fareed's situation. Yet Hikmet was terribly impressed with both Fiona's fame and feistiness. That prompted Hikmet to tell his wife about Fiona. He thought he would try to use the rapprochement between him and Fiona as a pretext to try and mend his alienation from his son, Ahmet. Later he asked Ayshe to let Ahmet know how Fiona handled herself and how impressed he was.

———

Fiona studied the list assembled by the "team," as she referred to it, which included friends and family. As she cross-checked the information of one source against all others, she managed to eliminate one potential suspect after another, except for Simra. She went to her notes and reviewed the statements about Simra from Nad, Deniz, and Naz. She suspected that either Nad, on one hand, or Deniz and Naz, on the other, were not telling her everything about Simra. She went back to them and asked for details of their statements.

She cornered Nad first. "Nad, I want you this time to tell me all about Simra and this time you need to tell me every single detail. You mentioned that you gave me those details in the past. I have a strong feeling you left out some. Listen, Nad, this is not a joke or an exercise in protecting the feelings of others. You need to tell all, regardless of whether they sound personal or incriminating. I need to hear every single detail."

Nad had not expected Fiona to rightly conclude that she had not told her everything. "Fareed told me that Simra and Murat belong to two anti-government leftist organizations, and the one Simra belongs to is the more extreme of the two. They both hate my father, General Hikmet, and what he stands for. They're planning to take revenge for the eleven leftist members who disappeared a year earlier. The general belief is that they had been kidnapped at the instigation of Hikmet."

Fiona looked at Nad pointedly. "You should not have kept this from me, Nad. This is immature behavior. We are talking about Fareed's life here. I think Simra is one of our potential suspects. And for you, you have the potential to learn a lot and lead, in the future, but you cannot lie by omission."

Before Fiona could talk to Naz and Deniz, Hikmet contacted Fiona to let her know that Aslan had been apprehended, having been accused of desertion. Hikmet went to see Aslan, where he yelled at him and used demeaning language, telling him that he was not fit to be an airman and that he had tarnished the image of the air force and the armed forces in general.

Yet, when it came to Fareed's disappearance, Aslan denied knowing anything about it. In the fast and intensive give-and-take of the interrogation, Aslan said, "It is Nadidé I would like to kidnap, not her friend. What can I do with him? I am not a homosexual!"

General Hikmet called Fiona and informed her that he was convinced that Major Aslan had nothing to do with the disappearance of Fareed.

Fiona gathered everyone and repeated her suspicions that Simra and Murat were the only two with apparent motives to kidnap Fareed. It was Tolga who added that under such circumstances, he was convinced that Nad and Hikmet were their real target, and that Fareed was kidnapped either by mistake or as bait to get to General Hikmet.

Despite Aslan's erratic behavior, he had managed to take control of the extreme supporters of the junta. They were the extreme right wing of the right wing of the armed forces, with a fundamentalist nuance. They wanted Aslan released on bail, an exceptional situation in the military judicial system in Turkey.

In order to pressure the junta, the supporters of Aslan started releasing embarrassing information about the junta's activities. They published names of individuals that members of the junta had abducted and tortured, years before the coup took place. Supporters of Aslan wanted to show, with corroborating documents, that the junta mistreated many groups, to elicit violent reactions and gain public support, for the junta in turn to rationalize their takeover of the government.

The junta ordered the release of and issued a pardon to Major Ata Aslan. Aslan was not only free but free to travel and to act. It was a disappointment to everyone in Fareed's circle, as well as in Hikmet's.

The British and the American embassies in Ankara continued to act independent of each other. At the same time, they both thought similarly about Fareed's disappearance: They both thought of it as a distraction from their more important issues. Yet they felt they had no choice but to put some assets into the game. They intensified their spying on all the suspected parties.

CHAPTER 17

It was time for Fiona to go back to Ankara. This time, she was more prepared. She knew that the Americans and British were not cooperating, and she figured she could use the Irish ambassador McCray more productively. This time, minutes after meeting with Petry, he asked her first to be briefed by Major Hinton about what had transpired since her last visit.

She listened to Hinton intently and learned a lot, although no concrete results were produced. She decided that her concentration should be on Petry since she was convinced he was the decision-maker while Hinton was the leg man. When Fiona went back to see Petry, he started the conversation by asking about her meetings with Major Hinton.

"Well, he was incredibly detailed and helpful, without necessarily revealing his sources, which is expected," said Fiona. "This time he was a perfect gentleman. What I did not appreciate last time was his attempt to stroke my hand and arm."

"Major Hinton is always a gentleman and an officer. I doubt

he did such a thing. I don't doubt that you believe that it had taken place; it is just that I believe you may have misconstrued his intentions," said Petry.

"I am a middle-aged female, and I am not in the habit of misconstruing such advances. They have happened before and I took care of them," said Fiona.

"What did you tell Hinton, if I may ask?" said Petry.

"I told him that the last time somebody did what he did, he was dismissed from the neurosurgery department and ended up becoming a prison doctor, and I inquired from him if being a military attaché qualified him to become a prison guard," said Fiona.

"Good God, I will not be able to help you out without Hinton. Please be gentle with him," said Petry.

"What did you expect me to do, tell him it was okay to stroke my arm as long as he did not massage other parts?! No, all I said afterward, after he apologized, is that I would keep his indiscretion to myself if he would control himself in the future. The reason I am telling you this is because if I were not to tell you now, it would be harder for you to believe me if it were to happen again."

"Fair enough. I saw your husband's picture and he is a good-looking lad."

"He is not a lad, and yes, he is a good-looking middle-aged man; he is one year my senior," said Fiona.

"I think there is no harm in sharing with you that Princess Margaret had a crush on him. Unfortunately, he insulted the princess; he told her that just because he was raised in a refugee camp did not mean he was indiscriminate in his choices of companions. Obviously, that was the end of her interest," said Petry.

"Since we are on the subject and you are the one who brought it up, all that I can say is that the princess missed out big time. It would have been memorable for her, I am sure," Fiona said.

Petry looked at her amusedly and said, "I have been wondering why you are so composed and almost tranquil. I almost get the impression that you are not as anxious about the situation with Major Hinton as one might be."

"What do you want me to do, tear my hair and shed streaming tears to prove that I am boiling on the inside?" said Fiona.

"Please don't misunderstand me. Dr. Burke, allow me to say that you are a highly intelligent, determined woman, and you do speak your mind clearly and expressively. You have my deepest respect. I think we are going to work well together, and I have great hope that together we will find your son, safe and well. I would like Major Hinton to join us right now, if you don't mind," said Petry.

Major Hinton joined Fiona and Petry and repeated his admonition that although they might be able to share mostly everything that related to her son, they were not at liberty to share any information about their sources. Fiona said that she understood completely and that she expected them not to ask for her sources either. Both Petry and Hinton agreed, but not before they looked at each other, showing further surprise at Fiona's assertiveness.

"My information indicates that the kidnappers have nothing to do with the government or General Hikmet. The kidnapping has been perpetrated by an extremist socialist party. While the party is small and focused, they are determined to take revenge from the government for kidnapping eleven socialists; hereto their fate is unknown," said Fiona.

"Where did you get all this information from?" asked Hinton with a sulking voice.

"No sources—this is what we agreed on, didn't we? The question is whether your information matches mine or not, not whether my sources match yours," she said with widening eyes.

"For the most part, they do; we have one up on you. We are certain your son is alive. Do you know the name of the party involved?" asked Hinton.

"Are you sure my son is alive? This is the greatest news so far. We surmised this much analyzing the situation, but we don't know it for fact. My relative, Dr. Tolga Chakir, concluded this much and I concur that Fareed was kidnapped inadvertently but now is being used as a bargaining chip. They so far have no reason to harm him. Oh, by the way, the party we are talking about intentionally chose to remain nameless," said Fiona.

"Yes, we are sure. This time, since the ambassador does not object, we will share with you how we know. We have already tapped one phone, but unfortunately the phone is deliberately out of service now," said Hinton. "Going back to the party, I think you are absolutely right, now it figures; they have no name. We have been asking of our sources this exact question. Everyone speaks of this group, but nobody has a name for them."

"Gentlemen, I have a proposal for your consideration: What if I choose a name for them, for reference purposes? Could we name them the KIDFA group?" said Fiona.

"Where did you get this name from?" asked Petry.

"It is very simple, KID is for kidnapping and FA is for Fareed, my son."

"This is a very appropriate name, don't you think so, Hinton?" said Petry.

"A splendid choice," Hinton agreed.

"I suggest that you coordinate with the Americans to call them by the same name. One of their tactical methods is to have the different intelligence agencies use different names for them, which may serve to make it more difficult for agencies to refer to them in precise form, leading to confusion. They are in the business of using misinformation and disinformation as a tactic. They hope that their efforts, using such methods, will help in preventing the different authorities from taking any coordinated action against them," said Fiona.

Petry looked at Fiona and asked if she would consider postponing her flight back to Istanbul and having dinner with him and his wife. "I don't mind admitting here, in front of Colonel Hinton, that you are a most intriguing and intelligent lady. What you just said a minute ago is usually the language of the intelligence agencies, and yet you said it with great confidence. This is why it would please me, and I am sure also my wife, to host you for dinner," said Petry.

"Your wife. I thought—"

"Yes, my wife. We are not yet divorced. We are civil and cordial to each other and hoping to finalize our divorce shortly. I know well that you socialize with a number of our friends," said Petry.

Fiona apologized and told Petry that she was helping with a serious procedure in the morning. As an afterthought Fiona looked at Petry and said, "Your wife. So the news media was not wrong. It was not your friends. It was all over the news."

"You have lived in England for quite a few years. We English are rather civilized. Yes, my wife and yes, we are getting a divorce, but we are both friends and waiting to celebrate our daughter's twentieth birthday."

Fiona wished Petry good luck and decided not to add anything. The give-and-take with Petry did develop into mutual respect, after a bumpy start, which was much to Fiona's liking. She wanted to get the British more involved and she thought they were getting there gradually. Above all, while not showing it, she was elated it was confirmed that Fareed was a subject of kidnapping and not murder or assassination.

———

When Fiona got back to Istanbul, Leila, Nad, Naz, Deniz, and Tolga were waiting for her. Fiona started by saying, "The meeting in Ankara went well and I have great news to tell you: Fareed has been confirmed alive as of yesterday. British intelligence tapped one of the kidnappers' phones; unfortunately, it seems the kidnappers realized that much, and the phone is now out of service."

Nad ran toward Fiona and hugged her with tears on her cheeks. Leila put her hands on her face and started crying. Naz and Deniz teared up. Fiona told them to cheer up instead of crying and asked them to get to work. Fiona then hugged Tolga and thanked him for his analysis.

"The Irish ambassador, Sean McCray, left you a message to call him," Leila told Fiona.

Fiona immediately called him and was invited again for dinner the following evening. He had news for her. "The Americans are convinced that the kidnappings were the doings of Hikmet, and the American ambassador Hester and the CIA station chief gave instructions to pretend to be looking for Fareed but instead to do nothing tangible. You see, the Americans like Hikmet and they support him and the junta all the way," said McCray.

"The Americans are playing a game and I know why," Fiona said. "The Americans want to confuse the issue by intentionally connecting Fareed's celebrated kidnapping to General Hikmet. By so doing, they are not accusing the junta directly but sending them a signal to stop their kidnappings. Those kidnappings are becoming an embarrassment to the US government."

McCray apologized to Fiona and agreed with her analysis, then inquired about the British efforts and the efforts of the Turkish government. Fiona told him that the Turkish government had done nothing, but General Hikmet was trying to help in earnest.

McCray added, "All embassies have their budgets. Looking for Fareed may prove costly in the long run, and the cost of it may cause the British to abandon their efforts when they reach their limit. In this case, you should try to have the Americans foot the bill and the British do the legwork. It has happened in the past, especially when it involved dual citizens."

Fiona had no idea if such was possible and did not have a clue what to do to make it happen. That night she summoned Nad, Leila, and Tolga, reminding them that none of them was an intelligence officer, yet to try to think of a way for the Americans to foot the bill and for the British to do the legwork. During the discussion, the conversation shifted and Leila asked Fiona if she was being paid for the procedures she was doing in Turkey. That question gave Fiona an idea.

"Considering that I am still a permanent US resident and a known graduate of the world-renowned UCLA program, what if the Americans were to pay the United Kingdom health system for the procedures I am doing here for free, and the UK health system in turn transfers the payments to the British embassy in Ankara? The source of the money could be concealed yet designated exclusively for the effort to free Fareed," said Fiona.

All three liked the idea and Fiona said that she would think about it, and find out a way it could be executed. When she went to see Petry the following week, she broached the subject at dinner. He at first said there was no need for that. But then he suggested to Fiona to donate her time in the name of the UK health system. By so doing, they could justify asking for additional funds from the British government to cover the cost of her medical procedures.

Fiona went a step further; she met with US ambassador Hester. She told him that the British were willing to pay fifty percent, based on the fact that she was a British citizen, and she wondered if the United States would pay half since Fareed happened to be a US citizen, never mind that he was a citizen of three other countries.

That was the plan that everyone agreed upon, in the end. The American embassy wanted a cover for not doing anything. Fiona and the British wanted to secure enough funds to cover the costs for the long haul. Ambassador Petry told Fiona that the additional American contribution would guarantee the effort for at least two years.

Fiona was very pleased, yet she knew that they had not made any progress in tracing the whereabouts of Fareed. Naturally, that was her next phase.

At the same time Petry and Hinton were seriously working on freeing Fareed, Fiona wanted to buttress the efforts of the British. McCray could play a larger role in a clandestine fashion, she concluded. He needed to be continuously informed about the American and British plans without his interest being noticed by either. By Hester and Petry underestimating McCray's potential and being ignorant of his relationship to her, McCray could spy on their plans and share the information with her. She explained this to him.

"What do you suggest?" said McCray to Fiona, chagrined.

"I suggest that you make yourself ever present at all kinds of diplomatic functions. There you can pick some hints as to what is going on. Such hints will guide you toward your follow-up steps. I won't venture to advise you about what you need to do. I believe you will do the right thing by your own choice once more information comes to light," said Fiona.

"Dr. Burke, you understand that I will not solicit or elicit any information. All I can do is to listen to conversations that take place openly, and which do not require explicit or implied confidence on my part," said McCray.

Fiona assured McCray that he was describing exactly what she had in mind. She told him that his low profile would give him a greater opportunity to glean information from all kinds of open sources.

When Fiona saw McCray next, she asked him if the embassy had a security department. McCray told her that they had one security man. She asked McCray if the security man knew how to tap phones. He told her that tapping phones was very elementary for security personnel.

"I think we can move to the next step. We believe we know one person who is talking to one of the suspected perpetrators. Could you consider tapping one of the perpetrator's mother's phone?" asked Fiona.

"I don't believe I will," said McCray.

"Listen, Mr. Ambassador, if they ever find the device, they will never suspect the Irish embassy; they will suspect the Americans. You see, the device is a limited-use American-made piece of equipment. The Turks managed to receive a dozen devices from the Americans," said Fiona.

What Fiona had not shared with McCray was that General Hikmet had provided Fiona with the device on the basis that it was going to be used to record calls to Fareed's phone. McCray was convinced in the end, although Fiona refused to divulge the source of the equipment.

"The person of interest in this case is Simra's mother," Fiona told him, and provided him with her name and address. When the embassy's security man tried to tap Simra's mother's phone, he found out that she did not have a phone of any kind. Fiona had to think fast.

"Why don't we have Naz and Deniz go visit Simra's mother and find out how she got in touch with Simra?" Nad suggested, when Fiona brought up this issue with her. Fiona thought it was a great idea.

Naz and Deniz did just that. Fortunately for them, their names were familiar to Simra's mother, Afak. They told her that they wanted to contact Simra, and that they missed her. Afak revealed to them that she was in touch with Simra but could not call her as she did not have a phone of her own, and that Simra used a public phone to call her, from Europe. Simra called Afak's neighbor, who generously summoned Afak to the phone whenever Simra called.

The information provided by Afak was enough to alter the original plans. The Irish security man tapped Afak's neighbor's phone.

The conversations between Simra and Afak were innocuous, revealing nothing about the whereabouts of Simra. After three phone conversations, Fiona and the security man could hear a Germanic language spoken in the background, but they could not tell if it was German, Dutch, or something else.

Nad sent copies of the recordings to Ahmet, who confirmed that the conversations recorded were German, with a Bavarian dialect. He also could tell that there was an ice cream vendor on a loudspeaker, trying to sell ice cream.

With this information relayed to her, Fiona called Ahmet. "Can you possibly engage the services of a private eye to find out further details about the location?" she asked. He agreed.

The Bavarian private eye, after checking out over fifty ice cream companies and talking to tens of ice cream wholesale managers, managed to secure the needed information. He identified the exact vendor and the square where the ice cream was being sold. It was in Munich. At the same time, the private eye found out that there were over fifteen public phones in that square. It would have been an expensive endeavor to tap all fifteen phones until they could record Simra and be able to follow her. Regardless, the private eye refused to tap any public phones.

At that point Fiona thought her best chance was with Petry. She met with him and Hinton in Ankara, where her plan was to shame them to extract more effort from them. They told her that they had identified two of KIDFA's members, but so far, they did not know their whereabouts. When Fiona inquired and Hinton confirmed that the two were one male and one female, she said, "I think I know who they are. I believe that only one of them is a member of KIDFA. The other was a member of Vatan Partisi."

"I am afraid he is now a member of KIDFA," said Hinton.

"Nevertheless, they are Simra and Murat, and they are engaged to each other. I can give you their last names and where they are now in Europe, if you promise to pursue them there," said Fiona.

"I see what you are saying Dr. Burke, why not. Do you agree, Major?" said Petry to Hinton, who agreed.

"We can proceed provided that you will agree to share with me all the information you manage to secure about them and from them," said Fiona. "After all, you would not have known anything new about KIDFA's real identity without my help."

Petry and Hinton agreed. Fiona told them that Simra and Murat were in Munich. She gave them the name of the square, and the fact that Simra used one of fifteen public phones to call her mother. Fiona gave them Afak's name and the name and phone number of the neighbor.

"Good God!" exclaimed Hinton. "How do you continue getting such detailed information? Are the Americans helping you out?"

"I have my sources and you have yours. Suffice it to say my sources are better than yours," Fiona told them.

Petry looked at Hinton and Hinton at Petry. Petry promised that they would follow her leads and would share with her all new information, if her leads proved accurate. Before long, Petry involved the British embassy in Bonn, Germany.

The British embassy tapped into each of the fifteen phones, and appointed two Turkish-speaking agents to listen in on the phone calls. In no time, by listening in when Afak's neighbor's phone was in use, they identified the exact phone used in the square, in Munich. Once identified, the phone was physically monitored.

In the meantime, Fiona secured a picture of Murat from Ramzi and Nader, and Simra's picture from Naz. She gave the two pictures to Hinton.

The plan was for Simra to be followed to her apartment. They did not want German police to arrest them for fear that the two might clamp down and refuse to release Fareed or at least refuse to relay his whereabouts. After ten days of shadowing the two, British intelligence could not find anything about Fareed's situation. Simra and Murat were by themselves. They were recorded talking about Fareed but exchanged no details about him.

Hinton relayed the bad news to Fiona.

"I'll try to corner Simra and Murat and shame them into helping me," Fiona said in response. It was her only option.

She flew to Munich with Ramzi and Nader. By agreement, Simra and Murat were followed by British intelligence all the time, who in turn conveyed their address to Fiona.

Ramzi and Nader knocked on Simra and Murat's door. They, to Simra and Murat's total surprise, entered the apartment, warmly hugging Murat and greeting Simra. The meeting was tense since nobody was supposed to know where Simra and Murat lived. After a few minutes, Ramzi said to Murat and Simra, "We are here about Fareed. We know that you have him. Not only do we know that you have him, but we know that the Turkish, American, and British intelligence services are looking for him. If you are caught, you may be extradited back to Turkey, and you know what happens to you there."

They had barely finished listening to Nader and Ramzi when Fiona, by design, knocked on the door. Her being there was even a greater shock to Murat and Simra. "I don't need to remind you that he is my son, and if I have to, I will kill you both to free him. It is your choice—either he is released while I am here, or you will have to suffer the consequences."

Simra spoke first. "Fareed was not the intended target; he was kidnapped by mistake."

"Don't give me this nonsense, Simra. If this this is the case, why have you not released him? It has been two months!" yelled Fiona.

"Every time we tried, something happened. When he first was taken away—" Simra was interrupted.

"Taken away? Stop this damned nonsense. He was kidnapped. When you want to describe things, be real and describe them as they are." Fiona waved her hand dismissively. "Let us cut all of this useless talk. How soon can you release him? Can you do it in fewer than two hours?"

"I think so," said Simra while Murat kept quiet.

Simra said that she would call right away. Fiona said that she had to go with them and that she would not allow them out of her sight, and asked them if they were carrying any money. Fiona took all the money from them and then asked Murat to take off his belt and his jacket.

"What?" Murat asked. "I don't understand."

"Without any money, you cannot go far, and without your belt, you cannot run fast," Fiona replied.

Fiona and Nader took them to the same public phone they always used. Ramzi was left behind; in case Fiona and Nader did not come back in one hour, he was to call their contact in British intelligence.

Fiona knew that a British Turkish-speaking agent was there watching within hearing distance. Simra made one phone call, using money given to her by Fiona. The phone call barely took three minutes.

Fiona and Nader took Simra and Murat back to their apartment, then Fiona left right away to meet with the British agent while Ramzi and Nader kept watch.

"All Simra said was to implement plan 42," the agent told Fiona. "And seemingly when the other party asked her something, Simra said to try the full plan, if possible, and half the plan if not possible, but to do it right away."

Within ninety minutes, Fiona, Nader, Simra, and Murat went back to use the same phone. This conversation was also very brief. "Fareed has been released three blocks from his apartment," Simra told Fiona.

When Fiona went to see the agent again, he told her that he had called the embassy in Bonn, and they managed to intercept the second conversation between Simra and another woman. The other woman told Simra that the whole plan—both parts—had been executed.

"Simra told me that Fareed has been released," Fiona told the British agent.

"Already?" the agent said, surprised. "This is great news."

When Fiona found Tolga's phone to be busy, she called Ayshe and told her that Tolga and Leila needed to go to Fareed's apartment.

"Nad coincidently went to Fareed's apartment to deliver clean sheets and pillow covers," Ayshe said. "What was there had gotten damp and dusty due to the unexpected heat wave."

Fiona managed to get through to Tolga and Leila to let them know about Fareed. They told her that Nad was supposed to have gone to Fareed's just to drop off the laundry and then head back to their place, and that she was at least an hour late. They had called Fareed's apartment again and again, but nobody answered the phone.

"Please go to Fareed's apartment," she told Tolga and Leila. "If you miss Nad, leave a note for her to wait for them at your apartment."

Tolga and Leila went and could not find Fareed. They did not know what was happening. They were doubly surprised as they did not find Nad either.

Tolga called Fiona at the same phone where she was waiting with the British agent. "Go back to your house, and leave Leila behind at Fareed's apartment," Fiona asked Tolga. She expected Fareed to be at one house or the other. Tolga did not want to split the group. He, Leila, and everyone else went to his and Leila's house. As they arrived, they saw Ayshe getting out of her car, and in seconds Fareed got out also.

In the meantime, Fiona went back to Simra and Murat's apartment, and giving them their money and belt, told them, "Leave town before British intelligence or the German police get hold of you."

Leila and Tolga hurried to leave. "Fareed has been freed in front of General Hikmet's house instead."

Fiona was puzzled. "Why there?"

CHAPTER 18

Fiona, Ramzi, and Nader went back to Istanbul. They were met at the airport by Tolga and Leila. Fiona could see two faces drained of color. "What is wrong?"

Teary-eyed, Leila looked at Fiona. "Fareed is fine and healthy, but he is very distraught—Nad has disappeared."

"What do you mean, disappeared?"

"She was supposed to change Fareed's sheets and pillowcases, but she never got to the apartment," said Leila.

"My God, when did this happen? Does Ayshe know, and General Hikmet?" asked Fiona.

"No, we were waiting for you. We don't know them that well. This is a little too much to handle and we didn't know what to do," said Tolga.

Ramzi suddenly said, "I think I know what happened. They told us they never wanted to kidnap Fareed. Nad was the original target. Originally, something went wrong and somehow they kidnapped Fareed inadvertently, or possibly to use him as a bait to get to Nad. I think Fareed may be able to shed light on this aspect; he may have gleaned something from the conversations he may have overheard while abducted."

Fiona straightened. "Where is Fareed? I need to hug him and speak to him before I summon the strength to go see Ayshe. This is just beyond belief."

Fareed was at Tolga and Leila's house babysitting Nermin. Fiona hugged Fareed when she saw him and could barely let go.

"I am sorry, Fareed; I am sorry about Nad. Don't worry; we will find her just like we found you. I must see Ayshe and let her know right away. It is not fair, not to have told her right away. After all, Hikmet has a thousand times the resources we have," said Fiona.

Ramzi and Nader stayed with Fareed and tried to calm him down. He told them he had a severe headache and was not able to think straight and needed to lie down. Later, he had an extremely high fever. They called one of Tolga's internist friends, who checked Fareed's vital organs and functions.

Turning, the internist told the group, "Fareed seems to be run down, suffering from acute exhaustion. But he should make a full recovery."

"He's been missing his girlfriend," Leila said.

"That makes sense. Fareed's state of mind probably over-whelmed his weakened body," the internist said. Otherwise he did not think there was anything physically serious with Fareed.

———

Fiona left to see Ayshe, who looked concerned and agitated. "I've called Fareed's apartment and Leila's flat over ten times but could not get anybody to answer the phone," she said.

"Ayshe, you are like a sister to me. I just came back from Germany. Fareed is out and safe, but he is beside himself, as we are all. Nad is missing," said Fiona.

"What? Missing!" said Ayshe as she stood up, confused.

"She did not make it to Fareed's apartment nor to the Chakirs' flat. Friends of Fareed think that the same people who kidnapped Fareed and then released him also kidnapped Nad. You see, we believe they never intended to kidnap Fareed in the first place," said Fiona.

Disturbed, Ayshe went to the phone and called General Hikmet. He was in a staff meeting. She asked them to get him out of the meeting.

A moment later, he got on the phone. "What is the meaning of this, making me leave a staff meeting?"

"Your daughter has been kidnapped by the same people who kidnapped Fareed. Yes, they let Fareed go and kidnapped Nad," said Ayshe.

Hikmet rushed to see Ayshe to find Fiona there. Fiona explained all the details that led to the release of Fareed.

"There is something wrong," he said to Fiona. "There is something that does not make sense. Why would they release Fareed and kidnap Nad? Why didn't they keep Fareed and kidnap Nad as well? There is something missing here. The whole thing does not make sense. They know that we know who they are—why free Fareed? I don't think it is the same group!"

What Hikmet did not know was that Fareed was kidnapped by mistake, so to Hikmet's thinking it was not logical to release him. That made no sense to Hikmet. Hikmet was unaware that the

British had influence with the leftists, who were pressured to release Fareed.

Fiona was quietly suspicious that the British involvement might have been the catalyst in freeing Fareed, and much less her own involvement. "Let's all calm down; we're not thinking straight, including me," she said. Although blindfolded while abducted, Fareed had gathered possibly damaging information about KIDFA. "You should see Fareed. He looks like a weathered lizard, as if somebody drained the blood out of his body. This has been heart-breaking, through and through, for everybody. We've got to find Nad, or otherwise we will go crazy. I am not leaving town before we find her," said Fiona.

Fiona did not want to tell Hikmet that she had met the kidnap-pers. She wanted to consult with Petry first. She went back to see Fareed. Leila was there with Nermin. Leila told Fiona that Tolga and Ramzi had taken Fareed to the hospital. He was dehydrated and not feeling well. He needed to be hydrated.

Fiona rushed to the hospital to find Fareed in the emergency room with a 41.5 Celsius temperature. He was practically steaming and with severe head pain.

Fiona stayed next to Fareed. As they dripped some liquids into his system, his temperature dropped by one degree. That was the first sign that he was responding after having been rehydrated. It took Fareed three days to be released from the hospital.

———

Fiona left to see Petry in Ankara, unknown to Hikmet or anybody else. This time she took Ayshe with her. On the plane, she told

Ayshe that she would not leave town until Nad was released. Fiona felt she needed to get Ayshe involved and to provide her with as much support as possible.

"Ayshe, I love Nad as if she were my own daughter. Promise me to stay strong, and the two of us will work together to free Nad," she told Ayshe on the flight to Ankara.

Ayshe held Fiona's hand with both of hers. "You don't know how much I appreciate your involvement and help. As much as we hope and expect Nad and Fareed to be permanently together, you will remain like a sister to me under all circumstances. You are a source of strength to me and to the whole group."

In Ankara, Fiona told Petry and Hinton that she had planned to have them eat crow since she was the one who freed Fareed, but now she told them that she was just as unaccomplished since Nad had been kidnapped. After a clearly tense Ayshe was introduced to the two, Fiona noticed that Ayshe attracted Petry's attention. Petry and Hinton agreed with Fiona; they said that the Turkish government would put ten times more assets into searching for Nad than the British could.

Petry asked Fiona if the British security agent in Germany had done a good job.

"Yes, splendid," she said. Fiona again caught Petry looking intently at Ayshe.

"As an afterthought, the Turkish government may want to keep things unpublicized and as such spend less effort; they would not want to open the issue of the eleven kidnapped leftists. This is why I will do my best to secure more money for the embassy to triple or quadrable our efforts in looking for your daughter," Petry said, addressing Ayshe.

Fiona noticed the switch of attention, from her to Ayshe—
and more importantly, the switch in the nature of the attention.
It was not a businesslike attention; it was nuanced with greater
empathy. Ayshe must have noticed the same as she started looking
back at him. Fiona chose to pretend that she noticed nothing. She
wanted to encourage Petry's added attention—anything to help the
situation.

To screen his sudden interest in Ayshe, Petry said to Fiona, "I
will tell the foreign office that you were satisfied. The security agent
called me as soon as he discovered they were going to free Fareed."

Petry's statement sounded odd to Fiona. She was the one who
had told the agent that Fareed was being freed within two hours,
and based on his reaction at the time, he had not discovered Fareed's
release on his own.

She expected Petry to say that the security agent had called
him as soon as he heard the news from Fiona. Furthermore, as
soon as Fiona had finished her call from the square in Munich, the
public phone was grabbed by another person and kept busy for a
long time. The agent had to wait for more than a half hour before
he could call Petry.

"What time did he call you?" asked Fiona.

"Nine thirty in the morning," said Petry.

"That is eight thirty Germany time. Simra did not tell us
anything before eight thirty Germany time. You bastards—you
knew in advance. You made a deal with the leftists and had me go
to Germany as a cover-up. You deal with those people all the time,
don't you? Don't try to deny it. I may not have freed my son, but I
am not a fool," said Fiona.

Hinton looked at Petry and Petry at Hinton. Hinton left the room.

"No, you are not a fool, far from it," Petry said. "You see, we are in a bind. The Americans are in bed with the junta and we do not command matters the same way we did before the second world war. The junta executed tens of thousands and some of them are dual British–Turkish citizens. We needed information about them, and the leftists have been providing us with such information. They managed to keep some of their networks working, even inside the military camps they are held at. They don't deserve to be called just camps. Some of them are more like concentration camps. We have managed to save the lives of many of those dual citizens, with their help. We did not mean to conceal things from you, and we thought the result would please you, and I am sure it has except for the kidnapping of General Hikmet's daughter," said Petry in a low and humbled voice.

"Thank you, Mr. Ambassador. This is why we are here, to free my daughter. I would like you to stay on this subject. I don't care about what happened in the past except being elated Fareed has been freed. Nad needs to be freed and that is what matters now," said Ayshe, looking at Petry with a sideways glance.

Fiona thought to herself and could not decide who was signaling whom, Petry or Ayshe. Petry was a handsome and debonair forty-five-year-old upper-crust gentleman. He exhibited many of the traits of a titled upperclassman but was sensitized enough to switch to a more egalitarian demeanor, when the circumstances warranted it. It seemed like it was warranted in the presence of Ayshe since he did not want to play upmanship toward her.

Fiona looked at him and said, "Then I expect you to work as hard to free Nad as you did to free my son. I am sure you do not mind adding more to your initial accomplishments." She hoped he did not miss the double meaning. "We are all stricken with grief and guilt, and I do not want to hear again that the Turks have more assets than you. No, you have more useful assets than they. You know exactly who kidnapped her but are reticent to act in order to protect your sources and your helpers. You are collaborating with them, no doubt. Mr. Ambassador, if you had planned to cross Niagara Falls on a tightrope, you couldn't but have known how to balance the bar. I can't and I don't need to balance it for you, especially when I am being manipulated."

"I like your hyperbole about Niagara Falls," said Petry.

"This is not a hyperbole, it is a metaphor or simile; at least this is what they taught me at University College Dublin. Didn't they teach the same at Oxford?" said Fiona sarcastically, her tone condescending.

"Why do I feel I am always in trouble with you?" Petry fired back. "I like you and respect you, but I feel I cannot win. I promise you I will think about your suggestions long and hard. You see, Major Hinton was smart, he left the room some time ago, leaving me to twist in the wind in your presence and that of Mrs. Hikmet. I will have my chauffeur drive you in my Bentley, and I thank you, nevertheless."

Fiona said, "Be fair and open—it is only me that doesn't mind having you twist in the wind."

As he was saying goodbye to them, Petry took Ayshe's hand and kissed it, saying, "Mrs. Hikmet, first I want to share with you my thoughts: The group that kidnapped your daughter has no interest in harming her. They want to exchange her. I also want to assure you we will do our utmost to find your beautiful daughter and bring her back to you and her fiancé, and to General Hikmet.

Please give him my regards."

"Thank you, but I won't tell my husband anything about this meeting. He has no clue we are here. I am sure you will convey the same refrain to Major Hinton," said Ayshe.

Petry's interest was visibly piqued by Ayshe's double meaning. Petry's file of Hikmet had told him well in advance of the visit about the estrangement between Ayshe and the general.

CHAPTER 19

The British managed to record enough phone conversations not only to irrefutably conclude that the same leftists, KIDFA, were the culprits, but to have enough evidence to threaten them with and pressure them to release Nad. It was not entirely true that the real reason behind the British dealing with the leftists was their desire to save many of the dual citizens. The British had decided shortly after the military coup not to seriously oppose the leftists. They wanted them to exist to fight the extreme measures adopted by the junta—measures of kidnapping, torture, and mass executions that involved single and dual citizens.

The British moved to pressure the leftists without necessarily weakening them. They made it known to KIDFA that they knew that they were the ones who kidnapped Fareed, and now Nad. While KIDFA had released Fareed to get the British off their back, they were less likely to release Nad since her father was the object of their revenge and a potential conduit to releasing the eleven.

When KIDFA conceded to release Fareed, they shadowed

Nad's movements and were confident that they could easily kidnap her. In the end, that was exactly what they did, and they did it despite the tight constraints the British had imposed upon them. They did not want to free Fareed before they kidnapped Nad if they could help it. British pressure on KIDFA propelled them to free Fareed with only outside hope to kidnap Nad before they could free Fareed. The circumstances of Nad heading to clean Fareed's apartment played well into the hands of KIDFA. It was not the plan they had devised.

The taxi Nad had taken developed a mechanical problem two blocks away from Fareed's apartment, an area KIDFA had been watching. The car was in a distinctly exposed area. They could see her from Fareed's apartment where they had just delivered Fareed to be released. Simra's reference to the "whole plan" or "half the plan" became known to Fareed, having heard the team speak with each other. Half the plan referred to releasing Fareed before kidnapping Nad and the whole plan was to release him after they had kidnapped Nad.

The team designated to release Fareed sensed that they had an opportunity when they unexpectedly saw Nad clearly in the open; they tied Fareed up and proceeded to abduct Nad and dragged her to Fareed's apartment, only after they had walked Fareed out of the apartment.

The team that had released Fareed and conveniently found Nad and kidnapped her hurried up to catch up with another team that was supposed to attempt to kidnap Nad in front of her house. They got there, with Fareed, in time to alert the other team that they had already kidnapped and hidden Nad. That was why they released Fareed in front of Hikmet's house.

———

Three days later, when Fareed got out of the hospital, he was more alert and was slowly returning to his energetic self. He was informed about Nad, that she had been kidnapped by the same group with whom Simra and Murat were associated. He was most disheartened and agitated at the thought of not being able to be with Nad, and with the fact she was kidnapped.

"Don't worry," he told everyone. "The kidnappers meant to exchange Nad and not to harm her." He told them he was dehydrated because he tried to go on a hunger strike and was bruised because the group had moved him frequently, close to fifteen different times. He said the group did not torture him at all, and he took solace in this fact, hoping they would treat Nad the same.

He recalled something that his memory had not recollected earlier, upon his release. He recalled that as they were taking him out of the apartment and shoring him up down the back stairs, he had heard two very faint female voices, some distance away.

"What are you saying, Fareed?" asked Tolga. "Are you saying that they released you and abducted Nad at the same time?"

"I believe this is exactly what happened. I am sure now it is the same group, and the link to them was Simra and Murat. What a mistake to have them let go. I think the voices I heard were Nad's and Simra's. Simra and Murat must have taken the first plane back here as soon as they were let go by my mother and proceeded to organize my release and Nad's kidnapping."

———

Petry wanted to cover his behind. He contacted Ambassador Hester of the United States, asking if he knew of any dual American citizens the junta was holding. Hester confirmed that there were ninety-two. When Petry offered Hester help in releasing some of them, Hester accepted without asking how and how many. He gave the names to Petry, and Petry passed the names to the leftists. Within two weeks seven Turkish–Americans and three Turkish–British dual citizens had managed to escape, along with eleven leftists.

The leftists were using Petry as much as he was using them. The money that Petry was paying them was necessary for them to flee the country; they were broke. The junta had confiscated almost every penny the leftists had and had frozen their real estate assets. The leftists, in order not to reveal their dire need for money to the British, pretended that the payments represented a small bonus to them, for helping in the release of the dual citizens. In fact, it was the only money they could lay their hands on. They used the money to reach some of the European countries that were providing asylum to victims of the junta.

Hikmet met with Fareed at Tolga and Leila's house. He immediately started asking Fareed all sorts of questions. Fareed told him that all the time he was kidnapped he was blindfolded. He could not see or hear anybody distinctly. Only on one occasion, his blindfold got loose before they tightened it, during which he saw the tips of a female pair of shoes.

He also repeated himself about hearing two faint female voices, too faint to recognize, as he was being dragged out to be released. They released him after they drove him through back streets and alleys. He knew he was in alleys from the feel of the cobblestone ride.

Fiona inadvertently told General Hikmet that her hectic schedule, especially flying to Ankara, had exhausted her and that she was ready for a drink. She offered Hikmet a drink. Hikmet accommodated Fiona by trying what she was drinking, Irish whiskey. He nevertheless took notice of her mention of the round trip to Ankara. Fiona apologized and excused herself and said that she wanted to take a nap to be able to think straight afterward, and for Hikmet to visit with Fareed.

Hikmet instead was observing and gauging Fareed. After a long conversation, Hikmet started to soften toward Fareed. He noticed his good looks, but above all he noticed that Fareed was a serious and caring person. Fareed exhibited a clear sense of loss and overwhelming feeling of pain as a result of Nad's disappearance. Hikmet told Fareed, "You and I will find Nad even if I have to use half the Turkish army to look for her."

It was the first endearing expression by Hikmet toward Fareed, mentioning him in the search for Nad. Fareed took note of that. He told Hikmet, "I am confident we will find her, with your help. Thank you."

Hikmet left after he shook hands with Fareed. Fiona woke up from her nap and showed renewed vigor. She said, "Somebody needs to organize the group. Let us start now."

Fiona resumed her command of the group. She reminded everyone that Fareed had observed the tips of a woman's shoes. "Can anyone find somebody to produce a rendering of the part Fareed observed?" she asked. Deniz said she knew someone who could.

"Fiona, have you ever done prior investigations?" Tolga asked. "You sound like an investigator."

Fiona laughed, reminding him that she was a neurosurgeon, and that from time to time she was indirectly involved in autopsies of crime victims and crime perpetrators. Above all, Fiona reminded everyone that she was still in charge, a condition she had imposed on the group when Petry insulted her about the Irish and the Palestinians. Early on she was clearly angry at Petry and intended to complain about him to the foreign office. She had mellowed in the meantime.

While Fiona and the British were sure who the perpetrators were, they were both extremely careful not to share such beliefs with the military government. They were weighing if Hikmet could be trusted in that regard, even though the matter involved Nad's kidnapping. Hikmet did not think that the same group had perpetrated both kidnappings, but Fiona and the British knew that if the group was identified to the junta, it would lead to the execution of a significant additional number of leftists already in prison.

In the meantime, Hikmet was still trying to narrow down the list of suspects. Aslan had said that he was not interested in Fareed since Aslan was not a homosexual. Hikmet thought Aslan was implying that he could have been interested in Nad, a gorgeous woman who was once promised to him. Hikmet instigated the issuance of a civilian APB for Aslan.

It was not hard to locate Aslan. He was not hiding and felt confident that the government would not dare apprehending him for fear of a scandal. When the police found him, he was making love to a prostitute.

The prosecuting attorney's office did not think Aslan had anything to do with Nad's kidnapping. But Hikmet insisted for them to interrogate Aslan. Aslan had money but psychologically was in the dumps.

"I decided not to bother with Nad," Aslan told Hikmet, "and with my newfound wealth I could procure the best-looking prostitutes, ones that are anywhere between seventeen and nineteen years old." Aslan was confident that Hikmet would not harm him, even with his loose talk about prostitutes, due to their prior association and common criminal acts. "Some of the prostitutes are more beautiful than Nad."

Hikmet spit in his face.

———

Talking to the inner circle, Fiona asked, "We know the two kidnappings are completely related. What I am not sure of, despite Simra's explanation, is whether Fareed's kidnapping was inadvertent, or was it planned as a stepping-stone toward kidnapping Nad?"

Fiona left everyone to think within those perimeters, in the hope of creating a dialogue and extrapolating some practical answers, leading to taking the proper steps to free Nad. Fareed spent the night at the Chakirs'.

In the morning Fareed met with the sketch artist. He described to her clearly the details of the tips of the woman's shoes he had seen, and she came out with what looked like a credible sketch, identical to his recollection. What was particular to that pair of shoes were the stitches. They were unusual stitches in that they were farther away from where the leather and the sole came together. Everyone was alerted to such a fact.

Fiona met with Hikmet again. Their relationship had developed into one of mutual but varying respect. Fiona was suspicious of him. He could not consciously accept the relationship between Fareed and Nad. Both were Muslims but Fareed was not a Turk.

Fiona told him that she was about to disclose the names of two individuals—but before she did that, she needed to have his word that he would be most considerate and fair in treating them. They were friends of Fareed and Nad and they might or might not have been involved. "Promise me that if they are found not to be involved, you are not to persecute them based on their leftist views," she told him, her only condition. Hikmet fully agreed, and asked Fiona if they were found by his own team, and would she want to be involved in their preliminary interrogation.

Fiona was surprised at Hikmet's question. She declined, but as an afterthought, she recalled that Nad had told her that when her father swore on the Koran, he always kept his promise.

"Swear on the Koran not to bother Simra and Murat solely based on their leftist leanings," she said. At first, he declined but relented in the end.

Fiona felt relieved. She suggested to have him assign a couple of smart investigators to find out where Simra was and if she had the same kind of shoes Fareed had seen. Hikmet followed Fiona's advice.

Meanwhile, Tolga came out with a new possible relation-ship between the two kidnappings, after Fareed had told him that Simra and Murat were aware he was suspicious of them. He theorized that Simra and Murat were aware that Fareed knew of their intentions to harm General Hikmet directly or through kidnapping Nad, before they actually carried out Nad's kidnapping. They kidnapped Fareed first to keep him silent about their intentions. They did not care what he would tell after the kidnapping of Nad, since kidnapping

Nad, with Fareed being free, would have revealed their identity.

"You mean to say that Fareed was not a target at all?" said Fiona. "They intended to keep him away until they could kidnap Nad, and then it did not matter if he were let go. In the end, they let him go under pressure from the British. Nad happened to show up at his apartment and there they had their ideal opportunity!" Fiona paused. "But this means, if the shoes turn out to be Simra's, that they came back, kidnapped Nad, and got out of the country for the second time, and out of harm's way because they expected their identities to have been revealed by Fareed or through their actions."

Tolga nodded approvingly.

Fiona went on, "Yes, in general I agree with you, Tolga, except that we don't know what they will do if their demands are not met. I don't want to mention what others have done under such circumstances. Let us make sure of her safety first, ninety-nine percent sure. She is not only Fareed's love; she is also like a daughter to me. Although I don't know her well, I have a strong feeling that she is versatile and able to lead, if trained properly and challenged," said Fiona.

Tolga and Leila checked with Fareed, who confirmed that his thoughts were slowly leaning toward Tolga's analysis. On the other hand, everyone was baffled that no demands had been relayed despite the fact it had been three weeks since Nad was kidnapped.

As far as Fiona and her group were concerned, the facts were coming together. The perpetrators included directly or indirectly Simra and Murat. The decision by the group was made for them not to tell the government anything relative to Simra and Murat, for fear the military would take revenge on their relatives, especially the partially blind mother of Simra.

They also found out that Simra did not come from wealth. The fabrication facility Simra mentioned did not belong to her father; it belonged to her uncle instead, who had no dealings with her difficult father whatsoever. They believed that Simra introduced herself to Naz and Deniz in a contrived fashion, being financed by KIDFA, in order to befriend Nad and later kidnap her, for Nad to be used as a bargaining chip.

The inner group, made of Fiona, Leila, Tolga, and Fareed, had a decision to make. It was not an easy one. They wanted Nad back but at the same time they did not want to endanger her life or the lives of innocents in the process. Furthermore, they wanted to be careful not to become exposed to the wrath of the junta. Fiona, who emerged as the undisputed leader of the group, needed to devise a new master plan.

CHAPTER 20

Fiona needed to think both defensively and offensively. She needed the whole group to be immune to the possibility of any action against them by the junta. She knew it was all about Nad, the daughter of one of the most influential people in Turkey. The association of the group with Nad, being General Hikmet's daughter, may have provided the group protection against routine matters. Fiona needed a surer level of protection for the group, one that could protect them under extreme circumstances.

Fiona decided to widen her circle of contacts.

She offered two medical schools to train their physicians in some of the procedures she and her husband were famous for. Upon those schools accepting her offer and after she had done two lectures, she called Ameer. She told him that her Turkish colleagues had relayed to her that the mother of a junta member had a new case of a long and inflated neurovascular aneurysm, next to an existing and long arteriovenous malformation. In some cases, this combination created an unusually complicated situation, one of a dozen procedures Dr. Shaheen was the leading expert in.

Fiona suggested to Ameer for her to offer his services to operate on the junta member's mother in Istanbul. She was smart enough to first secure a report from the head of the Istanbul University neurosurgery department that said that her condition was terminal and untreatable. She was expected to die shortly without surgery. Before Fiona attracted Ameer's medical services, she shared the report with the patient's family, particularly the junta member. Only then did she present the possibility that her husband could offer some hope, remote as it may have been. The family opted to choose surgery. Ameer knew that her post-operative chances of survival were more like fifty/fifty, but Fiona wanted to create a higher degree of invincibility against any potential junta ill feelings toward the group. Ameer gave her the go-ahead, and Fiona informed the dean of the medical school at Istanbul University about Ameer's offer. He was elated at the prospect of Dr. Shaheen operating in Turkey, especially at Istanbul University hospital.

Ameer flew to Istanbul and brought along three of his top nurses and technicians. He started his preparations right away. In the process, Fiona contacted the junta secretariat and the ministry of health; she intended to have everyone in power hear about her husband's effort to save the life of the mother of one of the junta leaders. Ameer agreed to be interviewed by a major Istanbul newspaper. The headline said, *World-renowned neurosurgeon will try to save mother of council member.* Dr. Shaheen's picture and Fiona's were prominently displayed in the paper, as she was to be his assistant in the procedure. Fiona and Ameer were interviewed several times on radio and TV. On one occasion the owner of a famous restaurant and a supporter of the junta refused to charge the whole group of eight for dinner. Fiona was sure she had accomplished what she had planned.

The whereabouts of Simra were unknown to everyone, except possibly for Simra's mother, Afak. Fiona decided to contact Afak. Based on the opinion of Deniz and Naz, Fiona was convinced that neither Afak nor Simra had figured out that the confirmation of the identity of Fareed's kidnappers came through Afak. Fiona conveyed to Afak, through Deniz, that her life might be in danger, being Simra's mother, and that she needed to leave the country, and that Deniz would pay for her travel to wherever she wanted to go.

After Deniz's third visit to Afak, she accepted Deniz's offer. Deniz had convinced Afak not to use the phone for fear it might have been tapped. Afak told Deniz that she usually used her neighbor's phone because she could not afford the international calling monthly fee. Deniz had established a rapport with Afak earlier. Deniz offered to relay messages to Simra at no cost. Afak agreed. In no time, Deniz was in possession of Simra's phone number, at her work.

Fiona advised Deniz not to call Simra herself, but to use someone Simra did not know. Deniz's contact, Belgin, misrepresented to Simra that she was her mother's neighbor, and that the police had tried to recruit her to spy on Afak, putting Afak's life in danger. Later, Belgin told Deniz that Afak was joining Simra in Germany.

Fiona had hired two private eyes in Germany; they followed Afak and Simra from the airport and secured Simra's address and her place of work. With such information in hand, Fiona had to think about what was next.

Contrary to what Ambassador Petry thought, neither the

Turkish police crime unit, specifically assigning four detectives to find Nad, nor the Turkish military, using over five hundred military police and officers, managed to identify or trace the perpetrators. The government finally went to look for Afak, to find out she was not there.

Ameer performed the operation on the mother of the junta member; it was successful. Before Ameer left for London, he met with Fareed and asked him to come back to London.

"I know that you love Nad and Nad loves you, but you are going against a system that may end up crushing you both and ending your lives, without regard to who you are. I am pleading with you to come back," Ameer told Fareed.

Fareed looked at his father and said, "I will never abandon Nad. If I do, it will haunt me the rest of my life. I will never leave this place voluntarily until I find Nad. This is my kismet, and I am willing to live by it."

Ameer looked at Fareed, hugged him and said, "I fully understand. My thoughts are with you every single minute and my hopes are for a safe release of Nad. Good luck."

———

One day after Afak arrived in Germany, Hikmet received the offer of exchange. He casually told Fiona that much. In his office at the base, Fiona lost her cool.

"Are you out of your mind? You haven't told any of us that Nad is alive. What kind of man are you?! Our hearts have been bleeding for the last two months and you just ignore us and ignore our love for this beautiful and sensitive creature? You are not only stubborn;

you are totally inconsiderate."

"Dr. Burke, initially the council did not want an exchange, but they changed their mind. You see, officially I am the head of nothing in the armed forces; unofficially, not much can move without my approval. I didn't want to say it, but I made them change their mind. Yet we have a problem," said Hikmet.

"And what is that, may I ask?" said Fiona sarcastically.

"Two of them died in prison," answered Hikmet.

"Two of whom died in prison?"

"Two of the eleven."

Fiona chuckled, looking at Hikmet suspiciously. "Died, you said? You mean tortured to death."

"Dr. Burke. We are in an underdeveloped country; soldiers sometimes don't follow orders," said Hikmet.

"Excuse me, General. In underdeveloped countries soldiers are scared to death; they follow orders or they die, like their victims usually do. They, like their prisoners, are afraid they will die if they make the slightest wrong move. If you were to give them a clear order, they would obey it blindly, but this is neither here nor there. Will you be making the exchange with nine prisoners, instead of eleven, provided they accept your offer? Will you?" she asked, raising her voice.

"Yes, we will. It was part of the deal between me and the council," Hikmet said.

"Make sure that they stick to this bargain. I have a feeling the other side will accept. They need to know for sure that the two are dead and have been for some time, before Nad was kidnapped. Have they been dead for some time?"

"Yes, it has been more than a year. It goes back to the first three months of the council's takeover," he said.

"Will you promise me that you will keep me informed about Nad's situation all the time? I don't care what is secret and what is not. All I care about is Nad. General, have mercy on us. I need to sleep peacefully, my son needs to sleep peacefully, and everyone who loves Nad needs to sleep peacefully, especially Ayshe. We only want Nad to come back, no more and no less. We have no other agenda. She needs to come back safe and sound to help us put our lives back to where they were, to love her, smile at her, and she to smile back at us. Is this too much to ask? Is it?" said Fiona. "Let me leave before I lose my cool. I hope you are true to your word and the council is true to their word. I am leaving!"

Right away she went to see Ayshe. She hugged her tightly upon meeting her. She said to her, "Nad is alive. I just finished visiting with Hikmet. She is alive. Oh God, she is alive. They are trying to work out a deal," said Fiona.

Ayshe started crying uncontrollably. "We bring them to life just like our parents brought us into this world, and they are the only ones we love more than ourselves. If they disappear, we disappear with them, and if they die, in a way we die with them. In one way, we are the prisoners of our own creations—that is, if we behave like normal human beings."

Fiona asked Ayshe not to say anything to Hikmet unless he opened the subject.

Fiona hurried to see the rest of the group. They were eating a pizza for dinner. Fiona entered and right away said, "I have good news for you. Nad is alive. The junta received its first demand for an exchange. I think KIDFA initiated their demands after Simra's mother arrived in Germany, and I think Simra knew that she was vulnerable through her mother. She was afraid that her mother would be harmed after the exchange took place. We just lucked out. Deniz did a good job. They want all eleven prisoners for Nad. The problem is that it looks like the junta tortured two of them to death."

Everyone stopped eating, listening to Fiona. Fareed put his head in his hands. Fiona ran to him, wrapped her arms around his neck, and said, "Go ahead if you feel you need to cry. They would be tears of joy. It is okay; I cried in front of Hikmet when he told me about the potential exchange. What we need to do is try to make sure it will happen."

Fareed could not sleep that night. It was a mixture of joy and dread. He was afraid that the exchange would not work.

————

The following day Fiona summoned everyone at midday. "I have just talked to the prime minister of Ireland, and he agreed to be involved," she said. "I will let you know what else we need to do."

Tolga said, "How about Germany? They have quietly negoti- ated tens of exchanges with the Soviet Union. They are masters at this game."

Late that afternoon, Fiona told the group that, at her request, the president of the University of Heidelberg contacted Germany's chancellor's office, and the chancellor agreed to be involved. She told them that she needed to propose the logistics of the exchange, to ensure a safe process and that she did not know what to propose but for everyone to think about methods of exchange and ideas for a later discussion.

The following day, after she secured permission, Fiona contacted the German designated negotiator. She proposed to him that the nine would be flown to Germany and upon the release of Nad, he would release the nine into the custody of their friends, who were living in Germany. Additionally, the Germans would give the nine prisoners permanent-residence status. The negotiator turned the proposed exchange down. He wanted both Nad and the nine leftists to be flown to Germany and for the exchange to take place there.

"And if there is a glitch, any glitch in the exchange, what will happen?" asked Fiona.

"Then they will be flown back to Turkey," he said.

"You must be kidding. This means that there is a possibility the Turkish government will have Nad freed and proceed to put the nine prisoners back in prison. KIDFA will not go for it," Fiona said.

She asked for an additional half hour. She called the Irish prime minister and proposed to him that the nine be flown to Ireland. Fiona would then verify that Nad was released and if so, the Irish government would fly the nine to Germany, and if there was a glitch, Ireland would be ready to keep the nine in its prisons for seven years, and to be released after seven, or until an earlier mutually acceptable deal was reached and executed.

The prime minister agreed to such arrangement.

"Will you put it in writing?" said Fiona.

"I will," said the prime minister.

Fiona then called the German negotiator and asked him if they were willing to give the nine permanent-residence status if Ireland were to deliver them to Germany, and that Germany would have no say in the negotiations. The negotiator had to consult with his government first, and then went back to Fiona with an approval.

Fiona had one more step to take—for the junta to accept the deal, especially accepting that Fiona would be involved directly. At first, the junta balked at the arrangement, but when the member whose mother was operated on by Ameer and Fiona realized who Fiona was, he changed his vote and tipped the balance in her favor.

Fiona asked all involved to give her three days to work the logistics, step by step. She took the first flight to Germany, waited for Simra at work, and confronted her unannounced. She was open with Simra. "I know your friendship with Nad was for one purpose and one purpose only: to kidnap Nad and to use her as a bargaining chip," she said. Fiona then explained the whole plan to her and told her that the prime minister of Ireland was expecting their call to confirm their acceptance of the arrangement, and that if Simra wished, she would be provided with a ticket to go to Ireland to meet with the prime minister. "There are only nine left," Fiona added, and gave her the names of the two who were deceased.

Simra and Fiona put a call to the prime minister's chief of staff, and he in turn confirmed the deal and promised to have it in writing within one day, to deliver to Simra. The same routine was handled with the German negotiator. He agreed to give the nine asylums in Germany and make them permanent residents. He promised to have the office of the chancellor put the offer in writing.

Fiona went back to Turkey, where she was met by a car and driver provided by General Hikmet and was driven right away to see him. They went over the agreement and the logistical plan together.

———

The following day, the German and the Irish governments delivered their respective agreements to Simra through the Irish consulate in Frankfurt.

The nine leftists were flown to Ireland. The leftists took Nad to Fareed's apartment in Istanbul, then called Fiona to let her know that as soon as their nine members boarded the flight to Germany, they would let her know where Nad was. Fiona said no. She told them that since they had the letter from the prime minister of Ireland, they should consider it a done deal. The worst that could happen would be that their men would stay in Ireland. She told them that the written promise by the prime minister to fly them to Germany was as good as gold, and that the most that could go wrong was a possible delay.

"Otherwise, I will not advise the prime minister to fly your comrades to Germany," she told Simra. Simra relented and told Fiona that Nad was already at Fareed's apartment.

Fiona, Deniz, Naz, Fareed, and Leila hurried to Fareed's apartment to make sure that Nad was there before advising the prime minister to fly the nine to Germany. Within fifteen minutes the group was three blocks from the midrise building in which Fareed lived. The whole area was cordoned off with no fewer than thirty military vehicles.

Fiona approached one officer to inquire about what was going on. He went to check with his colonel. The colonel approached Fiona. "Dr. Burke. We have found Nadidé Hikmet. She is safe and she is on her way to her home."

"I need to make a phone call," said Fiona.

"I am sorry, I cannot let you do that. I have my orders. You and your friends are under arrest for betraying our state secrets," the colonel said.

"State secrets! What state secrets? I was working with General Hikmet and the council; how could I be betraying your state secrets? What I knew came from your top generals," she said.

"But you shared them with the terrorists," the colonel said.

The colonel signaled his junior officers to put the handcuffs on Fiona and all the group members. The only one who was spared was Tolga. He was babysitting Nermin.

Nad was being escorted to her home by the army. "Take me to Fareed, I want to see Fareed first," she mumbled.

They tried to subdue her but to no avail. In the process, they scratched her face and neck and caused her to have a nosebleed. In the end, they had to call General Hikmet. He advised them to relent and to take her to see Fareed.

When Tolga opened his apartment door holding Nermin in his arms, he could not believe his eyes. There was Nad. After he hugged her, he asked Nad what she was doing there as Fiona and the rest were on their way to Fareed's apartment.

Nad looked at him, confused. "I have not seen Fiona. I was rescued by the army. They are all over Fareed's apartment. Where is Fareed? I want to see him," she said.

"But Fareed, Leila, Naz, and Deniz are with Fiona. They wanted to make sure you were safe before advising the prime minister of Ireland to send the nine to Germany," said Tolga.

Nad told Tolga that she was aware of nothing while being kidnapped. Tolga told her that the military must have tricked Fiona in order to take credit for rescuing her, and to deny Fiona's involvement and hard work.

Nad called home and talked to her mother. Ayshe was so happy and was beside herself. When Nad asked her if Fareed and Fiona were there, she said she had not seen them. Nad then called her father. He was the one who told her that Fiona, Fareed, and the others were in custody. When Nad yelled and asked why, he answered that it was out of his hands and that he could not sway the council otherwise.

Nad hung up and looked at Tolga. "They are all in custody," she told him.

"You mean Leila, Fiona, and Fareed are all in prison?" exclaimed Tolga.

"Yes, they are, as well as Naz and Deniz. They want me to forget about Fareed; I will never do that, not for one second. I will die before I do that. Mark my words."

Nad asked the officer waiting outside to take her home, and told Tolga to go hide before the soldiers realized who he was.

A comrade of Simra, Nejat, who was watching Fareed's building to make sure that Nad was picked up by Fiona, called Simra and told her what he had witnessed. Simra told him that she was about to call the prime minister of Ireland and if he did not hear from her in two hours, to execute plan 59.

No sooner than Simra had hung up talking to the prime minister and learning that he had received no instructions from Fiona, she called Nejat. There was a knock on her door. She hurriedly told Nejat that since Fiona and her friends and family had been taken into custody, to execute plan 59 right away. Simra's phone went dead. When she opened the door, German police took her into custody.

Nejat shared Simra's instructions with his other comrades and the execution of plan 59 was carried out. It was pure and simple. The plan was to assassinate General Hikmet or any one of the council members, plus any four-star general, even if they were not members of the council. The details of plan 59 were already set as a backup plan in case the exchange failed to take place.

When Fiona became involved, the leftists' confidence in her satisfied them that they did not need to carry out the assassination. The four teams chosen commenced their surveillance of General Hikmet and another four-star general not on the council. Both were chosen because they traveled to locations vulnerable as sniper targets. Both Hikmet and the other general were having romantic affairs that they kept from the police and military security, and as such each was traveling alone to see his respective lover.

Although ready to go, sniper action was a backup choice. Their first choice was a side-road explosive device, as each drove his vehicle unprotected. The leftists' surveillance teams had secured Soviet roadside devices. They dug a small hole on the roads the two generals took and installed a special explosive element in each. The devices could be magnetized to latch to the bottom of vehicles and demagnetized remotely. They contained an explosive element to also be triggered remotely.

That day General Hikmet and the other general, General Hameedbey, had driven over such devices repeatedly. The leftists tried to remotely magnetize the devices several times as the generals' cars passed over them. Military security was aware of such devices and put in countermeasures. The leftists did not know about the countermeasures, and the process did not work as planned.

The leftists abandoned this method and were desperate enough to assign an assassin as a potential sacrificial lamb. Some of their sniper positions were compromised and abandoned as the army spread hundreds of troops all over the place, having anticipated a reaction to the government violating the understanding of the exchange. Despite all of this, the leftists were determined to act.

The plan was for them to puncture the tire first and after the car stopped, the assassin would be able to shoot General Hikmet in the head, after he emerged from the car. This time, however, Hikmet stayed inside the car. The assassin had no choice but to try to hit Hikmet through the small back window of his special-made car. They were ready with four different Hungarian sniper guns, each with a silencer.

Hikmet had just finished a meeting with the council and was on his way to see his mistress. The plan worked, and the bullet hit Hikmet through the small window.

Hameedbey, who was attending the same meeting, was only five hundred yards behind Hikmet. He stopped to help, as did a military truck traveling in the same direction. In the confusion of trying to help General Hikmet, the soldiers drove Hikmet to the hospital in Hameedbey's car.

Hameedbey was strangely and inadvertently left by himself. This was when the leftists saw another opportunity.

With no one around, they abducted General Hameedbey. The assassin was not sacrificed, but the leftists ended with an unexpected bargaining chip.

Istanbul and the whole of Turkey were in shock. Nobody imagined that someone was daring enough to undertake such an act.

———

The news reached Nad and her mother. Nad had been trying her best to go see Fareed, Fiona, and everyone else, in prison. They did not allow her in. Nad grew despondent.

When Ayshe and Nad heard the news of the assassination attempt on Hikmet, they were in disbelief. Fareed, his mother, and her friends were in a military prison, and now her father was close to losing his life. Nad did not trust her father and she might not have respected him, but she still loved him.

Nad and Ayshe ran to the military hospital. There, the facilities were first-class, particularly for a four-star general. They were met by the chief neurosurgeon, Dr. Benay. He offered his sympathies and told them that the bullet hit the base of the skull, but that Hikmet was in stable condition. Nad thought she recognized the term, the base of the skull. She asked to use the phone. She called Tolga and asked about Fiona's sub-specialty. He told her as far as he could recall, it was skull base surgery.

"Thank you. Thank you, Tolga. This is most helpful," Nad said.

He did not have any idea why she was that excited.

CHAPTER 21

Nad collected her thoughts. She was thinking of Fiona, how Fiona interacted with others and maneuvered to achieve her objectives. Fiona had managed to take advantage of the unthoughtful comment by Petry about babies born to Irish and Palestinian parents.

Nad went to see Tolga. Suddenly, she was not as nervous. She told Tolga how much she appreciated and admired Fiona's efforts and interactions. "I think she possesses a keen and quick analytical mind. I would like to try to parallel what she did in freeing me and Fareed. I think I have learned a few things from her, and I would like try to apply her own methods now that she is in custody." She continued, "She always worked according to a plan, and she took the initiative whenever she could but also reacted well when she was surprised by a statement or action from an opposing side. I want to do the same. I want to have a plan, a detailed plan, one that you and I can discuss."

Tolga, more than Leila, was the one Nad felt she could discuss detailed plans with. He was very analytical and perceptive himself. She described how Tolga had used his complaints about being interrupted by his students to get to the fact that Leila was Fareed's cousin, not his girlfriend.

Tolga looked at Nad, surprised, as if he were witnessing another character, or one with undiscovered bravado. "Your words seem to represent a genuine change; it sure is a surprising and pleasant transformation," he told Nad.

She gave Tolga a serious look and then smiled with an air of confidence. She said in a low but firm voice, "You mind if I sleep here tonight? I can cook dinner, help with Nermin, and think to myself. My mother is a distraction. I can discuss my thoughts with you as they pop up in my mind!"

Tolga looked at Nad, somewhat concerned. He thought the transformation he was witnessing was too sudden and erratic. It was too much, to happen in less than one day. He told her that sure, she could sleep in Fareed's room.

Nad made herself busy, cooking and holding on to Nermin, altogether calmer than Tolga had ever seen her. "You know, Tolga, under each circumstance, Fiona used her strong attributes first and if she had none with specific advantages, she would use the weakness of her enemies to reverse things. I will try to do the same."

"What are you talking about? You are talking so much differently than you used to," Tolga remarked.

"What I am talking about is quite simple. My father needs a procedure. Such procedure is done by a skull base surgeon, and who is one of the top two or three skull base surgeons in the world? It is none other than my future mother-in-law, Fiona Burke-Shaheen, the mother of Fareed Shaheen."

"You and Fareed decided to get married?"

"No, you are missing the point. I will let everyone think Fareed and I are engaged; this way I can call her my future mother-in-law, and work to try to barter her neurosurgery talent for everyone's release from prison," said Nad.

"I am getting it but are you sure you have not had anything strong to drink? You sound different. Are you trying to tell me that you are willing to blackmail the government, including your father, to release everyone, or otherwise your father will not be provided with Fiona's professional talent?" said Tolga.

"Yes, Tolga, I am different, and I will be different from now on. I will think first, plan second, and scheme third. Oh, by the way, if I get to marry Fareed, will you then be my uncle?" Nad teased.

"What are you talking about? You are shifting from one serious subject to a lighter one. I am too young to be your uncle. I will be your and your husband's cousin-in-law. How about that?" said Tolga.

"I will just call you cousin. Give me Nermin. I want her to sleep with me. Somehow, I feel that she will be in Leila's arms very, very soon," said Nad, almost in a giddy mood.

Nad took Nermin from Tolga and went to sleep, in Fareed's room. Tolga was still thinking about what had gotten into Nad to change so drastically and so fast.

———

In the morning Nad fed Nermin and cooked breakfast, singing and whistling. At breakfast, she was mostly thinking rather than eating.

"Tolga, we did not finish our conversation yet. I am leaving soon to meet my mother at the hospital. There I will initiate my bargain, namely Fiona's world-renowned services in exchange for releasing everyone. What do you say?"

"Nad, do you know what you are doing? You may be bargaining with your father's life to release Fareed, Leila, and the others," said Tolga.

"At least, I am going to give them such impression. You just wait and see," said Nad.

She took off to meet her mother at the military hospital. As usual, there were a dozen officers in the reception area, all in consideration of Hikmet having been a target of assassination. Nad also had a dozen of her family members, also there in honor of Hikmet. When she met her mother, she told Ayshe not to comment on what she had planned to do or say.

"I have a detailed plan and if you comment on it, you will spoil everything. Do not say anything. Do not agree with me or disagree. I will give you a hint when I want you to agree with me. Will you do that for me, Mother?" asked Nad.

"Sure, if you want me to, I will," said Ayshe.

"I want you to say nothing even when you disapprove of my statements completely, okay?" said Nad.

Ayshe agreed.

Nad asked for Dr. Benay. Benay came out and after Nad greeted him, she led him to the highest-ranking officer waiting in the reception area, three-star General Aydin. Nad introduced herself and Dr. Benay to the general. She told Aydin that Dr. Benay was in charge of her father's treatment, including the procedure they were trying to schedule for him. She asked General Aydin if he did not mind introducing Dr. Benay to all the officers waiting. Aydin was more than happy to do that.

That move was straight from Fiona's book. She had told Nad that to help herself win the argument or action, she should take control of the situation. That was what Nad was trying to do.

After Aydin obliged Nad, she said to him, "I want to thank you for introducing Dr. Benay. I always want everyone to know that here in Turkey we have some of the top physicians in the world, and Dr. Benay is definitely one of the most distinguished among those highly rated physicians."

Her statement pleased Benay to no end. It also pleased Aydin due to the nationalistic tone she was advancing. She then took Benay to the side and asked him if he knew of any surgeons that specialized in skull base surgery.

"Sure, there are four or five," said Benay.

"Are there some outstanding ones in Turkey?" asked Nad.

He nodded. "We have some outstanding skull base surgeons in Turkey, including myself, if I may say so; worldwide, there are a few that are absolutely great, one in London, two in the States, and one in Sweden."

"Who is the one in London? I understand that there is one who has performed close to four hundred skull base procedures."

"Well, that has to be Dr. Burke. She and the two in the United States are the only ones who may have done that many," said Benay.

"Dr. Burke! Are you sure? Dr. Burke is going to be my mother-in-law," said Nad.

"Oh my God, you are marrying an Englishman? She is still relatively young, but she might as well be my mentor. I know her well—that is, professionally," said Benay.

"Oh no, I am marrying a Palestinian; he is the son of Dr. Burke and Dr. Shaheen," said Nad.

"The same Dr. Shaheen who is a vascular neurosurgeon? I did not know they were married. I always thought they were just colleagues," said Benay.

"They are married for sure, and my fiancé is here at Boğaziçi University. Dr Burke is currently visiting him. Do you think she may be able to help with my father's upcoming procedure?"

"What do you mean? She is the best. Sure, she can be of great help. Your father's procedure is very intricate and requires highly experienced hands."

"You see, Dr. Benay, I am sure she would like to help, but she cannot. She is in prison here in Istanbul. She is being accused of divulging state secrets," said Nad.

"In prison, why? What are you talking about? This is ridiculous, what does a doctor like Dr. Burke have to do with state secrets? This must be a mistake," Benay said.

"You know if my father was awake, he would have solved this in a split second, but since he is not, maybe you can do something," said Nad.

"I am incensed and insulted. Why can't our government do the right thing? They always have to mess things up. I will talk to the dean of the college of medicine first. Let me find out," said Benay in a hushed voice.

Nad was feeling good about herself. She felt she was successful in her initial efforts to possibly get the medical community involved. Within hours Benay was back in touch. The dean of the college of medicine at Istanbul University was in the process of contacting the university president.

Nad did not wait to receive further information about the

efforts within Turkey; she called Ameer and informed him that Fiona and Fareed were in prison. Ameer got steaming mad. Nad told him not to worry. All the government planned to do was kick them out of the country, but even that was totally unacceptable to her.

She asked Ameer if he did not mind relaying the news to his and Fiona's colleagues and having them put pressure on the UK government to formally ask for their release. Nad then emphasized that they had to be released unconditionally. Ameer agreed with Nad's tactics, and he went to work immediately.

———

The following day, upon learning that more than 120 letters had been sent to the British prime minister from physicians all over the world, and that a greater number of letters and phone calls had gone to the secretariat of the junta, Nad approached General Aydin and asked him if he could accompany her to talk to someone at the office of General Evren, the head of the junta.

Aydin first hesitated. He did not want any nonessential dealings with the junta. When Nad asked Aydin to call the secretariat first and ask them if they would receive the daughter of General Hikmet, Colonel Beikal, chief aide to General Evren in Istanbul, accommodated Nad. He said they were happy to receive her.

They were under the impression Nad was going to discuss her father's medical condition. Instead, when she met Colonel Beikal at the junta's Istanbul offices, she told him that she was there for her future mother-in-law, not for her father. He was surprised but listened to Nad carefully. She asked that Fiona, Fareed, Leila, Naz, and Deniz be released. She told him that one of the main reasons was that Fiona needed to operate on her father.

She could not tell if her request reached Evren or not. Colonel Beikal told her that he would have an answer for her within days. Nad told him that her father was scheduled to have his operation within forty-eight hours, and that if the aide did not mind, she would wait in his reception area until the whole issue was resolved.

While there, she managed to call the British ambassador in Ankara. She introduced herself as General Hikmet's daughter and Dr. Burke's future daughter-in-law.

Ambassador Petry took the call. He obviously knew what had happened to General Hikmet and he knew well who Nad was. He had reviewed Hikmet's file several times since meeting Ayshe. It also was all over the news, but he had not heard that Dr. Burke was in prison. Nad informed him that she was waiting for Colonel Beikal. He was surprised, angry, and thought that the junta was behaving stupidly. He obviously gave no hint of the mutual feelings between him and Ayshe.

While Nad was in the reception area, waiting, the junta had received opinions and complaints from the medical community in Turkey and from several places around the world. Nad overheard the sergeant handling the switchboard say that it was Ambassador Petry who was on the line. Shortly afterward, Colonel Beikal went out and told Nad that Dr. Burke and Fareed would be released within hours. She asked Beikal if she could borrow the services of one of his staff. Nad was provided with a secretarial sergeant to help her out.

She proceeded to dictate a letter that said that the document was an agreement between the Turkish government and Dr. Fiona

Burke, Fareed Shaheen, Leila Chakir, Nazle Tekin, and Deniz Sedef. The agreement stipulated that all the named individuals were innocent and were to be freed immediately, and that the government of Turkey would exercise no retribution against them or their immediate families, now or in the future.

When Beikal looked at it, he laughed. "You must be joking."

"No, I am not. You see, Colonel Beikal, Dr. Burke is refusing to be released without this agreement, and my father is in dire shape," Nad told him.

"I can tell you that this government has never signed an agreement like this, and I do not think they will now. Come to my office tomorrow at eight in the morning and I will give you our answer," Colonel Baikal said.

Nad hurried to go home. From there she called the Irish ambassador, McCray, and told him what had happened to Fiona Burke.

"I plan to be there in Istanbul this evening, and in the meantime, I'll ask to see the foreign minister tomorrow, who happens to be in Istanbul," McCray said.

Nad asked him if he did not mind if she called him in a couple of hours to check on his progress. Ambassador McCray said that he did not.

When Nad called him back, he told her that the foreign minister had not gotten back to him.

"Can you call me upon your arrival in Istanbul?" Nad asked, and McCray agreed.

That evening McCray told Nad that he heard from nobody.

"Why not accompany me in the morning to see Colonel Beikal?" Nad suggested. To her surprise, McCray said yes.

McCray then did something unexpected: He called Petry and

told him that he was to see Colonel Beikal the following morning. He did not tell Petry that he had not been invited to see Beikal. To Petry, he asked, "Do you mind telling Beikal that the British government also demands the unconditional release of Dr. Burke and her son?"

Petry agreed.

"Can you arrange a similar statement from the British prime minister? I'll ask the same of the Irish prime minister."

Petry again agreed to try.

The Irish prime minister was scathing in his criticism of the junta. He described Dr. Burke as "One of our finest citizens, apprehended without cause and mistreated as a common criminal." The British prime minister was more circumspect: "I trust the Turkish government will see fit to free Dr. Burke, her son, and her friends when they find out that they have made a mistake, and we hope that their release will happen within the shortest time possible."

———

In the morning McCray told Nad that he was demanding the release of Dr. Burke and her son but also conveying to Colonel Beikal that the British government demanded the same.

Nad thought that an opportunity had just presented itself. She did not tell McCray that the junta had already offered to release Fiona and Fareed. She wanted Leila, Naz, and Deniz to be released at the same time. Otherwise, their future without proper leverage could be very harsh.

She showed a copy of the letter she had given Beikal, to McCray.

"This is a very strong and demanding letter, young lady," he told her.

"No, no, Ambassador McCray, you know them as well as I do; they let you out one day, and they put you back in prison the following day, especially if you happen to live in Turkey, don't you think?" asked Nad.

"I cannot say much. I am a diplomat," said McCray.

"Exactly, you don't have to say much other than demand the release of your citizens, Fiona and Fareed, but you can hand a copy of my proposed agreement to Beikal and ask for a response, as if you are inquiring about a demand already known to you," said Nad.

McCray chuckled. "Oh my God, you sound like your future mother-in-law: charming but somewhat devious. You knew all along you were going to spring this on me." He paused. "I will do it. I will pretend that I have approved the letter in advance, but if Beikal asks me anything about it, I will say that it is your letter and I have nothing to do with it. On the other hand, I can say that it sounds reasonable. How about it, Miss Hikmet?" said McCray with gazing eyes.

"Oh, you are so understanding, you don't have to say anything, just hand them the letter. I have only one minor request: Hand him a copy of my letter, which includes the names of all the detainees, before you briefly tell him that you demand the immediate and unconditional release of only Dr. Burke and her son," said Nad with a smile.

"I cannot believe it; did you and your future mother-in-law go to the same school or is it just she has coached you so well? This is so interesting and almost amusing, a diplomat is being played by two beguiling women."

"What is beguiling?"

"Deceptively charming. That is what it means to me," McCray said.

When the two of them met with Colonel Beikal, he inquired about why the ambassador was there. The ambassador told him that he knew Miss Hikmet and her father well, and that he was giving her a ride, after having heard the disturbing news.

"After all, she will be marrying a half-Irishman by birth, a full Irishman by citizenship," McCray said as he handed a copy of Nad's proposed agreement to Beikal, without adding any comments. He gave Beikal seconds to affirm that he was being handed a copy of Nad's agreement. "Colonel Beikal, I am here to convey to you the dismay of the Irish and the British governments; I spoke to Ambassador Petry yesterday and he authorized me to make this simple statement on their behalf, as Dr. Burke and her son are also equally citizens of the United Kingdom as well as Ireland."

Beikal had a written answer to hand to Nad. It looked as if when he heard Ambassador McCray, he decided not to hand it to her, and asked to be excused for ten minutes. It took more than forty-five minutes. He came back and said that the government was willing to release everyone, but to offer "no further retribution" only to Dr. Burke and her son.

"Well, what is the value here?" Nad said. "Dr. Burke and Fareed have the British and Irish governments to defend them; my friends, Leila Chakir, Nazle Tekin, and Deniz Sedef need these assurances more. They are Turkish citizens."

"I think this is a minor matter. What will it cost the government to give those poor souls such assurances? They are only three young women. Let us compromise. Let us say that you will not seek retribution for ten years," said McCray.

Beikal again asked to be excused. When he came back an hour later, he offered five years. Nad asked to be allowed to consult with McCray. He realized what Nad was doing. McCray told Beikal that he needed to consult with Ambassador Petry. On the phone, McCray coached Petry to say yes grudgingly to the counteroffer of five, as if Petry had been in the loop from the start. McCray had caught on to Nad's schemes; at every juncture she was trying to give Beikal the impression that McCray was in on the deal from the start. McCray extended the scheme to include Petry.

They came back to Beikal, and Nad said, "Well, this is not a good deal but under the circumstances of needing desperately to have Dr. Burke operate on my father, I accept."

Before she left Beikal's office, she had a signed agreement by one of the junta members, the same general that was scheduled to be present during Hikmet's procedure.

On the way to the prison, McCray told Nad, "I hate to keep expressing my astounding surprise, Miss Hikmet, but there is something very unusual which took place at Beikal's office. I have been ambassador for five years, and I have never experienced anything that has gone so smoothly. Turkey is known to have inherited one of the most entrenched bureaucracies—from the Ottomans—the world has seen. Junta or no junta, things went way too smoothly and there is something going on that I cannot put my finger on."

McCray and Nad left Beikal's office smiling. McCray asked Nad if she was looking for a job. When she told him that she would be graduating as a mechanical engineer in less than two months, he looked at her and said, "You really fooled me, I thought you were studying political science or psychology. Engineering! Did you know you performed better than ninety percent of the professional negotiators? Where are we going from here?"

"How about we head to prison, where I can hug my fiancé. He is officially not my fiancé, but you can't tell them he is only my boyfriend. I can imply it but in general it is not an endearing concept here in Turkey. They prefer fiancé," said Nad.

"I know it. It is hard to keep up with you and your future mother-in-law. It reminds me of what the Irish had to do to survive under the British," McCray joked.

When they got to the prison, the staff were not prepared for the release of the five. Nad showed them the signed letter and told them they had to be released right away for Dr. Burke to prepare to operate on her father the following day, and for them to call Colonel Beikal to authenticate the letter. The prison warden came out and told her that he had already been sent a copy of the letter. They just needed to take care of some formalities.

"This is fast, how did you get a copy so fast?" asked Nad.

"Let me look at it. Isn't it the letter that Beikal negotiated with Dr. Burke? Yes, it is. A copy was faxed to me," said the warden.

"I knew it. I knew it; I knew it went way too fast. They were negotiating with you and Dr. Burke at the same time. It is obvious that both you and Dr. Burke insisted that your friends be released. I didn't know that. We need to find the details from Dr. Burke before we start giving out conflicting scenarios," McCray said.

Nad said, "Why? We know they signed my version of the letter. It must have been inclusive of what Fiona was negotiating for her to have already accepted its terms."

Fiona and the four were surprised they were being released so soon. Beikal had not gotten back to Fiona to respond to her latest counteroffer, and never informed her that he had concluded a deal with Nad. They were totally cut off from all other outside contact. When Nad saw Fareed, she ran toward him, hugged him, and kissed him passionately. At the same time, the prison personnel gave her indignant looks.

Ambassador McCray shook hands with Fiona. "Congratulations on your release, and congratulations on a fine choice of your son's future wife. She did it all. She is so smart but a little bit devious and yet most charming. She needs to tell you what she has done; you will be most proud."

Fiona looked at the ambassador first and then Nad, nodding with a smirk. Fiona realized then that Colonel Beikal had reached an agreement with Nad first, and subsequently stopped his negotiations with her.

Nad could barely let go of Fareed. She told him, "I was stupid to think that you had anything to do with Dania. She is beautiful but I know you love me, and I love you and I will never accuse you of loving anybody but me. I know that now. I want you first to say that you forgive me."

"Nad, in the name of God. I never stopped loving you, and I will never stop. Stop blaming yourself. What you are talking about is centuries ago. Just let me be with you and you with me and the past is not important. We need to start enjoying each other, instead of spending our time in prison," Fareed said.

McCray heard the exchanges. "Why are you underplaying what you have done? When I tell them the way you conducted the negotiations, they will be even prouder of you, if this is at all possible. After what you have maneuvered, no fiancé or friend will deserve an iota of apology. I want you to stop it until you tell them everything. You were just wonderful."

Fiona hugged Nad and whispered in Nad's ear, "Don't apologize to men. They start taking you for granted. This applies to my son too. You have not done anything wrong, just a small misunderstanding. Did I tell you that you look wonderful, and you are wonderful, and I missed seeing you more than anybody else?"

Leila, Deniz, and Naz hugged Nad. They were floating on air. When they read the agreement letter from Beikal, they could not believe what they were reading; it was beyond their wildest expectations.

Leila asked everyone to hurry to go see Tolga and Nermin. Tolga handed Nermin to Laila and the three hugged each other. The reunion was surreal and very emotional. Tolga hugged everyone and was pleasantly surprised when he read the agree-ment letter.

Fiona rested for less than an hour before she prepared to leave for the hospital. Nad told everyone that she was going to sleep with Fareed that night. When Naz and Deniz looked at her sideways, she said, "I know what you are thinking. We will both sleep in our regular clothes. I just want to hug him and for him to hug me all night. I have missed him so much. Like Fareed said, we are spending more time being kidnapped and in prison than being with each other."

Through all the confusion Nad had forgotten to call her mother. But she did late that night. She told Ayshe that all were released unharmed and that she negotiated an agreement, according to which they and their families would not be touched by the government for five years. Ayshe then asked if Fiona was going to operate on Hikmet.

"Of course, Mother. This was the main reason behind my hard

work. Fiona is already on her way to the hospital. Ameer is scheduled to scrub with Fiona. He is on his way to London airport, to fly over to Istanbul. Dr. Benay has already convinced the ministry of health to issue Dr. Shaheen a temporary medical license, almost on the spot. I will come and pick you up in the morning and we will go to the hospital together."

CHAPTER 22

The following morning Nad and Ayshe were at the hospital. They saw Fiona and exchanged warm greetings. Ameer had arrived the night before. No sooner than Ayshe greeted him warmly and Nad gave him a hug, Fiona saw Ambassador Petry enter the lobby. It was most surprising as it was seven fifteen in the morning. At first, Ayshe was apprehensive but after she introduced him to everyone Nad took Fiona to the side. "He is very handsome but nowhere as handsome as your husband."

"Leave him alone. He has been going through a divorce for the last five years and still he and his wife are bickering about splitting their assets," said Fiona.

Within minutes Petry asked to speak to Ayshe alone, which surprised everyone. Everyone had thought he would approach Fiona, not Ayshe. As he and Ayshe left together, Nad asked Fiona if Petry had met her mother before. Fiona had to admit that Ayshe had met Petry once in Ankara when the two were seeking his help in looking for her. When Fiona also confirmed that she knew him well, Nad commented, "You would think that he would want to include you in any conversation."

Within fifteen minutes, Petry and Ayshe got back. Ayshe's face was more somber than usual, and she carried a large envelope. Nad could not wait. She took her mother to the side and inquired about her concern. Ayshe asked Nad to wait and that she wanted to share the contents of the envelope with everyone at the same time.

Petry had already left when Ayshe asked that they all go into a conference room. There, Ayshe told them that before Hikmet was a subject of an assassination attempt, he was planning to kick Fareed out of the country. "What you need to understand about my husband is that while consciously he attempts to understand the situation, from time to time he gets those right-wing fundamentalist fits; it seems he cannot help it," she said.

"What? He wants to kick Fareed out of the country after all of this, after we reached one agreement after another, with him? I thought he warmed up to Fareed, in the end?" said Fiona.

"I cannot believe this. This is crazy. If he kicks Fareed out, I am going to leave with him. I will not stay here." Nad sat up straighter, clenching her fist.

Ayshe looked at Nad quietly and said with a chagrined look, "I am afraid he made detailed plans for you also, Nad. He was planning to confine you to the base for as long as he needed to accomplish his objectives. His anxiety has worsened as your relationship with Fareed strengthened. He cannot stand the prospect of you marrying Fareed, although no one has said anything about it. He is possessed; he just cannot fathom someone who has not been Muslim Sunni and Turkish for three generations to marry his daughter. He has a mental block about this stupid formula of his. Now you understand what has been happening! Your father and I have been alienated from each other for more than ten years, mainly because he is over-whelmed with such crazy ideas that surface intermittently."

"What do you mean, Mother?" said Nad. "What are you talking about here, in front of everyone? I see you every night going into the same bedroom."

"You are forcing me to speak out in the open, Nad. You must have forgotten, our bedroom has another adjoining bedroom, where your father slept alone for all that length of time, before he moved to the base recently," said Ayshe.

Nad became somber and somewhat deflated having heard something she had not thought of before, although she had sensed that the relationship between her parents was strained. Fareed hugged Nad and took her to the corner. He did not want her to get further agitated listening to her mother.

"I think I understand how you feel," Fareed told her. "I would have been shocked if I heard the same about my parents. You know Nad, someone once said that what goes on between a husband and wife is only known to them. Nobody from the outside can figure out in detail the true nature of a relationship between the two. I don't want you to blame yourself for anything. I think I would have not known the nature of the relationship between my parents if it weren't for my mother. I kept asking questions until my mother relented and assured me that their relationship was loving and solid."

Fareed took Nad back to join the others.

"Ambassador Petry was here also to give me damning informa-tion about my husband," Ayshe said. "He did not want to give it to Fiona because it was personal. I happen to respect him. He gave me this folder in total confidence although its contents are known to most of the diplomatic corps. He made it clear to me that he would not have given it to me if it were not common knowledge in the diplomatic community. Don't worry, I have already told him that I could not but share it with you because it is more than personal; it is ammunition. Like I said, it may help us scuttle whatever plans Ali has concocted. I am sorry, Nad, there is no other way. This is a matter of life and death. It is not a romance novel."

She took three pictures from the file and gave it to Fiona. Fiona looked at the pictures of three women who looked like they were in their late twenties. She asked Ayshe who they were supposed to be.

Ayshe pointed to each and said, "She is a Soviet spy, the second is an Israeli spy, and the third is in it for the money."

"In it for what? How do they relate to you or the British?" asked Fiona.

"They are all my husband's mistresses. The British and the Americans happen to know the details. The others just know that his liaison with them exists," said Ayshe.

Nad grabbed the rest of the pictures from Ayshe's hand. "My father has three mistresses. I don't believe it. When is this supposed to have started?"

"These three continue to be in the picture. There were others before them. His favorite was a twenty-two-year-old, who ended up leaving him and leaving the country when he tried to put her in prison," answered Ayshe. "At any rate, the plan is that we will use these pictures if any one of us or our friends are threatened. He will stop at nothing."

"Listen, everyone, this is becoming too testy and may be bordering on being unethical, if we end up mixing medicine with personal actions and reactions. I know what I am going to do. I am going to help operate on General Hikmet and leave. Fiona will take care of post-operative care. Let us hope none of us is forced to reveal these pictures," said Ameer.

Ameer and Fiona left in a hurry to disrupt the unpleasant conversation and to start the procedure. It took six hours. Fiona led the team, as planned. Ameer had to work on two vessels while Fiona did all the rest. The waiting room was full, contrary to the advice of the hospital. Other than Hikmet's immediate family and friends, twenty more cousins, uncles, and aunts showed up. There were twenty-two officers also waiting, including two generals, one a junta member.

When it was all over, Benay, Fiona, and Ameer went to talk to Ayshe and Nad, plus the two generals waiting for the results. Fiona took the lead. She told the four that the procedure had been remarkably successful, but that she did not expect Hikmet to fully wake up for forty-eight hours.

Nad and Ayshe moved into the hotel next door, at least until Hikmet woke up. Nad reserved a second room for Fareed; she wanted to make up for the two months of lost time.

Ameer went back to London. Fiona stayed behind to check on Hikmet. Within thirty-six hours, Hikmet woke up. He asked to see Ayshe and Nad. After Nad kissed her father ever so lightly, she asked if he wouldn't mind having Fareed come in. Fareed did. It was the second time Hikmet looked at him intently.

"How is your mother?" Hikmet asked Fareed.

Nad answered, "She is helping with another operation. Dad, did you know that Fiona was the one who operated on you? Fareed's father came all the way from London to help her out—did you know that?"

Hikmet said he did not know and added that he owed her and her husband a lot since they had saved his life. Nad told her father that she and Fareed would be there briefly every day, but that they would be spending most of their time trying to catch up on their studies as they needed to graduate in under two months. Tolga was scheduled to tutor them free of charge two hours a day. Nad was convinced that her father, despite what negatives she had heard from him and about him previously, was not beyond changing his attitude.

"Don't worry about me, just concentrate on your studies. My sister Fatima will be keeping me company here soon," said Ayshe.

Fiona arrived after finishing with the second procedure. She kissed Ayshe and Nad and said to Hikmet, "I am your doctor now. You must obey my orders. This is going to take you anywhere between six and eight months to recover. I am afraid I cannot stay here that long. I will be leaving in six days. But I will be returning for Fareed's and Nad's graduation. Don't worry, you are in good hands. You have first-class doctors and nurses here, at this fine military hospital."

Hikmet thanked Fiona profusely and told her to let him know if she needed anything. Fiona looked at him and said, "I am afraid I have a lot to ask of you. Today is not the time. If you are feeling much better by the time I leave, I may share a few things with you. For now, I want everyone out. Your attending doctor will examine you and she will report to me."

"She?!" said Hikmet.

"Yes, she is Dr. Benay's right-hand person, and she is as good as they come. I hope you don't mind. Things have changed, you know?"

After visiting hours at the hospital, everyone, except for Ayshe, gathered at the Chakir residence and celebrated for hours. They agreed that it would be the last lengthy celebration before graduation.

That evening Ayshe had a visitor, none other than Ambassador Petry. Petry went into the hotel room, sat at the dining table, and asked Ayshe to sit. "I am here to say what is on my mind and then leave, and for you to think of what I said, Mrs. Hikmet."

"From now on, when we are alone, call me Ayshe," she said.

"Ayshe, I am going to be brief because I am slightly lost for words. I am a forty-six-year-old man, and you are a forty-year-old attractive woman. Pardon me for mentioning your age, but we have a full file on your husband and the rest of the family. I was attracted to you the moment I first saw you, in Ankara. I am under the impression that you may also have feelings for me. I want to confess that I shared with you the file about your husband's girlfriends primarily to help you out but secondarily to test your feelings for the general. Excuse me for rambling, but if you do not have feelings for me, I will leave and you will never hear from me again."

Ayshe looked at Petry softly but intently. She slowly gave him a kiss on his cheek. "Is this answer enough for you? My feelings are strong, but they need to settle down and I need to work out the logistics. You will hear from me."

Petry stood up, smiled, and said, "Am I allowed to give you a kiss on your cheek?"

"Do it on the left cheek; the last time Ali kissed me, eleven years ago, he kissed me on the right cheek. By the way, I still don't know your first name although we have met twice," answered Ayshe.

Petry told her that it was Jeffrey, but she should call him Jeff in private. He then gave her a kiss on her left cheek and left grinning with an air of polite satisfaction.

Ayshe left right away to join everyone at the Chakirs'. She did not want the group to know how close she had gotten to Petry and so soon. She had not shared with Fiona or anyone else that she had made a second secret visit to Ankara to see Petry, all on her own.

After Fiona and Ayshe had visited him together, Petry had called her and offered to provide her information about Hikmet. The file he gave her in the morning was the evidence he had compiled to corroborate what he had told her during her secret visit to Ankara. Her pretense of surprise at what the file included was contrived to cover up the clandestine trip and their close relationship.

———

Before Fiona returned to London, she checked on Hikmet. Fiona told him that she had never planned to be involved in Turkish politics, but since she had gotten involved, she needed to finish with the issues that related to her. "You have betrayed me a couple of times. I need assurances that this time you will not betray me."

"After you saved my life, you expect me to betray you? I give you my word, I will try to help you as much as I can and I will always help you, knowing that you saved my life," said Hikmet.

"Listen, General, I am not going to stand here and tell you that the Turkish physicians could not have done as good a job as I did. I think they could have, but they wanted to be sure. They asked me to operate on you because I, my husband, and Dr. Nelson at UCLA have done more of this kind of operation than anyone in the world," said Fiona. "Let us dispense with this. I would like to leave you with the fact that I will only contact you when you are much better—and hopefully you will be much better before Nad's and Fareed's commencement. In the meantime, I want you to take care of yourself. See you in seven weeks."

This time Fiona made sure she said goodbye to everyone. On top of visiting with Nad, Tolga, and Leila, she spent time with Ayshe, Naz, and Deniz before she left. She had become close to them, and she wanted them to form a solid core to tackle any future challenges, like so many of the ones that had been popping up so unexpectedly and so dangerously.

Fiona met with Nad by herself for about an hour, just before she left for the airport. She reminded Nad that their job was not completely over. She told Nad that they should try to finish everything by having the nine Turks, now in an Irish prison, be flown to and given asylum in Germany. She reminded her that Simra was roaming free. Likewise, she told her that they needed to try to free General Hameedbey.

She then looked at Nad straight in the eyes and said, "Before I say anything else, remember not to arouse your suspicions about Fareed before you talk to him plainly and openly, okay? Now, freeing the nine is part of the deal and it is too potentially dangerous to each one of us, especially you and Fareed, not to fulfill what we promised the leftists. Never mind that the leftists tried to assassinate your father. They have not gotten their nine back yet. He will recover in a few months." She paused. "I want you to start helping in finding an acceptable deal—not at the expense of your studies, only in your spare time. Start the process and we may be able to finish it together later. I have full trust in you, and you have done a magnificent job freeing me, Naz, Deniz, and Leila. You should be proud of yourself. I am so proud of you, and again do not apologize unnecessarily to anybody, you hear?" she added.

As for Fareed and Nad, it was an opportunity to savor the moment—especially for Nad, after having been kidnapped and isolated for two months. Tolga and one other professor shouldered the task of tutoring Nad and Fareed for the finals. With Tolga's and the other professor's help, Nad and Fareed got caught up within five weeks. They were left with two more weeks to spare.

This was when Nad started to devote some time to finish the job. She was anxious to find some way to entice the junta in negotiating a deal with the leftists, for the purpose of transferring the nine and releasing General Hameedbey. She knew he was a lieutenant-general, yet he was politically neutral. He was not involved in politics nor was he a member of the junta.

The nine leftists were well-known specimens. Each one had been imprisoned in the past. They were all hard-core but not members of the upper echelon of the leftist opposition. If it were not for the abuse the Turkish military heaped on them, the leftist party's command was temporarily considering abandoning the release demand of seven of them. The other two possessed enough secrets to seriously hurt the leftists, if made to confess. The leftists were keen to get the two out before the junta would have them talk.

As Nad could not come up with anything especially useful, she asked her group to have a meeting that included Fareed, Naz, Deniz, Leila, and Tolga. Fiona was in London and Ayshe was not included since she was not a member of the inner circle. She was not considered liberal enough to belong all the way.

Nad shared with them the background of each of the nine leftists and that of General Hameedbey. Seven of the leftists were high
school graduates, now mostly assembly and construction workers.
The other two consisted of one engineer and one social worker.
They did not know but suspected that the engineer was the one
who possessed important secrets of the movement.

"I have met Hameedbey," Tolga said. "He was in my lab four
years ago, several times. I recall that he has a Ph.D. in computer
engineering from Berlin Freie University," said Tolga. He explained
that Hameedbey was the head of missiles, radars, and electronic
warfare.

Although the government had signed off on a document
exempting each member from prosecution for five years, the group
did not want to unduly challenge the government on that point by
making public what they knew about Hameedbey. They needed to
devise a detailed plan for how to use Hameedbey's importance in
order to put together a negotiable deal.

Leila reminded Tolga that he was working on a setup to block
Soviet detection and hacking of Turkish and Turkish/NATO electronic missile codes.

"How about if you pretend to the ministry of defense that
General Hameedbey could be of great help to your research project
against the Soviets? This way they may feel they need to negotiate
for his freedom real fast," said Nad.

Tolga jumped at the suggestion. "Your thoughts are similar to
mine. The junta does not want to appear weak by exchanging one
general for nine rebels—I think this is the stumbling point. We
need to highlight the fact that he is a special general."

Nad suggested that Tolga visit her father, who was no longer in intensive care, and mention his research to him to arouse his interest in the subject, as an initial step.

CHAPTER 23

When Tolga visited Hikmet, Ayshe was there. Tolga told him that Hameedbey was the top general in combating Soviet hacking capabilities, hacking that was taking place not only against Turkey but against NATO itself.

Ayshe had heard about the inclusion of NATO as a potential victim of all past and future hacking by the Soviets. She asked Petry if she could visit him in Ankara. He was more than happy to see her.

Petry excluded Hinton from the meeting despite Ayshe's telling Petry in advance that the issue concerned NATO. He wanted to be with Ayshe alone. He arranged a meeting at a secret house the British clandestinely used for their agents. When Ayshe talked about the importance of Hameedbey, Petry told her that he was aware of Hameedbey's special expertise, but that there was a more urgent issue, namely for the two of them to be together.

Ayshe agreed with Petry wholeheartedly. It was the first time the two had sex. Petry told Ayshe that he would take care of things with Hameedbey from his side, and for her not to worry except to enjoy the interlude. Petry also had unexpectedly good news to relay to Ayshe: His attorney and his wife's attorney had recently agreed on the split of the estate. His divorce should take place within weeks.

As they cuddled together, Petry told Ayshe that he knew that she and Nad needed his help in trying to enhance the chances for a prisoner exchange.

Ayshe said, "Yes, because it will remove a serious source of danger to Nad."

Petry promised to help as much as he could. He added, "I trust that you wanted to be here for me and I for you. I will do anything to make you happy."

Ayshe answered, "And for you I have done what was unthinkable to me, and which I am happy to continue to do without further hesitation."

———

Two days later Petry met with the Turkish foreign minister and informed him that the British were aware of the Soviet Union's escalation of their attempts at hacking NATO operations in Turkey, and that Great Britain was concerned that the Turkish armed forces did not have the top-notch personnel to defend against such efforts by the Soviet Union. When the foreign minister tried to disagree with Petry, Petry convinced him that he was not there to criticize Turkey but to ask diplomatically that they buttress their staff, especially at the very top.

At the same time, Petry advised that Hikmet put his request directly to the defense minister to engage the services of General

Hameedbey. Hameedbey's disappearance, by name, was not supposed to be known outside the top echelon of the military. As such, the assumption was that he was active in the armed forces.

When the foreign minister relayed Petry's message to the defense minister, the defense minister had already heard from Hikmet about the same concern. Hameedbey had become much more important than first thought.

Ayshe knew well that she needed to be secretive about the relationship, especially for fear that Nad would rebel against her. Ayshe wanted to stay close to the group, not only to help in attempting to conclude the exchange, but also to keep tabs on any hint about her personal relationship with Petry.

Yet Fiona's sixth sense alerted her to the fact that Ayshe was not acting normal. Fiona's suspicion was not about Petry but about Hinton. Fiona thought Hinton might have finally managed to hit on someone successfully, in this case Ayshe.

As Ayshe called Fiona for the fourth time, Fiona told her that she had got hold of some beneficial information that she needed to convey to Ambassador Petry. The exchange with Ayshe aroused Fiona's suspicions. Based on Ayshe inadvertently referring to Petry by Jeff, Fiona got to wonder if the more handsome and debonair Petry was the subject of Ayshe's interest. She told Ayshe in an attempt to cover up her new suspicions, "Petry is a gentleman, but pay attention to Hinton. He is a daring womanizer, from what I understand, here in London."

"Don't worry, Fiona, you have already forewarned me about his attempt with you, and how he tried to slide his hand up your arm," said Ayshe.

The trouble with such a statement was that Fiona had never

told anybody about her experience with Hinton except Ameer and Petry. It was obvious to Fiona that it was Petry and not Hinton, and that Petry would not have shared such details with Ayshe unless they had gotten close.

Ayshe's relationship with Petry, however preliminary at that point, could damage Fiona's relationship with Hikmet, if he were to find out. Secondly, if Ayshe and Petry had gotten close, could the group openly ask Ayshe to be a friendly liaison with Petry, particularly regarding the exchange? The exchange was most important for Fiona and everyone else because they were concerned that the leftists would carry through with their revenge threats if they continued to be dissatisfied.

In reaction to Ayshe's statement about Hinton and herself, Fiona thought of making a short trip to Istanbul, before Nad's and Fareed's graduation, but decided against it and instead concluded that it would be much more productive if she could extend her stay to two weeks around the time of the graduation.

Fiona had developed a simple but risky plan to use to her advantage. She arranged to meet with Ayshe on the second evening of her stay in Istanbul. Her approach was to open the conversation with Ayshe as if she was certain there was a relationship between Ayshe and Petry. She intended to put Ayshe on the defensive.

After she greeted Ayshe at her hotel room, she said, "Listen, Ayshe. My interest in this conversation is one thing and one thing only: the safety of Nad and Fareed. I know that Sir Jeffrey Petry is a handsome and proper British gentleman. I just need to ask you two things: When did it all start and how far has it gone?"

The question was a total shock to Ayshe. She hesitated to say anything for a few seconds. Her slow reaction was further confirmation of Fiona's suspicions.

Fiona added, "You don't need to let me know tonight. I am less interested in the romantic relationship than I am with the help we could accrue from your closeness with him. Listen Ayshe, the leftists are still mad, and I am here trying to protect Nad and Fareed, and beyond that, I don't care if you spend the rest of your life eating kebab, on one hand, or steak and kidney pie, on the other. I also sincerely want you to be happy."

Ayshe looked at Fiona. "Can I answer you later? I thought nobody knew, but seemingly word has gotten out and I am now in danger, if Ali happens to know!"

"Nobody knows. You see, Ayshe, you got confused; I never told you about what Hinton did. It was Petry who told you and he could not have told you such details if he had not gotten close to you. Maybe you want to change your mind and tell me what you need to tell me right now."

Ayshe opened up. She told Fiona that she and Hikmet had been estranged from each other for the last eleven years and that her relationship with Petry was fraught with danger on many levels. Above all, she was concerned about Nad's reaction, when she would find out. There was also the danger of Hikmet knowing. She said that it could be dangerous to her physically. What was more, any revelation may be a danger to Petry's career, resulting at a minimum in an automatic transfer from Turkey.

True to her nature, Fiona told Ayshe that being estranged from someone and yet living with him is a form of torture. Fiona added that she was more than willing to help her in any way in concealing her extramarital affair. "In other words, let us plan for the worst and hope for the best. The best defense is a good offense, to be used prudently and in a timely fashion," said Fiona.

From that point forward, Fiona's contacts with Petry would be separate from Ayshe's contacts so as to keep him in the loop selectively. Additionally, Fiona wanted to make sure that in the remote event of Hikmet finding out, she would be spared the consequences of his wrath, in order to continue with her attempts to conclude the deal between the government and the leftists using Hikmet as a conduit.

As a final point, Fiona told Ayshe that despite the fact she planned for them not to act together, she intended to coordinate matters with her, in order to secure Petry's help toward the exchange.

"If he and you manage to keep your relationship secret, Petry may be able to play a crucial role. Yet you must promise me that you will not share any of our conversations with Petry, unless and until I tell you to do so," said Fiona.

Ayshe reluctantly agreed to keep Petry in the dark about their cooperation. Fiona told Ayshe that if Petry got to know that she was keeping things from him, Ayshe needed to be ready with an answer.

"You can say something like this: 'I asked Fiona to keep my husband in the dark about our relationship, and in return she asked me to keep you in the dark about the potential exchange.'"

———

Two days before the commencement, Petry had run his usual ad in the help-wanted section of the designated paper, which said, *Structural engineer wanted, premium pay*. Ayshe did not have access to a secret phone to be contacted at, so by using the word "premium," Petry meant that he wanted to see Ayshe urgently.

As Ayshe got to the airport, a lady bumped into her and gave her a note telling her not to fly to Ankara and to go home. She was being followed.

Petry saw Ayshe the evening before the commencement. "I met with both the foreign minister and the defense minister, and they promised that they would make concerted efforts relative to Hameedbey," he told her. "In other words, to free him." Petry added that the leftists, both parties, promised never to threaten Nad or Fareed upon the transfer of their prisoners.

"I told you there is nothing I will not do for you. This is only the beginning," said Petry.

"And as I mentioned before, there is nothing I would not do for you," said Ayshe, before they made passionate love.

————

When Ayshe got to the commencement ceremony the following day, Fiona told her that Petry would be there to attend the graduation of the medical class, since the British were sponsoring the program of free operations carried out by Fiona and Ameer. There, Petry took the opportunity to tell Ayshe that Hikmet had had her followed, and that British intelligence had a lookalike use her plane ticket to fly to Ankara, to detour Hikmet's man.

"I bet Hikmet checked on you to find you at home, when he realized that your lookalike was not you. We know that he does not know who you may have been rendezvousing with; all he knows is that you had been to Ankara without telling him," said Petry.

Ayshe recalled that the day she was supposed to leave for

Ankara and after she returned from the airport, Hikmet had called
her out of the blue. He wanted to check on her whereabouts. She
was lucky she had returned home from the airport; otherwise, she
would have been followed all the way to Ankara and possibly to the
secret rendezvous house.

To camouflage Petry's presence further, Fiona made sure that
Hikmet heard that Petry accompanied her and Ameer to go to the
medical school's commencement. Hikmet was not well enough
to attend. It was Nad who told him that Petry was there, at her
commencement, accompanying Fiona and Ameer. Without Nad
having a hint, Fiona used Nad to emphasize to Hikmet that Petry's
visit was primarily related to the medical school commencement,
and that he had just accompanied the Shaheens to Fareed's and
Nad's commencement as a complement to his being there.

Fiona asked Ayshe for Petry not to accompany them to the
gathering they were having after both commencements were over,
although this was not Petry's and Ayshe's plan for the evening.
Ayshe was present at the gathering. Petry accommodated Fiona,
through Ayshe, as he could see the logic behind Ayshe's request.
Based on Ayshe's request, Petry suspected that Fiona knew about
his affair with Ayshe.

CHAPTER 24

Five days after the graduation, Hikmet was released from the hospital in a healthy but ginger condition. Tolga liked the idea of talking to Hikmet at his home and away from the stiff military atmosphere at the base. Ayshe had accepted Hikmet to recuperate at home. Hikmet, being an air force general, cared about the kind of research Tolga was involved in. When Tolga repeated mentioning Hameedbey's expertise, Hikmet took it in without comment. He later contacted the head of the air force and asked him if he could expedite their efforts in attempting to free Hameedbey. Before long, the armed forces decided that they had no chance of forcefully freeing Hameedbey since they did not know where he was being held. Their only hope was a negotiated exchange along the terms of the original agreement.

Fiona called for a meeting of the inner circle. She wanted to make sure everyone was on the same page. She then went to check on Hikmet at home. She found that he was progressing ahead of schedule and his mental alertness seemed to be normal. She reminded Hikmet that she had mentioned to him that there were outstanding issues between them, and they needed to decide about them.

"I am directly proposing that we try to exchange the transfer of the nine for General Hameedbey. I know he is not an important general but nevertheless, this will close a bad chapter for the government," said Fiona, pretending to be ignorant about Hameedbey's specialty. "After all, my understanding is that the Irish government is treating the nine as political prisoners, at a well-guarded minimum-security prison. They have sixty-one prisoners on a sixty-acre campus. The facility they are at is very accommodating. If it weren't for the fact they were cut off from the outside world, I am sure they would not mind living there permanently. In other words, they are close to being free and yet the government of Turkey is not willing to admit such a fact. The government just does not want to make things public when most of what the leftists wanted has already been given to them. Doesn't the government care about General Hameedbey in exchange for one final small advantage to the other side?"

After Fiona left, Hikmet called the head of the air force again to inquire if he had heard anything new. The air force chief told Hikmet that he assumed that he already knew the military council had decided to exchange General Hameedbey for the transfer of the nine remaining leftists. Hikmet had no idea.

Hikmet relayed the news to Fiona, and she to the whole group. Fiona told Hikmet that she was not anxious to be an in-between this time. She suggested that the council issue a press release, hoping that upon the council publicly declaring that Hameedbey had been abducted and that it was now willing to do an exchange, Simra,

Murat, or the other involved leftist leaders would contact her.

That is exactly what happened. Simra contacted Fiona, in an unexpected way, through Dr. Benay, who had no idea who Simra was. Her message was that she needed Fiona to do the operation.

Fiona told Benay, attempting to further cover up the nature of Simra's call, "Oh yes, she called about another complicated operation. I may need your assistance with that one. Tell her yes, I'll do the operation."

Fiona went to Nad and told her, "Listen, Nad, I want you to handle the negotiations here in Turkey and I will handle them out of Europe. This way, if they discover either of us there will still be a backup to continue with the efforts. We cannot afford discontinuing our attempts to conclude the original agreement and relieve you and Fareed from future danger."

Nad, smiling broadly, said, "Yes, with pleasure."

Among the first requests Fiona made of Nad was for Nad to find a way to contact Simra and Murat, face to face. Fiona could not think of a way to contact the two at the time.

While she knew that Simra was serious about the exchange, Fiona wanted to be ready to stop unpredictable Simra from scuttling the exchange in case a minor glitch surfaced. Simra was using a public phone and one that Fiona could not use to contact her back. Fiona told Nad that she was extremely busy and for Nad to call the same private eye, Gunther, in Germany and have him find either Simra or Murat, or both.

All of that was new to Nad; she was enjoying the delegation of duty and the trust Fiona was placing in her. When Gunther called Fiona and inquired why the switch in contacts, she explained to him that she had a backlog of sixteen medical procedures. He accepted her explanation. Fiona further asked him if he could continue to communicate with Nad and to tutor Nad in the process, by being elaborate and detailed. Gunther did not mind. He was very sharp. He first went to meet with Simra's last employer in Munich. He told them that Simra had done some work for him and that his company owed her a small amount of money, and since he did not have her address, could they forward his check to her? They did. Simra did not suspect anything sinister since she freelanced, working for a dozen different individuals and companies.

The purpose was to receive the deposited check back with a bank stamp showing the city and the branch. Within three weeks, all that information was in Gunther's possession.

She was living in Frankfurt. He then sent Simra another check, from another source, in care of the bank manager in Frankfurt. In his letter he once again claimed that the source owed Simra money but did not know where she lived. The bank manager called Simra to come to the bank and endorse the check. Gunther waited outside the branch; he followed her to her apartment and relayed her whereabouts to Nad and to Fiona afterward.

Fiona told Nad that the two of them had some work to do together. She also told her, tongue in cheek, that while the two of them were busy, Fareed needed to practice babysitting, using Nermin as a live model. It was music to Nad's ears.

"Why can't he learn on the job? Why does he need to train in advance?" asked Nad playfully.

"There are tasks one needs to learn early and others he or you can learn on the job. I guess which takes place when defines people. You and I can continue to help Fareed choose the proper order," said Fiona jokingly.

She also told Nad that her guess was that she and Fareed wanted to spend more time together, after all of this was done with. Fiona called it "unburdened time," but she hoped Nad would spare one week for the two of them to be together.

"I am already spending all my time with Fareed. He had plans that we spend all summer together, uninterrupted by any single event. I know Fareed loves it too," said Nad.

Fareed was routinely taking Nad back to the sea, where they once thought they were alone, while all the time Ata Aslan and his spies were watching them. This time around, Nad and Fareed were by themselves. They were uninhibited as they felt they and their love had defeated both Ata Aslan and Ali Hikmet. On top of that, they felt they were close to defeating Simra and Murat since they were supported by family and friends. It was a challenge that had led several times to the brink of death, but now they felt full of relief and liberation.

She never thought that the time would come where her father would not even bother to question the fact that she was sleeping at the Chakirs', with Fareed sleeping in the same apartment, in a bed next to hers.

When Ayshe visited with Leila and Tolga, she asked to see Nad's room. Leila told her that Nad and Fareed slept in the same room. Ayshe looked at Leila with an accusatory glare.

"Look Leila, this is the last thing I expected from you, to have Fareed and Nad sleeping together. This is unacceptable and you have done all of us a great insult, with potential bad consequences."

Leila said nothing at first and then asked Ayshe if she wanted to see Fareed's and Nad's room. Ayshe nodded yes with glaring eyes.

When Leila opened the bedroom, Ayshe was at first baffled. It did not look like any normal room she had known. There was one bed, with a wooden barrier next to it. When she looked further, she could see the layout of the room clearly. There was another bed on the other side. She also noticed that the barrier was ceiling high but with an eight-inch-wide opening at pillow level, barely enough for one hand to slip through.

"Look Ayshe, you put Nad in our trust and we feel it is our responsibility to provide the care you expected from us. At night, Nad must come through one door on one side of this room, and there is another opposite door on the other side. Neither Nad nor Fareed can go through an eight-inch opening. They may be able to kiss, rather uncomfortably, but that is it."

Ayshe looked at Leila, hugged her, and apologized to her first, and to Tolga the following day.

All of this was interrupted by Fiona, who called Nad from Frankfurt and asked her if they could meet in Frankfurt in two days. Nad didn't really want to. She was having lots of fun and relaxing with Fareed. Yet, she knew she needed to and had been expecting Fiona's call. She woke up Fareed, who in turn expressed his dislike for the whole idea. When Leila was told, she said to Fareed teasingly, "Listen, Nad will be back in in five short days. Your mother said you can have Nermin sleep with you, in lieu of Nad. How about it?"

"I know my mother means well. She is just not taking into consideration that Nad and I have been hiding from one party, being hurt by another, and being kidnapped by a third. Nad deserves to rest," said Fareed.

"But your mother went to prison for you and Nad," said Leila.

Nad, listening to the conversation, said, "Fareed needs to wake up. He will then realize that Fiona makes more sense than all of us put together. She has even reserved my ticket, arranged all the necessary logistics, all in no time. All I must do is go to the airport in two hours," said Nad.

———

Later, Nad was in Frankfurt, next to Fiona and Gunther. Gunther had sent his assistant to keep track of Simra. Within an hour they were knocking on Simra's door. Murat opened the door but tried to shut it before Gunther prevented him from doing that. It was a surprise for Simra and Murat to see Fiona again. It was a total shock when Nad appeared.

"Fareed sends you both his best regards," said Nad facetiously.

"You are still together?" said Simra.

"Together all the time, and we graduated last week. What did you graduate in, kidnapping?" said Nad.

"Well, Nadidé, you brought it upon yourself," said Murat.

"No, Murat, *you* brought it upon yourself. You decided to kidnap another general who had nothing to do with the council. You did the kidnapping after you reached an agreement with the Irish government stipulating that you would have no more violent activities upon the release of the nine. Instead, you kidnapped Hameedbey hours after the nine reached Ireland."

"Why are you here?" asked Simra. "We still have our comrades in prison in Ireland."

"In Ireland, that is no prison. It is a four-star hotel," said Nad, giving Murat a piercing look. "We are here to transfer the nine to Germany and to free Hameedbey from your unreasonable detention. If you want to, we can finish everything today. Otherwise, we will prove to the German government that your kidnapping took place after the nine were freed. This will be enough for both of you to be charged with kidnapping, stripped of your asylum status, and eventually sent back to Turkey."

Fiona broke in. "Listen, we are here to make a trade, not argue with you. You have very little time. It is possible that you will be put back in prison right after we leave empty-handed. They know where you are, and they are the ones who gave us your address. We have already been in touch with the German government; they promised to honor the old agreement and respect your asylum status," she added, lying, pretending that the Germans knew the whereabouts of Simra and Murat.

Murat asked for a minute to consult with Simra. They came out and said that they were amenable for a deal along the proposed terms, provided that the Turkish government would give them an absolute pardon.

Fiona said that she was tired of working with the Turkish government and that Simra and Murat either accept her terms or drop everything. Simra told them that a pardon had to be an essential part of the deal. Fiona signaled everyone to leave except for her, Nad, and Simra.

"Why don't you come back tomorrow? We may reach a com-promise," said Simra right away, not waiting for anyone's departure.

"You may be in prison by tomorrow and the deal would be totally inoperative. Look, I will try but if I cannot secure a non-retribution clause within the coming twenty-four hours, will you go through with the exchange?" said Nad.

Simra did not answer.

Gunther excused himself to talk to his assistant waiting a block away, pretending he needed to smoke. When he came back, he talked to Fiona on the side. Fiona nodded approvingly. Gunther again excused himself pretending he needed another cigarette. Instead, he talked to his assistant again.

A few minutes later, as the others were on the doorstep, the assistant arrived, pretending to be a German detective.

"Is Simra Gumus here?" the assistant asked.

Gunther looked at him. "No, it's the Shaheen family that is here."

The assistant asked Fiona for her passport, which she showed to him. "I see I was mistaken," the assistant said, handing Fiona's passport back. He apologized and left.

That convinced Murat and Simra to accept Fiona's and Nad's conditions. They called Tolga and asked him to see Ali Hikmet again, to check if he would be able to convince Hikmet to provide Simra and Murat with the same non-retribution agreement that was given to Naz, Deniz, and Leila. Despite Simra leaning toward an unconditional exchange, Fiona still wanted to secure the most from each side in case she needed to use the extras as bargaining chips.

Tolga had already updated the programming and coding setup to be used potentially by the Turkish armed forces to foil any new hacking by the Soviets. He asked to see Hikmet immediately, ostensibly to share with him the news of the updates. There, he told Hikmet about his improved and already installed coding system. In the process, he said that he needed General Hameedbey to check his work and that Nad had put everything in order, short of the five-year non-retribution clause. Tolga asked Hikmet if he could convince the council to agree to include such clause.

"Are you telling me that Nad is involved in the negotiations?" said Hikmet, totally surprised. "I need to talk to her. She needs to come here and see me."

"But she is in Germany," said Tolga.

"What, she went to Germany without telling me? How could she!" Hikmet said as he banged on his desk, incensed.

Tolga pleaded with Hikmet and told him that time was of the essence and that Nad had grown into a mature and intelligent young woman.

"I want to speak with her and Fareed when they come back," said Hikmet.

"But Fareed is not with her, he is here babysitting my daughter because my wife is helping me with some of the calculations. She also has her doctorate in civil engineering. Nad is with Dr. Burke," said Tolga.

"Oh my God, this is crazy. Let me talk to Colonel Beikal," said Hikmet.

He told Beikal that it was of the most urgent order. He impressed upon him that Hameedbey could be released any minute if the council agreed to give the two "terrorists," referring to Simra and Murat, five years free from retribution, just like they had given the others. He advised Beikal to tell the council that the terrorists sensed that Hameedbey possessed all the country's radar and missile codes and proprietary specifications, and that action needed to be taken immediately.

Within an hour, Hikmet secured the additional non-retribution provision. It was relayed to Fiona.

Fiona asked Nad to relay the news to Murat and Simra, in her and Gunther's presence. Fiona wanted Nad to be the star of the deal. Fiona, Nad, and Gunther went back to see Simra and Murat, for Nad to make her hopefully final presentation. Nad spoke slowly, succinctly, and assertively.

"Simra, you know that I don't trust you, but you have no reason not to trust me. I just spoke to my father, and he said that he would be able to secure a five-year non-retribution provision from the council. It is too late to make an official deal with the Turkish government. We have an unofficial deal with them. Fiona will be talking to the Irish prime minister to approve the deal. What do you say?"

Murat interjected, talking to Fiona, "We will go with the deal on one condition: You and Nad have to sign off, guaranteeing our understanding. I know it has no official importance, yet it's important enough to commit you and Nad to work on our behalf if something goes wrong. Nad is important in Turkey being who she is."

Fiona looked at Nad and Nad at Fiona. They were not prepared for Murat's condition.

It was Nad who said, "I will be happy to sign such a promise."

Fiona followed suit, but with her own condition: "Yes, I will sign off on an agreement which says what you want, but once the council signs off on the non-retribution clause, our guarantees will be null and void, and we shall include this in our agreement."

Murat thought for a long while. It was obvious from his expression that he wanted Fiona's and Nad's guarantees to be permanent. Yet in the end he agreed grudgingly. He asked for one more thing: to have the Irish prime minister talk to the Turkish government to confirm that they would sign off on the guarantee.

Fiona asked Nad and Gunther to stay with Simra and Murat. She went and contacted the Irish prime minister, and he agreed the deal and accepted to contact the Turkish government. Fiona then called Tolga and told him to secure the agreement of the council in writing through Hikmet. She emphasized to him how important it was to include the council's non-retribution clause.

Every party was agreeing to minimum measures but maneuvering for the maximum results. Murat and Simra advised their comrades to release Hameedbey in Taksim Square upon securing the document from the council, and for Hameedbey to announce his freedom there in the presence of the news media. Hameedbey performed accordingly. His statement was immediately relayed to the leftist parties by sympathizers within the press corps.

Tolga received the agreement in short order. With such expeditious action on the part of the Turkish government, they would not have needed any of Fiona's or Nad's guarantees or confirmation by the Irish prime minister. The document was also shared with the Irish prime minister and the German government.

All parts fell in place. Nad and Fiona finished and arrived back in Istanbul before the third day was over. Tolga had delivered the original copy to Simra's and Murat's "comrades" before Fiona and Nad got back.

CHAPTER 25

Fiona's and Nad's flight to Istanbul left hours after they were alerted that the nine leftists were already in the air, on their way to Germany. They wanted to celebrate the end of their troubles. When Nad first saw Fareed, she gave him a warm and almost endless hug and asked him if he had enjoyed sleeping with Nermin as much as he did sleeping next to her.

Before he could answer, Fiona said, "Listen Fareed, if I were you, I would think twice before I'd proceed with your relationship with Nad; she has gotten to be too smart and too sophisticated."

Ameer arrived the following day, to celebrate with everyone and to signal to Fiona that it was the end of the affair, and for her not to be away from him so frequently. Hikmet insisted on seeing Ameer and having dinner with him and all of Fareed's and Nad's friends. He said he wanted to thank Ameer for flying all the way from London to save the life of one who was opposed to his son.

Everyone was pleased with Hikmet's turnaround. There were more than twelve generals and colonels and fifteen of Hikmet's relatives plus a couple on Ayshe's side. Fiona, Ameer, Fareed, and the three ambassadors sparsely occupied one side of the custom square table. Hikmet's group occupied the other three sides. Upon the insistence of Hikmet, Fareed invited the Lebanese and the PLO ambassadors. Fiona invited the Irish ambassador.

The arrangement was odd in that all twelve officers sat on both sides of Hikmet. To Hikmet's left sat General Abdullah Pasha; on his right sat the only low-level officer, a captain. He was young, tall, and very handsome. Ayshe and Nad sat on the extreme left, next to the officers. Hikmet was in full control and seemed to be in good spirits. He introduced Fiona and Fareed and described in detail how the two together saved his life, and how Ameer dropped everything and flew over to Istanbul. The praise was excessive.

Hikmet went ahead to introduce the officers, starting from the outside in. When he got to General Abdullah Pasha, he emphasized the fact the Pasha could trace his Turkish and Sunni Muslim lineage for seven centuries. When he got to the captain immediately on his right, he asked him to stand up, which he did. There was no doubt about his impressive demeanor, posture, youth, and good looks. He introduced him as Selim Pasha, the son of General Abdullah Pasha.

Hikmet paused, looked at Selim, and said, "This young and honorable officer, the son of my most honorable friends, Abdullah and Gulya Pasha, has asked for Nadidé's hand—and I accepted."

The officers clapped after Hikmet's announcement, but the shock from the other side of the room was clear. Fareed's and Nad's family and friends were dumbfounded. They looked at each other in slow motion with ashen faces. It was a long and quiet two minutes, with complete silence after the clapping had stopped. Most of the officers noticed the shock on the guests' faces as they started to darken, propelled by a scene transformed from being cordially cheerful to deeply painful.

Ayshe was holding on to her knife and fork, not knowing what to do with them. Deniz's eyes were full of tears she was trying to prevent from spilling over. Leila and Tolga looked at each other in total amazement. Nobody moved and nobody said a word.

Hikmet held his lemonade in his hand and was about to make a toast. Suddenly Nad eased her chair back, got up, and walked slowly around the square table. She got to Leila's chair, next to Fareed's. Nad looked at Leila and signaled her, without saying a word, for Leila to go across the table and sit in Nad's chair.

Nad sat in Leila's chair, took Fareed's arm in her two hands, then rested her head against Fareed's arm and shut her eyes.

There continued to be silence in the room. Selim Pasha was standing all that time. Everyone was looking at Nad, especially Selim and Abdullah Pasha. Hikmet stood up, fixing to speak, when Ayshe intentionally dropped her knife and fork onto the floor, stopping Hikmet from speaking. She stood up looking angry but determined.

"It is a great honor for anyone to be related to the Pasha family," Ayshe began. "They come, like my husband said, from a noble lineage. Because of such lineage they will also be most prudent when they realize what has transpired this evening. Nad, our daughter, and Fareed Shaheen have been in love with each other for almost three years. We could have announced their engagement at any time, but we were waiting for the two to graduate. I think my husband owes the Pashas a sincere apology. He did not inform you that my maternal grandfather was Georgian and my paternal grandfather was Albanian, which means Nad has not been Turkish for three generations, like Ali wants everyone to be." She paused, then spoke again, her voice forceful. "Nad and Fareed will be engaged next week. I am her mother, and she is over twenty-one. It is her decision; I respect it and I will let her speak for herself."

Shock passed over the faces of the officers and the Pasha family. Ali Hikmet's face drained of color.

Nad was totally surprised and somewhat unprepared, especially at her mother announcing an engagement that had not been agreed upon. She stood. "Everyone here knows who Major Aslan is. My father wanted me to get engaged to him, I refused, and Major Aslan is now in an unhealthy situation because he was trying to marry one who did not love him. I respect Captain Selim and I appreciate his personal and professional credentials, but I do not love him. My one and only love is Fareed. I plan to get engaged to him next week and marry him in a few months. This is all I have to say."

Fiona and Ameer looked at each other, not knowing what to say or do in this whirlwind situation. Fiona was about to stand up and speak; instead she poked Fareed to do so. He spoke in Turkish.

"I want to salute Captain Selim for being interested in one of the most beautiful and honest human beings I have ever known. Nad's name is neither Nad nor Nadidé. It is Nad of Nadidé. It is a name I gave her, and she accepted. Just like they used to refer to Helen of Troy or Joan of Arc, she is likewise one of a kind, but above all she is my love and I know and believe I am hers. I can say that I cannot live without her. I wish Captain Selim progress, good health, and happiness."

Fiona again was about to stand up and speak when Ahmet, Nad's brother, entered with his family. He was there late, having been privately approached by Ayshe on short notice to fly over and join her and Ayshe in celebrating Nad's and Fareed's graduation. Without having told anyone else, Ayshe wanted him to continue to join forces with her against Hikmet.

"What is going on?" Ahmet said when he found everyone silent.

"I think it is your turn, Ahmet. It is your turn as her older brother to announce that Nad and Fareed are getting engaged one week from today," said Ayshe.

Ahmet hurried toward Nad, stood her up, kissed her on both cheeks and forehead, and said, "Nothing gives more pleasure than to see my sister happy, and I believe she made the right choice. I had the honor of being lectured by Fareed's parents and, as physicians, they are my idols in every respect, great physicians and great human beings. Let us drink juice in celebration."

"We also have champagne for those who prefer it," Ayshe added.

Ahmet kissed his mother and nodded to his father. Champagne was brought out against the preference of Hikmet, a strict practicing Muslim. By then, Ayshe was clearly in control. It was a most strange and challenging atmosphere. Most of the guests did not know what to do. The dynamics of the gathering were overwhelming. After an interval of several minutes of silence and the sipping of champagne and lemonade, Ayshe, emboldened by Hikmet's fumbled attempt, stood up and started speaking.

"I have already shared the potential of this decision with my two children. This is an important and sad piece of news for them and for me. Yet I never told them when. What happened tonight was an insult to me and to my motherhood. My husband of twenty-plus years tried to announce the engagement of my daughter without first consulting with her or me. This is not the first time he has done things of this kind. I have had to endure similar insulting incidents through our married life. This will be the last one." She stood up straighter. "In honor of Abdullah and Selim Pasha and to preserve my own honor, I have decided to divorce Ali Hikmet as soon as tomorrow morning."

If there were any room left to pile on additional shock, it was surely filled. Fiona, barely having been relieved of her own astonishment, sensed the potential danger that might befall Nad and Fareed. She felt she needed to say something. As she did not want Hikmet to associate her plans to Ayshe's actions, she went toward Ayshe and said in a loud voice, "I am sure you don't mean it. It is true General Hikmet should have consulted with Nad and yourself first, but we have all corrected his mistake and scheduled Nad's engagement to Fareed. There is no harm done. I hope you will reconsider."

What Fiona did not know was that Ayshe had talked to Nad and Ahmet shortly after Petry had given Ayshe the pictures of Hikmet's mistresses. She told them then that she could not take it any longer and that her agonizing state of mind would lead her eventually to divorce Hikmet. The other thing that she withheld from everybody was that she had told Petry about her plans and Petry had prepared all sorts of countermeasures for Ayshe to consider, in case Hikmet decided to take revenge against her, Nad, or Fareed. When Ayshe signaled Fiona that her decision was final, Fiona went to the living room to make a phone call.

General Abdullah Pasha stood up next to his son and said, addressing everyone present, but mainly Ayshe, "I know that you are an honorable and sincere family. We are too. If we had known, we would not have taken the liberty of asking for Nadidé's hand.

For that, we apologize. I wish Nadidé and her fiancé the best. Please excuse us as we feel it is time to leave with our best wishes to all."

All the officers present left with Abdullah and Selim Pasha. Members of Ali Hikmet's family and Ayshe's family left soon after.

Fiona's call to her administrative assistant in London concluded, during which Fiona asked her to try to have the chartered airline company they had contacted when Fareed was in a coma prepare another chartered flight to take her, Ameer, and Fareed out of Turkey. Within three hours, the three of them were at the airport waiting for the chartered plane to arrive. Nad was there to see them off; Fareed had insisted that she accompany them, and she agreed. Fiona told Nad that they would all be back as soon as they felt safe from any potential wrath of Hikmet.

As the chartered plane touched down, Ayshe arrived at the airport. Fiona told her that under the circumstances she should not have bothered.

"You do not need to leave," Ayshe told Fiona. "Instead, it will be Hikmet's turn to defend his own behavior."

Fiona was confused.

"The pictures of Hikmet's mistresses are scheduled to appear in the papers in the morning," Ayshe said. "Not only that, but two of them will be identified, one as an Israeli plant and another as a Soviet plant. I think Hikmet's days of being in control of the shadow council are over. You don't need to leave; the file has already been transferred by Jeff to the minister of defense. He is sure NATO will insist on the removal of Ali. Jeff assured me of that."

Fiona looked at Ayshe and said, "Jeff? You mean Ambassador Jeffrey Petry?"

Ayshe blushed, realizing that she again had revealed the

sequence of her actions and the informality in referencing her lover, the ambassador. Fiona could tell that it had all been orchestrated by Petry, including having Ayshe wait for the right circumstance.

Fiona looked at Ameer and Fareed and asked, "What are your thoughts, having listened to Ayshe?"

Nad interjected. "This is a no brainer; you don't need to leave." Nad then looked at her mother. "I presume Ambassador Petry is willing to defend Fiona, Fareed, and Ameer, if need be."

Ayshe answered, "For sure. After all, they are citizens of the United Kingdom and you have my word. Jeff—I mean the ambassador—will do anything and everything possible to protect his country's citizens."

Fiona again looked at Ayshe and said, "The United Kingdom—interesting! In the past you used to refer to it as England!" She knew Ayshe was using terms commonly used by Petry and not Ayshe.

Ameer then spoke. "Let me go back to London and pretend that we all left for London, but before the plane flies me back, it can drop you off in Izmir, away and with whereabouts unknown to Hikmet, for you to watch events as they unfold. London as the final destination of the flight should camouflage our plans, should Hikmet look into it. If asked in the meantime, you can spread the word that the chartered plane company did not have a kerosene account in Istanbul, only in Izmir. I can come back next week for the engagement, if there is going to be one. How about it?"

Fiona agreed, and she, Fareed, and Nad left for Izmir. Before they left, they agreed with Ayshe for her to spread the news that they had returned to London. They were sure that if Hikmet became suspicious about their plans, it would take him a few days before finding their general location, and even longer to find their exact location. Ayshe was planning to call a distant aunt Hikmet had never met, to host the three.

———

In the morning, to the surprise of Ayshe, she got a call from Hikmet's aide-de-camp.

"Hikmet is amenable to a divorce if you really want it," the aide-de-camp began, "but he will not accept Nad marrying Fareed. Regardless of Nad's foreign lineage, Hikmet insists his daughter marry a three-generation Muslim Sunni and a three-generation Turk, such as Selim Pasha." He was also open to Nad marrying somebody other than Selim Pasha but of the same pedigree, the aide-de-camp told Ayshe. The rationalization was that Nad was his blood and Ayshe was not.

Ayshe was most disappointed by Hikmet's message. She did not know what to do. As usual, she headed for her favorite coffee shop, in Taksim Square, to think things over.

At the coffee shop, she could not come up with any plans to defy Hikmet. Legally, he had no say since Nad was over twenty-one, but considering who he was, legal and illegal were blurred in his psyche and in his actions. Ayshe had no choice but to contact Petry.

She first took one cab, changed to another and to a third, before she headed for the airport. By then, she was sure she had evaded the man who was supposedly shadowing her for Hikmet. When she got to Ankara, she also took three different cabs to get to the British embassy. The security guard there recognized her and proceeded to take her note to Petry, saying that she would be at the secret safe house. Petry arranged for her to be chauffeured there, and he dispatched three cars in the same direction, using two as a decoy. Petry himself used the same car selection plus two empty cabs to get to the same safe house. He did not use any official trappings, like raising the British flag on any of the cars. There, Ayshe and Petry hugged warmly, with Ayshe projecting her concern and fear.

"What is wrong? Did anything happen?" asked Petry.

"I asked for a divorce from Ali. He claims he accepted my request to accommodate me, but now he is still adamant to stop Nad from getting engaged to Fareed next week. I announced Nad's engagement on the spur of the moment when Ali tried to announce Nad's engagement to Captain Selim Pasha, without having consulted with Nad or myself."

Petry tried to calm Ayshe. Ayshe told Petry that they needed to stop Hikmet before it was too late.

Petry reminded her that the pictures of Hikmet's girlfriends were scheduled to run in the papers that same afternoon, and all that had changed was that she announced her intention to divorce Hikmet before the news appeared, instead of waiting till after they were to run. "There is no problem here. You will be interviewed by the press. You can say then that you learned of Hikmet consorting with spies the previous day. Don't mention anything about Selim Pasha. It is all very simple."

"But what about Nad? What if Ali takes some sinister action to prevent her from getting engaged to Fareed?" asked Ayshe.

"He will not. I have other steps in my arsenal but this time I am not going to share them with you. It is best that you know nothing about it, trust me," answered Petry. He added, "I want you to go home and pretend that you are not concerned about anything and that you are already completely and fully successful with your plans to have Nad and Fareed get engaged next week, and let me do the rest. I will advise you in general as to each successful step I have taken."

Petry's plan was easy: He was tapping General Hikmet's phones, all approved by NATO, since Hikmet was consorting with a Soviet spy. British intelligence surmised that Hikmet, as a result of the articles in two papers, was going to do nothing officially. Hikmet called Major Aslan and advised him that he needed him to be a liaison between him and a group known as the Young Lions. The Young Lions were considered by British intelligence as an ultra-right-wing Islamic group, to the right of the junta. The junta had no Islamic-leaning tendencies in the first place. If anything, they were one hundred percent secularists.

In no time, the group proposed to and received approval from Hikmet to kidnap Fareed, hold him for up to a month, and then deliver him to one of the European countries. They wanted to put the "fear of God" into Fareed to convince him, once and for all, to drop his relationship with Nad. When Petry heard about their plan, he was somewhat relieved that Fareed was the target, and not Nad. In the case of Fareed, the British had every right to go to the limit to protect one of their own citizens.

Petry knew he had to act fast and decisively. Petry sent Ayshe a female messenger, who briefed Ayshe and told her that Petry and Hinton wanted to meet with her and her group. Ayshe arranged the meeting. It was held at a hotel suite in Istanbul.

When Petry got there, the inner circle members knew well that Petry was Ayshe's teammate, if not lover. Hinton took the floor. He explained to them that Fareed was going to be kidnapped, but not to worry, he would not be in any danger and his kidnappers would release him in short order, no more than two days. Petry did not tell them that British intelligence had intercepted the plan of the Young Lions to kidnap Fareed. The kidnapping was no more than a fake one to abort the real kidnapping plan by the Young Lions.

When Nad asked for details, Hinton told them simply to have trust in him. The plan did not sound logical to anyone, and when Nad was told about the plan, she showed serious concern. Petry then called Nad. "You have to trust me and Major Hinton. This is going to be really successful, and it is going to stop Hikmet once and for all, for real this time."

Fareed was kidnapped, albeit a contrived kidnapping—and so was Aslan, who was kidnapped in earnest.

The setup was successful in portraying that Aslan was there as the kidnapper of Fareed, acting on behalf of the Young Lions. Aslan could not help himself; he did repeatedly scold Fareed while Fareed was being tied up. Once the setup was documented with pictures and film, the British freed Fareed, with all the so-called evidence clandestinely shared with the press.

The documents revealed the relationship between Hikmet, Aslan, and the Young Lions. When the group saw the picture of Fareed and Aslan together, they thought Fareed had been kidnapped by the Young Lions, and not by British intelligence. It was an extreme undertaking by the British. While they had carried out similar activities in the past, this one was done with an added incentive. Petry did it to please Ayshe.

CHAPTER 26

It took Petry two days to ask for an urgent meeting with the foreign and defense ministers. He wanted to gauge the reaction of the government to the press reports. Petry confirmed to the foreign minister that a general was heading the Young Lions but intentionally chose to pretend that he did not know the identity of the general. He did not want to show his cards as him having developed into being Hikmet's nemesis. The following day, Hinton shared with his Turkish counterpart that Hikmet was that general.

The statements by the government made it clear that Hikmet's days in the armed forces were over. Even before Hikmet was officially dismissed from the air force, Fiona, Fareed, and Nad felt comfortable enough to fly back to Istanbul after staying in Izmir for two nights. Ayshe, Fiona, Nad, and Fareed got together, in a giddy mood. Without anyone discussing Ayshe's announcement of Nad's and Fareed's engagement, Fiona wanted the engagement ceremony postponed, under the circumstances. Ayshe said no; the biggest mistake would be to appear as if they were accommodating Ali Hikmet.

Fiona proposed that it should be a family affair; Ayshe said that everyone knew by then that she had filed for divorce and that while she was not pushing for a large engagement ceremony, she still wanted her friends and Fareed's and Nad's friends to attend. Ayshe had another ulterior motive: She felt that it was time for Petry to be next to her, albeit to appear in his capacity as a friend of Fiona and Ameer, surely not as her lover. Ayshe's divorce attorney was trying to contact Hikmet to make it an amicable divorce, so as to have Nad's engagement ceremony proceed in a joyful mood.

Fiona was conscious of the fact that she did not want to connect Nad's above-board relationship with Fareed to Ayshe's clandestine relationship with Petry. She felt that Nad and Fareed deserved to cement their relationship by first getting engaged, all in a peaceful and joyous atmosphere, and without any ambiguities that might arise if Ayshe's relationship were to stumble. But Ayshe, having been denied proper companionship for eleven years, felt differently. She felt that she had wasted young years of her life and could afford to wait no longer.

Hikmet was still a source of worry. Outside the military, his Islamic right-wing feelings were strong, through associations he had nurtured and led over the years. Fiona decided not to leave such issues in the hands of Ayshe. She was determined to put Fareed and Nad's interests as a priority. She contacted Petry and asked if she could see him.

When she met him at the embassy, she told him, "Listen, Mr. Ambassador, I am not here to beat around the bush. You know that I know that you and Ayshe have gotten close. This is not why I am here, and neither is this important except that I wish Ayshe all the happiness, happiness enough to hopefully compensate her for the lost love and years she has gone through. I am here to make sure that no one, above all Nad and Fareed, are under any threat from General Hikmet or any of his associates."

"I hear you well and now I choose to comment on your second point, pertaining to Nad and Fareed. General Hikmet is under base arrest, and he is being investigated for consorting with not one, but two spies. I don't think you are justified in worrying about him. His relationship to the Young Lions has not been officially revealed and if it were, he would be in the most untenable position any Turkish general has ever been in. The members of the junta would then have to take punitive actions against him. Furthermore, they are anything but Islamists," said Petry.

"With all due respect, Mr. Ambassador, we have believed in such rationalizations in the past and we lived long enough to be disappointed. I don't want to be disappointed again, at the high cost of making the life of two young budding lovers more miserable than they have been over the last three years," said Fiona.

Petry looked at Fiona almost condescendingly and said, "The problem here is that you don't know half of what I know about Hikmet. First, I have the proof that he planned, without being able to carry it out, the most recent kidnapping of Fareed. Secondly—and this is the first time I've shared it with anyone outside our intelligence apparatus—I know that General Hikmet had siphoned off around fifty million dollars to finance the Young Lions and other groups like them. When I share this with the military council, they would then be forced to reveal the same and there would be no chance that Hikmet would be out of prison for at least twenty years."

"Then let us use those two crimes against him right away. Living in limbo is not a good feeling for me. I have one son and one son only and I want to protect a new daughter, for I love her as much as I love Fareed. In other words, Mr. Ambassador, I want to be open with you and ask you not to keep those crimes hidden, and for you to use them to protect everyone, including your relationship with Ayshe."

Petry looked at Fiona and told her that he had expressed his favorable opinion of her in the past, and nothing that was said today indicated anything else other than that his prior opinion of her did not do her justice, and that she was one of the most perceptive and intelligent women he had ever met. He added that he would see her in two days, at the engagement party, and that he may have news for her then.

———

The engagement party did not end up being a small affair. There were half a dozen members each from two medical schools and three hospitals, around ten people from each of the Irish, British, and American embassies, Fareed's and Nad's classmates, and twenty relatives of Ayshe but only six from Hikmet's side.

Hikmet was not there to be seen. Ahmet called him, upon the advice of Ayshe, to ask him not to attend. When he asked why, Ahmet told him that he should not celebrate an engagement that he did not support. Ahmet also reminded him that if he were to attend in the company of several air force policemen guarding him, it would not be the image they intended to project for the engagement.

At the engagement party, Petry tried not to eye Ayshe; she was much less experienced in secretive and clandestine affairs. He tried to conceal any potential interactions by spending more time talking to Fiona. There, Petry told Fiona that he would be meeting with both the foreign minister and the defense minister to impress upon them that the British had irrefutable evidence that Hikmet had planned to kidnap Fareed and instigated the whole affair, and that Hikmet had embezzled around fifty million dollars, to finance his political and illegal causes.

Fiona told Petry, "I am counting on you, and I am confident you will perform as promised. I am so sure of that that I am going to relinquish my suite at the hotel for your own use tonight. Be very careful; there are ten colleagues of mine from our hospital in London, and a couple of them know who you are!"

Petry said nothing and the implication was clear to him. He expected to be joined by Ayshe. Fiona, Fareed, Nad, and Ameer were staying with the Chakirs for two more nights.

———

The following morning, Hikmet advised his attorney to represent him in an uncontested divorce proceeding. Little did Hikmet know that he was going to be further charged with attempted kidnapping and embezzlement, all instigated by the same man benefiting from the divorce: Petry.

After spending the evening fruitfully at the hotel, Petry relayed his charges against Hikmet and supplied the two ministers with solid and damning evidence, much of it through the London banks Hikmet used. The first person he called afterward was Fiona, who, true to form, upon hearing the news from Petry, started planning the next step.

Things moved rather quickly. Hikmet was already under base arrest. Yet Hikmet was shrewd and knew how to proceed. He told his interrogators that there was such a group as the Young Lions, but it had gone off course due to Aslan's extremist views and unstable psychological state.

When Petry heard about Hikmet's embellishments, he contacted Ayshe and asked if she could help. She, in response, hired three helpers to look for all hidden documents at their house. During the second day of the search, one helper removed several wooden panels in Hikmet's bedroom, to find a trove of documents pertaining to the Young Lions' codes, their activities, and their financial dealings. When Petry looked at them, he told Ayshe not to reveal their existence until they thought things over.

"But I could use those documents to blackmail Hikmet with," Ayshe said. She wanted Hikmet to agree to Nad marrying Fareed, and to put his approval in writing.

When she was allowed to visit Hikmet, she told him where they found his hidden documents. She gave him an ultimatum: "Either agree to Nad marrying Fareed, in writing, or risk the documents to be given to the military prosecutor." She stayed silent, waiting for his answer.

Hikmet nodded, accepting the bargain right away, and later signed a legally prepared document that not only stated his approval of the engagement but stipulated that if sentenced to a minimum of ten years, fifty percent of his assets would be split three ways, between Ayshe, Nad, and Ahmet.

CHAPTER 27

Although the headlines projected a sad situation, where Hikmet was facing a trial and possibly a long sentence, the details were much more positive to Ayshe and Nad. For one thing, the press took note of the fact that Nad and Ahmet were serious critics of their father. Ayshe was even more opposed. Fiona figured rightly that despite all of the written and verbal guarantees, the surest guarantee for Nad and Fareed was to marry, and marry as soon as possible before something happened to stop it.

Fiona knew that she had one especially important task to do. It was her ultimate desire that Fareed and Nad get married for real, without further impediments or delays. Fiona could not help but to think of all the suffering Nad and Fareed had gone through. Both had had near-death experiences.

Initially Fiona wanted Fareed to make his own choices and reach his own decisions, without interference from her or his generally self-sidelined father. It was Dania's abuse of her housekeeper that had repulsed Fiona's senses and gradually involved her in treating Imelda and trying to save spellbound Fareed. The affection Fiona had for Nad, and the disdain she'd had earlier for Dania, made the challenge much more deserving. She promised herself to meet it when she would remind herself of once being threatened with having an abusive mother of her own grandchildren.

Just like she used to prepare for a critical neurosurgery, Fiona started to itemize her plan, step by tiny step. Her objective was to have an unforgettable wedding. It was not a case of arrogance or showing off. She wanted the wedding to be memorialized in order to compensate for the past and to add to the bond Fareed and Nad had for each other.

All the planning and the execution had to remain secret, the full details of which were only known to Fiona. The first objective was to produce a wedding, proudly done to represent both Turkish and Palestinian cultures. As the thoughts streamed through her mind, she thought to herself that the Irish culture also needed to be represented. When she bounced the idea off Ameer, he told her that including the Irish culture in everything relating to Fareed was only natural. Fiona liked the idea of her own culture to be presented at the wedding, and to have Fareed connect to his half-Irish roots on his most memorable day.

For things to remain secretive, she contacted her sister, Emily. Emily, in Dublin, was far removed from the affairs in Turkey, other than having been intermittently briefed by Fiona about what was happening. Fiona had already bounced off her sister several ideas as she sought her help. Emily was overjoyed to help with anything related to Fareed. He was more like a son to her, especially since she had never had children of her own.

Fiona spoke to Ayshe and asked her if Nad could spend two

months with her, in London. When Ayshe asked if Fareed would be there, she was surprised that the plan called for Fareed to spend the same two months in Dublin. The plan was that Fareed would visit London once every two weeks, taking the earliest flight out of Dublin every Friday, and returning to Dublin on the last flight every Sunday. Nad would have the same program every two weeks, from London to Dublin and back. Fareed and Nad would be together every weekend.

Ayshe had questions showing on her face. She was thinking of cultural expectations. As Fiona figured what was on Ayshe's mind, she said to Ayshe, "Don't worry, we live in a four-bedroom house and so does my sister, and yes, they will be sleeping in separate bedrooms."

Ayshe could not understand why such a complicated plan, and why they would spend together only two days a week. It did not make sense to Ayshe but having so much trust in Fiona, she decided to ask no further questions and to agree to Fiona's plan.

Emily knew what she needed to do, and that was to make sure that Fareed was fully occupied with one major task—to learn Irish traditional dancing, and learn it well. When Fareed arrived in Dublin, he wanted to restart the same routine he'd had when he visited his aunt three years earlier, this time to buttress his horseback riding by himself. His aunt told him that Fiona had a program and a schedule and for him to follow it to the last detail, and that such program met with Emily's approval. The plan was very simple: four hours of Irish dancing, four days a week.

As to Nad, she was staying with Fiona and Ameer. Her schedule included Turkish dance training for three hours a day, and another two hours of Irish dance training, four days a week.

When Fiona briefed Nad about her schedule, Nad tried gently to convince Fiona that Turkish traditional dancing was not for a girl like her, but for less sophisticated girls. Fiona asked Nad to try it for a week. When Nad tried it, she more than liked it. It was different than the amateurish dance most Turks engaged in. It was fully choreographed and elevated to a high standard. The choreographer was none other than the former choreographer of the Royal Ballet in London. Per Fiona's advice and his inclination, he designed dances to elevate the form to a theatrical level. In trying to produce the best he could, he engaged the services of one Turkish choreographer and another Georgian choreographer.

Nad tried both, and she got to like both Turkish traditional dancing and Irish dancing. As the lead choreographer gauged Nad's attributes, he softened the movements but undulated them further. He believed the changes reflected her personality better than his original design. He thought of her as having a firmly smooth walk and aerated presence. As he developed an admiration for what she represented, he decided also to consult with a flamenco dance choreographer to improve his original design. The flamenco choreographer undulated the dance steps further. He wanted her dance to be as expressive as possible, at every juncture.

As to the Irish dancing, Nad found it most interesting and refreshing, even though at first, she had a hard time suppressing her above-the-waist lack of movement, including eliminating the movements in her arms and hands. Once she managed to separate her Turkish dance rhythms from her Irish dance rhythms, things started to fall in place neatly.

————

It was a grand time for Fiona and Nad. They spent several hours together every day, mostly in the evening. On some occasions they would shop together and cook together. In short, they bonded further using new platforms. They loved spending precious time together and speaking openly to each other.

Two months later and one month from their wedding, Fareed and Nad went back to Istanbul. Nad was looking forward to sharing with her mother how much she had enjoyed being in London, with Fiona, and visiting Fareed every weekend. Fareed went to resume staying with Leila and Tolga. Nad decided to spend two days a week with her mother and the rest sleeping next to Fareed, still separated by a barrier.

Ayshe did not pay much attention to what Nad was describing. When Nad pressed Ayshe to let her know why she seemed to be in a bad mood, Ayshe told her that Petry was being transferred to become the British ambassador to the Soviet Union.

"You see my predicament. I don't want to leave you behind!" said Ayshe.

"Leave me behind, why?" asked Nad.

"I am getting married to Jeffrey," said Ayshe.

Nad said nothing. She was surprised at the quick progression of her mother's relationship with Petry. She asked her mother if she did not mind if she could sleep at the Chakirs that night, instead of staying with her. When her mother told her that she was in agony and that she needed her, Nad told her that she was not able to think clearly as events were moving too fast, and that talking to Fareed would help her sort things out. Ayshe unenthusiastically agreed and Nad promised to be there in the morning.

———

That evening, Nad spoke about her mother's plans to marry Petry, in the presence of Fareed, Tolga, and Leila. She then asked for their advice.

Tolga was the first to respond. "It's okay to consult with Fareed, since the two of you are scheduled to marry, but I do not feel it's proper for me or Leila to give an opinion about Ayshe's plans."

Nad said, "I don't want you to say whether it was a good idea or not; I am asking you what shall *I* do since my mother asked me the same question."

Fareed looked at Nad. "I am wondering since your mother is marrying Sir Jeffrey Petry, would she become Lady Ayshe Petry? How about you, will you become Lady Nad since you are her daughter?" He paused. "We all know they have bonded, for lack of a better word, and now they are getting married. This is all for the better; marriage is much more acceptable in Turkey than a love affair. She can move into the ambassador's residence and you and I can move into your house."

"Fareed, my mother will move to Moscow since Petry is being transferred there."

"So, we can visit her once a month. You can fly there in ninety minutes. Please, Nad, be reasonable. You are not worried about Moscow or the fact that she is getting married, you just cannot figure out your feelings. I would have the same strange feelings if my mother ended up being with someone other than my father."

Nad agreed with Fareed. To Tolga and Leila, she said that she understood their hesitation to express an opinion. "Can I share with you my experience in London, learning how to dance Turkish and Irish dancing?"

Fareed looked at her, confused. "I only learned Irish dancing."

Nad nodded. "I know why—it's because I'm the only one to dance Turkish and Irish at the wedding."

"Why do you need to dance at the wedding at all?"

She laid a hand on his arm. "The bride's wedding dance is much more important than the groom's, but even so, ask Fiona—she knows all the details."

"Wait, Nad, do you mean that you are going to dance what you learned in London, and I am supposed to dance what I learned in Dublin, at our wedding?"

"Where else?" said Nad.

"I cannot believe that neither my mother nor my aunt said anything about training us to dance in preparation for our wedding. This is so strange."

"No, it is not. You should know your mother well by now; she loves to plan and execute perfectly, and if she has not been this kind of person, you and I would still be kidnapped," said Nad.

Leila and Tolga were fascinated to hear the details of Fiona's plan. Nad told them that her dance teacher was none other than the former choreographer of the Royal Ballet, and that he and the Turkish and the Georgian dance choreographers would be in Istanbul to integrate Fareed's dance, plus a one-hundred-man Irish dance troupe.

Fareed had not been given any details and was under the impression that his training was for the purpose of him and Nad forgetting about the bad things that had happened to them.

"Not only are you going to dance, but you will be dancing in your Irish kilt. I cannot help it, but the Turks will be asking if you wear a kilt all the time," said Nad playfully.

———

When they were awakened in the morning, Ayshe had just arrived. She told Nad that her father had given an interview from his base prison cell, in which he claimed that Ayshe had been having an affair with Petry ever since he was appointed as ambassador, four years earlier. She also told Nad that Petry was summoned to the foreign office in London an hour after the article appeared in the paper. Nad and Fareed put their heads together but could not come up with anything—until Nad's thoughts reverted to her most trusted source, Fiona. When they told Fiona, she asked to be given time.

Fiona called Ambassador McCray. "I don't need to explain to you that Irish ambassadors are not in the habit of defending their British colleagues. Yet, I want you to think of it this way, that you are defending me and my son, both Irish citizens," said Fiona on the phone.

When McCray inquired about what exactly she wanted him to do, she told McCray that she wanted him to read the article about Petry and to think of a forceful but diplomatic way to defend him. She added that she would call him back in two hours after he would have read the article.

Fiona called McCray back, and when he asked what she wanted him to do, Fiona read a proposed statement for McCray to issue: "I am compelled to answer the article which maligns Ambassador Petry and Mrs. Ayshe Hikmet (now divorced) since I am very much familiar with the history of their relationship. I know Ambassador Petry well and I know on firsthand basis that he and Ayshe Hikmet, other than having conversed with each other, had not had any type of relationship until she filed for divorce. The relationship that has existed since filing for divorce can be described as open, proper, and above-board."

McCray listened and said nothing at first. "Do you have a job for me if I am fired by the foreign office in Dublin?"

"No, but I have an explanation for you to give to the foreign office. You can tell the foreign office that Hikmet was also planning to accuse me, an Irish citizen, of having a relationship with Colonel Hinton, and that you wanted to stop this from happening—and what could be better than to stop it with Petry rather than wait for my accusations to have surfaced?"

"And how do you know that?" said McCray.

"I know it from Petry, and he knows it from the interrogation of the Young Lions. They confessed as to Hikmet's plan. The Turks had to share it with the British because it is information the Young Turks revealed while being questioned about the role of the Soviet spy, one of Hikmet's girlfriends."

"If Petry can share a copy of the relevant interrogation with me, I will then do it," said McCray.

In no time, Petry managed to send McCray the seventeen pages that related to the subject of Hikmet's intentions. McCray called for a press conference and read the statement prepared by Fiona. He also told the press that what prompted him to speak was the fact that Hikmet was preparing to issue more fabricated accusations and for the members of the press not to believe them.

By the time Petry got into London and met with the foreign secretary, a copy of McCray's press conference and statement was in the secretary's hand. He told Petry that things were reversed while he was on the flight to London. The plan to transfer him to Moscow, while it had nothing to do with the fabricated scandal, had been cancelled and Petry would stay in Ankara, so as not to give satisfaction to Hikmet or to relay publicly any erroneous impression of Petry's guilt.

When Fiona called Nad and told her about it, Nad called for a meeting with Fareed, Leila, and Tolga. She told the three what had transpired, and embraced Fareed in a hug, then kissed his lips. "That kiss was for Fiona. She never ceases to amaze me. I want so much to be like her. I will be someday, since she will be my mother-in-law."

Tolga looked at Nad and said, "But she lives in London, and you live here. Hasn't she told you that you will be part-owner, here in Istanbul, of a full-service engineering company called Chakir, Hikmet, and Shaheen? You see, Nad, Fiona not only plans *with* you, but she also plans *for* you. You will know when you get to the level of Fiona; this is when you start planning for yourself and for others. That day will come, I am sure. I can already see it."

CHAPTER 28

As to Fiona's efforts, she worked her way methodically toward the wedding. It was a labor of love, starting from the first moment she went back to London, with Nad. Fiona barely rested from her travails in Turkey. She wanted a grand finale, as she rightly believed that all involved had suffered inordinately.

From the start, most of the traditional dance groups she had contacted in Ireland and in England expressed their readiness at the prospect of performing in Turkey. In the end, after screening over six troupes, she selected three to negotiate with, and revealed to them that the performances were going to be in the most famous square in Turkey, Taksim Square. While the troupes were expected to perform Irish dances, with the direct involvement of the former Royal Ballet choreographer, they were also to train in how to synchronize and harmonize their dancing with Arabic and Turkish tunes.

Initially, all three Dublin-based dance groups turned down the offer. They had always danced to Irish music and had never contemplated dancing to any other kind of music. Fiona convinced them to first consider hearing from the lead choreographer. She had already hired John Simmons. Upon hearing Simmons's name, they were more amenable to listening.

She asked everyone to be on hold until she could choose the belly dancers. She hired the services of a famous Turkish belly dance instructor, Nesim Kaplan. Her instructions to him were to hire six dancers, three Turkish and three Arab. She told him that the criteria of choice in this case was not only that their performances were exceptional, but that they were readily able and inclined to learn new steps.

Kaplan interviewed around forty belly dancers and ended with ten finalists. Next they had to wait for a sample of the actual music and songs, all composed exclusively for the wedding. Being able to excel in dancing to custom-made tunes was going to be the *test célèbre* to choose the six finalists.

Fiona hired a songwriter in Lebanon to write half a dozen songs, in Arabic. She gave the songwriter the themes for him to build the songs around. She wanted the songwriter to promote passionate love, kismet, and the celebration of special and joyous occasions, all to be crystalized through the persona and life of a heroine called Nad of Nadidé. As the songwriter faxed her the songs with their English translations, Fiona would suggest changes. In the end, they agreed on three different songs.

She then shared the songs with a Turkish songwriter, who translated them into Turkish, with liberties to stick to the tunes but change the wording, if needed. After so many trials and corrections, The Lebanese and Turkish music writers came out with common tunes that Fiona liked. The poetic meters were Arabic. In the end the songs sounded the same to an Arab or a Turk, without the listener necessarily being bilingual. The songs belonged to a form called Turkish Arabesque.

The phrase "Nad of Nadidé" was the opener for the songs, as well as the refrain of the three songs. The singers made sure that the songs in both Arabic and Turkish were synchronized and the switch from one language to the other was made by repeating the refrain.

Six dancers were finally chosen. They were given copies of all the Arabic and Turkish songs. They wanted the dancers to commit the rhythms to memory, as they usually did, and to connect with such rhythms as if they had danced to them for many years. They tried hard, but when they demonstrated their new dances to Fiona, she could tell that the movements were not flowing smoothly.

They had consulted with a flamenco choreographer early on—one whose production she had seen, a magnificent, soft, and undulating flamenco dance in Madrid. She contacted him, Alfredo Bidania, and had him once again connect with John Simmons. She asked Simmons to have Bidania review the belly dances and have him try to soften the steps and body movement, to his liking. Bidania did, which resulted in a significant improvement and added sophistication to the belly dances.

Fiona then sent the songs to the Irish troupe. They tried to dance to it but found the arrangement cumbersome. Fiona then asked if the Irish dance group, instead of dancing to the music, could try to make the same music with their steps. When they tried it, it came out surprisingly well.

After each singer sang part of a song, the music stopped completely; the Irish troupe would then dance making the same rhythms with their tap dancing, just as the songs and music did. The Irish group's skepticism was eliminated, and they seemed to be happy with the new arrangement.

Simmons, the lead choreographer, all six belly dancers, and the Irish dance troupe were invited to a series of rehearsals in London, the purpose of which was to coordinate the different parts. Upon finalizing that segment, Fiona had Fareed and Nad join her again in London. There they met everyone and were shown the scope of Fiona's grand act. When Nad and Fareed were told that the wedding and musical act were to take place at Taksim Square, they wished her good luck to secure the square for such a private affair. She answered, "You think I would have gone to this trouble without having secured the square? I have just received the approvals of the mayor and the minister of culture."

All the dance and song participants arrived in Istanbul early in order to have a series of final rehearsals; this time with the participation of Nad and Fareed. Within the first two days, things started looking promising. Every participant had rehearsed their part well. By the fifth day of rehearsal, they danced as if they belonged to the same dance troupe.

––––––––

Mid-morning one October day, Fiona, Ameer, Ayshe, Ahmet, Leila, Tolga, Naz, and Deniz accompanied Nad and Fareed to be legally married. Ali Hikmet was noticeably absent as he was still under arrest. When the ceremony was concluded, Ayshe, Fiona, and Ahmet hugged Nad first and then Fareed. They were followed with Naz, Deniz, Ameer, Leila, and Tolga. Fiona then hugged both tightly, with tears of joy.

Nad looked at Fiona and said, "Considering what we all have gone through, I don't believe anyone but you could have saved our love and brought us to this moment. I cannot believe how lucky I am to have Fareed as my husband and you as my mother-in-law."

"What you have not appreciated yet is that I did not do all this work for Fareed's sake only," Fiona began. "I did it for you, me, and Ayshe, and everyone present here. I know that you will be considerate enough for me to share him with you. I have always had a rose in my vase, full of thorns. You are the rose, without any thorns, which will permanently replace the other rose—the one with thorns."

She again held them both tightly.

––––––

Fareed grabbed Nad's hand and told everyone that he and Nad, as planned, would be meeting the group for a two o'clock lunch. They walked to a luxury hotel nearby where they had reserved the hotel's largest suite. They went into the barely lit suite hugging, kissing, and caressing each other.

Nad told Fareed, "I know that you usually cannot go through the day without your marron glacé and you once told me that I am the real marron glacé. Before we go any further, you have not answered a long-standing question of mine: What did you mean when you called me fosilleşmiş kaltak, a fossilized bitch?"

"Good God, Nad, you must have been thinking of this for the last three years, for it to pop up on our wedding day!"

"Okay, if you are embarrassed to explain it to me, then what is the opposite of a fossilized bitch?" asked Nad.

Fareed posed first, then said, "Please Nad, let us do what we came here to do. We are now husband and wife and we have never had true sex."

Nad shrugged defiantly. "Okay then, I won't take off my clothes."

Fareed looked at Nad with amazement and said, "Is this the way it is going to be?"

"No, this is a one-time thing. Just answer me and everything will be fine."

Fareed sighed. "The opposite of a fossilized bitch is a wet princess."

Nad looked at him, stood quietly, collected her thoughts and said, "In this case, you have five minutes to make this princess wet. I cannot wait." She slipped off her clothes gently, in the dimmed lighting of the suite, and she looked at Fareed and continued, "Come, have your real dessert. Come and have your Turkish Delight."

He took his clothes off; he hugged, kissed, and caressed her. They made love for the first time for two hours, all-consuming and passionate.

"I now realize what I have been missing for the last three years. I dreamt about it all the time," said Nad.

"From now on I do not need my marron glacé anymore; it has been replaced permanently by Turkish Delight; it is called Nad of Nadidé," said Fareed.

CHAPTER 29

Nad and Fareed arrived at the restaurant to find no one there. The owner handed them a message asking them to proceed to the Chakirs' home. When they got there, Fiona was beside herself.

"Where have you been? We have been looking for you!" said Fiona.

Fareed looked at his mother, not sure what to say. "We were at the hotel."

"Did you already have lunch?" asked Fiona.

"No, we were just at the hotel," said Nad.

Fiona was wondering what there was to do to take so long at a hotel. Fiona had reserved a suite at a resort hotel, a long distance from where they were. "And what were you doing there?" she quipped.

Fareed looked at his mother with his eyes widening. "I felt like having marron glacé, but instead I had Turkish Delight."

"You are still hooked on marron glacé?" said Fiona.

"Not anymore, Mother. It has been replaced permanently by Turkish Delight," said Fareed.

"Well, one sweet thing for another—six of one, half a dozen of the other."

"Not this time, Mother. This Turkish Delight was special; it is called Nad of Nadidé."

Nad turned the other way, blushing. Fiona paused again, her eyes widened, and her lips turned up into a smile of resignation. She made one slow nod and expanded her smile, signaling that she understood.

As she turned back to face Fiona, Nad said, "I think Fareed is right, he could not wait; he wanted to get used to the new taste," giggling and covering her face with both hands.

Fiona said nothing further about the subject. She added, "I have bad news for you. The reason we are here and not at the restaurant is because the mayor is thinking of cancelling the wedding ceremony in Taksim Square."

"What, but why?" said Nad.

"Why? Well, it is the same story: General Hikmet and his friends are putting pressure on the mayor to cancel. They told the mayor that he has never done this to accommodate Turks in the past and yet he is making the square available to foreigners," said Fiona. "Listen guys, marriage is not about weddings; it is about what comes after the wedding. It is about loving and enjoying each other. If it is not to be, so be it. We will celebrate at Tolga's house or at your house. The guests will understand. I talked to Ambassador McCray, and I am waiting to hear from him."

The phone rang; it was McCray. He told Fiona that he had talked to Petry and Petry gave him two names of the ringleaders among the Young Lions. They were participants in the attempt to overthrow the council. They were very close to General Hikmet. The council members knew who they were but decided not to do anything about it for fear it would split the support for the council.

"What do you suggest we do, Mr. Ambassador?" asked Fiona.

"I am not suggesting anything. It is all up to you—your decision," McCray said.

Fiona looked at the faces of the group, trying to figure out what to do. She took Ameer into an adjacent room and told him what McCray had told her. For the first time, Ameer got involved. "I think McCray is, without saying anything, suggesting we blackmail Hikmet." He addressed the group and told them there was very little time. He shared with them what McCray had told Fiona.

Fareed looked at Nad. "I am afraid with three hours left, the only three people who can most effectively threaten Hikmet are Ayshe, Nad, and Ahmet." Nad then suggested that Ayshe was to call Hikmet first and for Nad to take the phone and threaten her father. Ayshe followed through by telling Hikmet that she knew who the leaders of the conspiracy were, and she named them.

Nad took the phone from Ayshe. "Dad, what I am asking you is that you take the phone and call the mayor and tell him not only that you and your group no longer oppose the wedding celebration in Taksim Square, but that you want the ceremony to proceed, with your full blessings. Otherwise, the two names will be given to the press."

Hikmet paused and said nothing for a long minute. He then said, "I will call him right away."

Fiona called the mayor ten minutes later to find out that Hikmet had carried through with his promise. The wedding celebration at Taksim Square was back on, in earnest. Fortunately, none of the artists had any hint of the cancellation.

The celebrations started at five o'clock, as scheduled. The invited guests—physicians from the two medical schools, Turkish artists of all sorts, ambassadors and their staff, and many others interested in this daring tri-cultural production—were joined by several thousand shoppers in the very heart of Istanbul.

The mayor was the main usher of the event, with three hundred policemen helping. The mayor guided everyone to clear a hundred yards on three sides of the square, and to have them face the stage, a makeshift hardwood stage that measured one hundred by one hundred feet.

The music started to play the tunes of the three chosen songs without any singing. The Arabic male singer started singing, to the surprise of some of the Turkish spectators, to the musical tunes, setting the melodies in motion. He was followed by a Turkish female singer, who also sang to the same tunes. After alternating between the two singers, the Turkish belly dancers appeared to undulate softly. Within minutes they were joined by the three Palestinian belly dancers, dancing harmoniously with the Turkish dancers.

They danced for ten minutes against the alternating Turkish and Arabic songs. As the dancers and the singing reached a crescendo, they stopped and separated, each three on one side. The crowd could suddenly see silhouettes and hear huffing in the background. The Irish dancers became visible to the crowd, in their Irish kilts. They walked forward until they got settled, up front.

With their firm but slow steps, the Irish troupe tapped the tunes of the songs, after they had been sung in Arabic and Turkish. They would pause and say one sentence in a hushed, deep, and elongated tone, "Nad of Nadidé." Slowly, the Irish troupe sped up their steps to continue tapping the same tune. The crowd loved seeing one hundred dancers, fifty men and fifty women, tapping music that the crowd related to and much appreciated.

The dancing stopped. Fareed appeared wearing his Irish kilt and green shirt with a Palestinian *keffiyeh* around his neck. He danced for three minutes solo, in front of the troupe, tapping the same tunes the troupe had tap danced before him. The troupe joined Fareed, dancing for another five minutes.

Fareed and the Irish troupe slowed their dancing, huffing the name, "Nad of Nadidé." They sped up; the singing resumed in Arabic and Turkish at the same time. The belly dancers came out dancing, first slowly and then faster. They undulated and then slowed down.

Nad came out in her traditional Turkish red wedding dress, took center stage, and commenced her choreographed Turkish dancing, in harmony with the other belly dancers. After another five minutes, Nad danced her way to Fareed and stopped. He folded her veil back. She danced for him, and he tap danced for her. She then leaned over backward to ease into his arms and paused.

The Irish troupe started huffing the musical tones before they resumed tap dancing, starting slow then speeding up, making music with their tapping. Fareed and Nad went into the front of the Irish troupe and tap danced ahead of them, he in his kilt and she in her Turkish wedding dress. The ceremony took one hour, and ended gloriously in a crescendo finale.

The crowds were elated at this phenomenal production. The mayor shook Fiona's hand warmly, followed by the four ambassadors, including Lebanon's. McCray had not expected Irish dancing to be in the picture. It was the best payback Fiona could have given him.

As the crowds circled around Fareed, Nad, and the performers, three figures stood apart, two together and one by himself, surrounded by four plainclothes military police. There were Simra and Murat, and twenty-five feet away was Hikmet, with his prison guards in the background.

Nad looked at them and paused. Fareed gave her a nudge on her back, encouraging her to go see them. Nad hesitated but then walked toward Murat and Simra first. "I forgive you. I do not want the love I have for Fareed to be diminished by any residual hate. It is nice to see you."

Fareed and Ameer then flanked Nad. Fareed encouraged her again toward her father. She looked at Hikmet silently then kissed his hand and placed it on her forehead, a revered gesture of respect in Turkey.

She repeated herself to her father. "I forgive you."

Ameer went back to join Fiona as Fareed approached Nad and escorted her back to the center of the stage. The crowds looked on, parting to give them a pathway back. There Fareed twisted Nad backward and gave her the juiciest kiss ever given in public, in Turkey.

The crowd liked what they saw. They clapped and cheered for a long, long time.

ABOUT THE AUTHOR

 WAGIH ABU-RISH is a Palestinian author and activist. His first novel, *Replenishing the Sea of Galilee*, was published in 2021, and he is currently in the process of publishing his first poetry book, *Joys and Lamentations from the Wind*. He spent much of his career as a businessman, specializing in acquisitions. During a long and varied professional career, he was a foreign journalist in Beirut, Lebanon, and an ad executive on Madison Avenue.

He has been active in promoting progressive causes, such as democratic practices and equal rights. Among those causes, he feels strongly about the need for the liberation of women in the Middle East, which he considers to be the most overlooked and abridged human right of all.

It is his hope that this novel, coupled with his first, highlights the themes he believes in. The most salient of which is the fact that most adherents are ignorant of the essence of their own religions. This applies equally to the adherents of Islam and to all other religions.

His other theme in this book is crystalized in the epigraph

at the front of this book, namely that dictatorships are arbitrary and capricious, even when their actions are unrelated to their own survival, in this case in relationship to a love affair.

Mr. Abu-Rish earned his bachelor's and master's degrees in journalism from the University of Houston and the University of Oregon, respectively. To learn more, please visit his website at www.wagihaburish.com.

To follow the author and get a free short story "Wadi Habab," sign up for Wagih Abu-Rish's newsletter at:

https://wagihaburish.com/newsletter-sign-up/

CPSIA information can be obtained
at www.ICGtesting.com
Printed in the USA
JSHW032347081222
34571JS00002B/8